About Three Authors: Poison Pen

VAL TOBIN

DEDICATION

To the memory of Rod Gardner. RIP, my friend. You are missed.
To my readers: without you, this would be just a YOP in the void.
To Bob, Jenn, Mark, Chanelle, Savannah, and Jack, always.

ACKNOWLEDGMENTS

Thank you to Andrea Holmes; Val Cseh; Michelle Legere; John Erwin; Alis Kennedy; Wendy Quirion; Diane King, owner of The Hedge Witch in Sharon, Ontario; Sergeant Kelly Bachoo, York Regional Police; Melanie Smith; Myra Lawson; Stephanie Sabourin, Media Relations Specialist, Niagara Regional Police; and Dan Savoie, Niagara Regional Police Service.

"The opposite of love is fear." Thank you, Doreen Virtue, for the knowledge you imparted through your books and classes.

Editing by Kelly Hartigan (XterraWeb) editing.xterraweb.com. Thank you, Kelly.

Thanks to Patti Roberts of Paradox (paradoxbooktrailerproductions.blogspot.com.au/) for the amazing cover and for beta reading.

*Success makes so many people hate you. I wish it wasn't that way. It would be wonderful to enjoy success without seeing envy in the eyes of those around you.—*Marilyn Monroe

Never underestimate the power of jealousy and the power of envy to destroy. Never underestimate that.—Oliver Stone.

i

CHAPTER 1

The place was a stone and steel palace. Whenever Conrad Barnes visited, which was often, the bile rose in his throat and his stomach churned with resentment.

But not today.

He parked his bike next to the fifteen-hundred-square-foot garage and hooked his helmet over the handlebars. On any other day, he would've stewed over the fact that the garage alone dwarfed his house.

But not today.

He almost whistled as he approached the glass-enclosed front entrance. With his head down, he exposed to the security cameras only the top of the long, blond wig he wore. He threw a quick glance towards the Niagara River, which fronted one thousand feet of the property on the outskirts of Niagara-on-the-Lake in Ontario. Coast clear, Conrad eased the glass door open and slipped onto the porch.

Before ringing the bell, he removed the wig and the women's bulky sweater he wore despite the warm, humid air and stuffed them into the backpack he carried. Next, he wiped his lipstick-coated mouth with a moist towelette. He shoved the soiled tissue and the rest of the packet into a Ziploc bag and then into the backpack.

Later, he'd burn the soiled tissue but planned to keep what remained of the packet—no need to be wasteful. The backpack he set in the right corner of the porch beside the front door. He ran a hand through his jet-black hair to remove the flatness from the helmet and wig. The pair of running shoes he'd stolen from their owner remained on his feet.

After weeks of snooping, he'd scoped out every camera at every angle in the place. Thankfully, Leon Patterson valued his privacy and the electronic eyes focused outward only. Inside, Conrad would be safe from such surveillance, but he kept himself pressed to the front doors once he'd removed the wig and sweater.

He drew the cuff of his white collared shirt over his right fist and rang the doorbell with a cloth-covered knuckle. While he waited, he stuffed his hands in his pockets. With his right hand, he clutched the packet of ground water hemlock root, his ticket to riches and fame.

After a few minutes, he repeated the bell-ringing process. As he considered ringing a third time, the door opened, exposing a bleary-eyed, bed-headed Leon Patterson.

"What the hell are you doing here at six in the morning? Did we have an appointment?" Leon yawned, his jaw cracking.

Conrad frowned. "Oh, no. Tell me we have an appointment."

They didn't, of course. Everyone thought Conrad was attending a massage conference in nearby Niagara Falls. He'd spouted off about it often to prepare for this morning. The conference existed—he'd timed his visit here to coincide with it. He'd even registered for the conference, booked a hotel room, and checked in. It made the perfect alibi for a professional masseur, and he'd return to the room after he finished here.

Leon scrubbed his face with his hands and then ran them through his wavy brown hair, spiking it up even more. "Didn't you have a conference?"

"Starts tomorrow." Conrad frowned as though puzzled.

"My phone didn't fire off a reminder."

"What the hell? Weird, man. It's in my appointment book. Sorry I woke you for nothing." He brightened as though struck with a brilliant idea. "Why don't I give you a free half-hour massage for the inconvenience?"

"I haven't even had coffee." Leon hesitated, squinting in contemplation. "But it'd be great." After another pause, he said, "I'll pay you. It's your job, and you should be paid for your time."

Yeah, Mister Money Bags has it to throw around. Conrad smiled. "Sure, I'll take your money."

Leon opened the door wide and ushered Conrad into the main foyer. An opulent living room with grey broadloom and French provincial couches, chairs, and loveseats in tan sprawled to his right. A glass coffee table, a glass hutch, and a large glass china cabinet added sparkle to the room.

Whenever he entered this house, he fought the urge to smash everything. He visualized taking a sledgehammer to all that fragile junk. If it weren't for this pompous jerk, Conrad would be rich, famous—happy. As it was, he struggled to pay his bills while Leon rattled around in an enormous mansion with only his sister Daphne to share it.

Pretentious. Who needs seven thousand square feet of home?

His desire for what Leon owned didn't strike Conrad as hypocritical. The little peckerhead had everything handed to him. Leon hadn't earned it, hadn't struggled the way Conrad struggled. How was that fair?

Forcing his teeth to unclench, he made his way to the kitchen, Leon padding after him.

"Shall we have coffee to wake you up?" Conrad stopped next to the cappuccino machine and inclined his head. "I'd make it for you, buddy, but I don't know how to work this contraption."

Leon, fully awake now, grinned. "No problem. Sit."

Conrad eyed the four rattan-backed barstools pushed up against the gleaming white island in the centre of the kitchen. He strolled over to a stool snugged up against the island near the embedded gas range. When Leon turned away to set up the coffee maker, Conrad covered his hand with his shirt cuff and yanked the stool out. By the time Leon spun around again, Conrad sat on the barstool, elbows on the island's granite top, chin resting on hands.

"I gotta say, I rarely wake up this early." Leon set spoons, sugar, and milk in front of Conrad.

"Where's Daphne?" She was at work, but he needed Leon to verify. Better to be safe. The last thing he needed was his future wife walking in on him murdering her brother—not that she knew she was his future wife. The housekeeper always arrived in the afternoon, so he was safe there, too.

"Work. She has the morning shift at the diner all week."

"Bummer. Wasn't she on the night shift last week?"

"Yeah."

The coffee maker rumbled and Leon retrieved mugs from the

cupboard. "She doesn't mind. We're sure the job's only temporary."

"You helping sell her book?" A big-name author such as Leon surely worked his magic for his sister even though he'd done diddly squat for his good pal Conrad. *Selfish.* The man was self-absorbed and selfish.

"I'm doing what I can, sure." Leon poured coffee and walked the mugs to the island. He snagged a seat next to Conrad and doctored his coffee with milk and sugar.

When Conrad didn't make a move to add anything to his coffee, Leon raised his brows. "Aren't you having milk?"

"Nah. I'm cutting out dairy." He wasn't. The less he touched in the house, the better. In a few minutes, Leon would thrash on the floor in death throes. Whether Conrad used dairy wouldn't matter to Leon ever again.

"You got a lactose problem? I didn't know that."

Conrad shrugged. "Neither did I."

He stifled the smirk before it displayed on his face and grinned instead. A glance at the time showed twenty minutes had passed—time to get this project underway.

"Hey, can I buy a copy of your last paperback from you?" That ought to shove Leon's ass from the room.

Delight crossed Leon's face. "Yeah, sure. Awesome."

"Can you sign it? Make it out to Beth Holmes and add today's date? I'm giving it as a gift."

"Sure. Be right back."

The moment Leon disappeared from sight, Conrad slipped the packet of powder from his pocket and tipped it into Leon's coffee.

Poison was a woman's weapon. As an aspiring author, Conrad often researched murder. After deciding to use poison, he'd visited the library in St. Catharines to figure out which one suited his needs. Water hemlock fit perfectly into his plans. It worked fast and would make Leon suffer before he died.

Served him right. He should have helped Conrad sell his novel. Leon had influence, but his petty selfishness made him keep all the fame and glory for himself. He wasn't even a talented writer. His editor did the heavy lifting. Conrad had read Leon's books and found the stories lacked depth. They weren't intellectually stimulating masterpieces like Conrad's novels.

"Here ya go." Leon reappeared and held up the book, front

facing out.

The cover showed a half-naked couple canoodling, glittering masks covering their eyes, the woman's wrists in handcuffs. He opened the book and displayed the title page. On it, he'd written *To Beth Holmes. Hope it spices up your nights. Leon Patterson.* Under the signature, he'd written the current date. The signature displayed exaggerated loops and swirls.

Conrad winced. Erotica. The man wrote erotica and made millions from it. Life just wasn't fair. He picked up his mug and raised it in a toast. "Thanks, buddy. Cheers."

Leon raised his mug and tapped it against Conrad's. "Cheers."

Conrad sipped, his gaze riveted on Leon's eyes as he drank the tainted coffee. No matter what, Conrad wanted to witness the light in the other man's eyes dim and flicker out. He'd read about killers who'd watched their victims die. What a rare and precious opportunity to observe the moment of death. This would be research as well as revenge.

Fifteen minutes later, the tremors started and Leon's mug crashed to the floor. His mouth opened and closed, opened and closed, and he made a pleading gesture with his hands. His eyes went wide and the aroma of shit rent the air. He tumbled from his chair onto the cold, hard floor, his groans filling the room as he curled into a ball.

"Gee, buddy," Conrad said, "don't you feel well?"

***

The whole thing took too long, and not only did Leon soil himself, he puked. Conrad almost missed the eyes going blank when Leon's flailing flipped him onto his stomach. Though it disgusted him, Conrad, who'd slipped on a pair of gloves, turned his victim over and kneeled on him, holding his face until life fled. When Leon finally lay still, Conrad rose, dumped his coffee down the sink, and washed and put away his mug.

He rushed up the short flight of stairs to Leon's office.

Bright sunlight streamed in through the floor-to-ceiling windows that provided an unobstructed view of the lush grounds and the glittering Niagara River backdrop. Almost every room in this house overlooked the Niagara River. Conrad seethed. This property was worth at least eight million. Soon it would be his—

well, his and Daphne's.

He'd already laid the groundwork. They'd dated twice. She hadn't allowed him to fuck her yet, but he'd get there. Once she was his, she'd fall in line. Stupid cow, using sex as a weapon, withholding it from him. He'd have to set her straight now she couldn't hide behind Leon.

With a shake of his head, he forced his attention back to the job at hand. Where was the laptop? Ah, there. The bag for it stood next to the desk. Leon had probably been working outside yesterday. His covered patio off the back of the house overlooked not just the pool, but the Niagara River. The deck even sported a television and wet bar.

Conrad snatched up the bag standing next to the desk and removed the laptop. As soon as it booted up, he logged on with the password he'd stolen from Leon. The trusting idiot. It'd been too easy. The moron had written it on a Post-it note and kept it right in his desk drawer where anyone could find it. Conrad had located it within seconds of nipping into the office on his way to the bathroom two weeks ago.

From the left pocket of his jeans, he retrieved a memory stick and stuck it into the first available slot. Now to find the files he wanted. This machine stored Leon's whole life. Conrad had asked him about backups, and Leon had replied that, sure, he backed everything up to the cloud before he shut down. But he'd saved all the original files on the laptop.

This included industry contact lists and works in progress—and one work in progress was a non-fiction book on online book marketing. The notes contained a wealth of strategies and secrets.

He found the folders he needed no problem, but security prevented him from accessing them. *Dammit.*

A glance at the time showed him hours remained before the housekeeper arrived, but he needed to return to his hotel room before room service showed up with breakfast. He opened the internet browser and checked the history to see if he could find the backup folder location. No joy on that front either. It, too, was password protected. Conrad copied the link for future reference.

Maybe Daphne had access and wasn't so careful about security. She always beta read for Leon, often the first person to read the completed work and provide feedback on it. Perhaps he'd provided her with copies of everything.

As Conrad powered down and tucked away the laptop, he scanned the room. His gaze landed on a smoky quartz rock, Leon's souvenir from an archaeological dig he'd participated in when researching for a novel. Yeah, he'd researched archaeologists for an erotica novel. Mister Self-Important wanted to be genuine.

Conrad snatched up the rock and stuck it in his pocket. *Mine. My trophy. My precious.* He snickered and headed to Daphne's office.

CHAPTER 2

Stately trees on either side of the peaceful country road screened the mansions behind them. Daphne Russel, driving a Mazda 3, approached the home she and her brother shared—a situation that must change soon.

She loved Leon, and the house was spacious enough, but she felt like a freeloader and wanted her own place. The last time she'd survived off the kindness of relatives was before she moved from her parents' place to attend university. That's why she worked as many hours as possible at a twenty-four seven diner in downtown Niagara Falls.

If she'd wanted more reasonable hours, she'd have found employment closer to home in Niagara-on-the-Lake. But then earning the money required to rent a decent place to live and move out would take months longer.

Since Warren, Daphne's ex-husband, worked only sporadically, she paid him support, which chafed. He insisted his band would hit the big time soon, but he'd said that for the last five years of their marriage. The cliché was akin to caricature—the wannabe rock star living off his woman and never catching the big break.

The groupies he'd slept with, when Daphne discovered their existence, pushed the marriage off the cliff on which it teetered. Did he think her an idiot? She refused to slave away at menial jobs so he could booze and carouse and sleep until noon every day.

But they'd sure had fun before and even, for a while, after they'd married. Warren knew how to have a good time. The

8

problem was, he didn't know how to get serious and didn't seem to care they were always broke. Music ruled his life, and, while she wanted to support his artistic pursuits, if he never treated it as a business, he'd never succeed.

She sighed in frustration. Lately, she constantly rehashed her life with Warren. Of course, she'd wanted to stand by her man. Daphne understood wanting to have a career in the arts. Her brother made a living as an author, and she received small revenues from sales of her novels. But it resulted from hard work and treating it as a business first.

"Love you. Love you. Love you," she muttered, and her tension eased. *Damn.* Thoughts of Warren had her repeating phrases. She'd gone a whole week without using the self-soothing technique.

How many times had Warren insisted he lived to write and play music? Yet he never promoted himself or the band. *Damn.* Here she was, back onto Warren. *Dammit, get out of my head.*

Thankfully, she'd arrived home. The rest of her stress released at the thought of the free evening ahead. The clock read only three o'clock. If he hadn't eaten yet, she'd pester Leon to stop working long enough to have dinner with her. They hadn't had a meal together in days.

Daphne spotted the police cars while halfway down the long, tree-lined driveway. The sun cast dappled shadows over the asphalt, the trees arching overhead reminiscent of a green tunnel. Ahead, on the roundabout by the huge fountain in the courtyard, sat two police cars, two unmarked cruisers, and an ambulance.

The blood froze in Daphne's veins, and her heart thudded against her chest. "Oh, God. Leon?"

For a selfish moment, she hoped Giselle Northrop, the housekeeper, needed the ambulance rather than her brother. Then guilt overwhelmed her, and she shoved the thought aside.

Daphne left the car in the driveway, almost forgetting to put it in park before jumping out, and rushed to the entrance.

The glass door of the porch and the ornate front doors stood propped open. A police officer positioned outside held up a hand before she reached the porch.

"I'm sorry, ma'am," he said, "but you can't enter."

"I live here. What happened? Where's Leon?" When he hesitated, she added, "My brother."

The cop, who looked younger than Daphne's thirty-four years, asked her to wait a moment and used a walkie-talkie to call into the house. "Detective Turner, the sister's here."

"What happened to Leon? Why is a detective here?"

"I'm sorry." His expression showed true sorrow. "Detective Turner will explain everything."

A tall man in a business suit appeared, and the officer introduced Detective Jacob Turner to Daphne. Barely registering the man's outthrust hand and grim expression, Daphne tried to push past him.

"I need to see my brother. Who's the ambulance for? Why do you need an ambulance?"

***

Jacob gripped her upper arms and held her still, assessing the woman standing before him. He recognized her brother's square jaw, but the doe-brown eyes and flowing black hair were all hers. The eyes held fear and worry.

"I'll explain, but first, please verify: you're Daphne Russel?" He eased the grip on her arms and then released them.

"Yes, yes. Let me in."

"I need to see identification." His voice was firm but kind.

Daphne dug into her purse and fished out her wallet. When she located her driver's license, she thrust it at his face.

"Mrs. Russel, I'm sorry. Leon died this morning. The death looked suspicious, so the homicide unit was called in."

The tech guys had reviewed video footage from the security cameras. The recordings showed a blonde woman on a bicycle approaching the house. For now, Jacob kept that to himself.

"Homicide?" The fear in her eyes turned to shock. "Who'd hurt Leon? You're mistaken. Please, let me in."

"When they've finished collecting evidence from the scene, you may enter."

"The scene?" Daphne's brows drew together, and she frowned, broadcasting confusion, puzzlement, more shock.

"The kitchen." Jacob hated this part of the job. Informing someone of a loved one's murder always affected him. For the sake of the victim's family, he must present a strong yet compassionate demeanor. Their lives would alter after he finished speaking to them. How he handled them influenced how they coped afterwards.

"Did he choke?" More denial.

Jacob shook his head. "Nothing's certain until they do the autopsy."

"Where's Giselle?" Daphne's voice broke and tears trickled from her eyes. She swiped them away.

"Home. She found your brother's body and called nine-one-one. I questioned and released her." Gently, Jacob pried the wallet from her hands and dropped it back in her purse.

"Why didn't you come and tell me at the restaurant?" Her tone was accusatory.

He stifled a retort and gentled his voice. "We were getting to that. First, we needed to secure the scene and interview the housekeeper."

"Let me see him. I need to verify it's him. What if she made a mistake? It might be someone else."

"Mrs. Northrop reported she's worked as a housekeeper for Leon for four years. She's certain it's him. I'm sorry." He took her by the arm. When he tried to steer her towards the driveway, she balked.

"Let me go to him." She gasped between sobs.

"I'm sorry, but the house is a crime scene. You can't enter. If you want to see him, you can call the coroner tomorrow and request a viewing." Jacob kept a light grip on her arm and spoke soothingly. "I must interview you, Mrs. Russel. Come with me. One step at a time, all right?"

Daphne struggled at first and tried to break free but when their gazes locked, she quieted. Her shoulders slumped.

"Okay," she whispered.

Jacob guided the wide-eyed woman to his car, a Ford Explorer. "You can help him best by answering my questions. First, do you want water?"

She nodded. "I'll get it."

He gave her kudos for trying and signalled to the officer standing at the front door. "Officer, please ask someone to get Mrs. Russel a glass of water. We'll be out here."

After that, she allowed him to ease her onto the back seat of the car. She sat primly at the edge of the seat, feet on the floor, hands folded in her lap, and head lowered. Jacob indicated she should slide over, and when she did, he sat beside her. He remained silent until the police officer returned.

The cop handed a tall glass filled with water to Jacob, who passed it over to Daphne. She sipped from it and then rested the glass on her thigh, clutching it one-handed to keep it steady. Jacob cleared his throat to attract her attention.

"What do you want to know?" She sounded weary.

He retrieved a digital recorder from his pocket. After turning it on, he rested it on the seat between them. "I'm recording this conversation."

When she gave a small nod, he stated the date and time, identified the interview participants, and then launched the first question. "You live here with your brother?"

"I already said so."

"I'm verifying for the record. This is difficult for you, Mrs. Russel, I know, but I need information if I'm to find who did this to Leon." Maybe using the victim's name would jar her into cooperating.

"Yes. Okay. I'm sorry." She heaved a sigh and, lifting her glass with a trembling hand, sipped water.

"When did you last see or speak to Leon?"

She rested the glass on her thigh. "Last night, before we went to bed. He was out all day—meetings about his book."

"Who did he meet?"

She frowned and her expression perked up as recollection dawned. "His agent. They had a dinner date."

"Date?" Jacob raised his brows.

Daphne's face clouded. "They're not romantically involved. She's his agent. It's business."

"Just trying to understand, ma'am."

"Oh, for God's sake. Call me Daphne. I'm not married anymore and am changing the last name. And ma'am makes me sound like an old lady." As soon as the words were out, she clapped a hand over her mouth. Hurriedly, she said, "Sorry. Please, I didn't mean to be so harsh."

"It's okay. Daphne." He smiled, hoping to ease her guilt and fear. "Let's take this one question at a time, okay?"

She nodded. "Can I ask you something?"

"Sure." He'd even try to answer truthfully.

"Why are you convinced someone mur—someone hurt Leon?"

Daphne hadn't been able to say the word. So much denial.

She'd have to get past it to deal with this. Jacob made a mental note to send a grief counsellor her way.

"There's evidence. The autopsy will verify, but the divisional detective deemed it suspicious enough to call in homicide."

"So you don't know for sure?" Her voice held hope, and he hated to squash it.

"I know enough to take this investigation seriously."

"Will you catch whoever did this?"

"I won't stop looking until I do." That wasn't a definite yes or no, but he could at least assure her the case wouldn't close until they caught someone. A time might come, if the trail grew cold, when he'd have to deprioritize it, but he'd never stop hunting.

Daphne swallowed and braced herself, her body going rigid.

"How can I help?" She whispered the words, but he heard them. He hoped the recorder caught them.

"You said you saw Leon yesterday evening. How did he seem?"

"A little tired but okay. Pleased. They're negotiating movie rights for his first novel. He said talks are going well." Her eyes welled up then, but the tears didn't fall. She retrieved a package of tissues from her purse.

Jacob waited to speak while she settled. "He has a good relationship with his agent?"

"Yes!" Anger flared in the word, and she made a visible effort to calm herself. "Yes," she repeated, her voice under control. "He likes her. They work well together. She loves his work—that's why she represents him."

"So no animosity? No friction?"

She shook her head. "As far as I know, their partnership thrived. Detective, his books made her rich. She has no reason to complain."

"He seemed in good health when you spoke to him?"

"Yes."

"What time did he get home?"

"Nine?"

"Are you asking?" He shifted in his seat, angling his body towards her.

"I'm not positive what time he arrived home."

"What were you doing at the time?"

"Getting ready for bed. I have the early shift this week and needed to go to sleep."

"What time did you leave for work?"

"Five thirty."

"Did you see him at all, hear from him at all, this morning?"

"No. You asked me when I last saw him. I told you. Last night. Then not again. Oh, God, never again." Her breath hitched on that last bit, but she continued. "I never spoke to him either. When I left this morning, the house was quiet, the kitchen empty. I assumed he was in bed, sleeping. Leon's not an early riser, so Giselle doesn't come in until the afternoon."

Daphne stopped speaking, horror dawning on her face. "She found him when she got here? Already dead?"

Before Jacob could respond, a commotion from the doorway had him rising to investigate. He tossed a glance back at Daphne. "Wait there."

But she'd heard the voices and climbed from the car. "No. It's Warren, my ex."

Jacob held up a hand, halting her. He kept his voice low and firm but kind and gentle. "Wait, Daphne. You can't speak to him yet."

She paled; her body trembled. Anger flitted across her face, but to Jacob's relief, she returned to the back seat of the vehicle. He rushed to the front entrance where a long, lanky man with shaggy, brown hair struggled to push past the officer on sentry duty.

"Mr. Russel. What brings you here?"

CHAPTER 3

"Where's Daphne? Where's Leon?" Warren sounded panicked.

"Answer my question first."

"Personal business. With my wife."

"She didn't mention expecting you."

Warren shrugged. "She wasn't, exactly."

"So, exactly, why did you come?"

"To ask for an advance on the support payment." His eyes shifted so his gaze focused beyond Jacob and down the front steps.

"Daphne?"

Jacob stepped closer to Warren. "You'll see her in a moment." He leaned into the open front door and called to the woman who hovered near the kitchen entrance down the hall. "Officer, make sure Mr. Russel stays outside but doesn't leave."

The police officer nodded and moved to Warren's side, motioning with her arm. "This way, sir."

"I want to talk to Daphne."

Jacob shook his head. "Later. When I'm done talking to her, I'll want to talk to you."

This day grew longer by the moment. The sound of a vehicle approaching caught his attention. A news van pulled up to the house.

"Shut the doors," he said to the sentry. "No one else in or out unless I say so."

***

Warren's arrival had unnerved Daphne. Why was he here? He shouldn't be here. Money. Must be. He never came around unless he needed money. Too often, he darkened her doorstep with his hand out.

I guess he's due. Typically, he pestered her at the beginning of the month and, oh, look, it was the beginning of the month. He'd likely burned through all his funds and wanted an advance on the support payment.

Why did it have to be today? Now? Didn't she have enough to deal with?

"Love you. Love you. Love you." *No, don't. Not while the cops are around. They'll think you're crazy.* She buried her face in her hands.

Hearing footsteps on the driveway, she shifted her gaze to verify who approached. She'd been grateful when the detective intervened, delaying the inevitable confrontation with Warren. Now, a frisson of fear had her holding her breath. If Warren confronted her, she'd break down. The first person she talked to about Leon's death shouldn't be her ex.

When Jacob Turner strode to the car, she exhaled in relief.

"Ready to continue?" he asked.

"Does it matter?" The words shot out before she could stop them. "Again, I'm sorry. I want this to not be real. It's impossible."

Her heart hurt, and it would hurt until the day she died. Even if they arrested someone for it, she'd always carry this ache with her.

"I'm sorry, Mrs.—Daphne. I'll try to make it quick. In the meantime, can we notify someone you can stay with?"

She contemplated. Robin Carson and Beth Holmes were her closest friends, but Robin hated to leave her house. Beth ran a bed and breakfast. She'd have difficulty stepping away, but one of her staff might take over for a few hours. Daphne didn't want to drive herself. Her whole body shook. She couldn't focus, couldn't concentrate.

"Yes. Elizabeth Holmes." *Oh, Beth*, she thought. *Please come and get me.*

***

Jacob took Beth's contact information from Daphne and assigned an officer to call her. One news van would become multiple vans—maybe even a helicopter. Leon Patterson had been a big-name author. The media would go crazy over his death. They'd overrun this house. He didn't envy Daphne the ordeal she'd endure over the coming weeks.

"All right," he said, distracting her as emergency personnel loaded the bagged body into the ambulance, two officers keeping the reporters at bay. "Let's pick up where we left off."

By the time Jacob finished his interview with Daphne, her ex, and Beth Holmes, his watch read seven o'clock. He had a long list of follow-up names from the witnesses. Most were friends and family, and others were colleagues or work associates of Leon's.

He'd also supervised Daphne packing a few items in an overnight bag to take to her friend's place. The police would spend days collecting evidence from the house. Banishment from her home on top of her brother's murder distressed her—you didn't need to be an empath to sense it—but he couldn't help it. Sometimes the tiniest item held the best clue.

First, though, he'd escorted her around the house to see if anything was missing. From this walk-through, he ruled out robbery as a motive. She'd only reported one item stolen: a rock made of smoky quartz that had sat on Leon's desk. Jacob didn't comment on it, but the killer had taken it as a souvenir. Nothing else seemed to be missing.

The worst part of the walk-through had been the kitchen. Daphne had fallen apart at the sight of blood and bodily fluids on the kitchen floor. The rest of the house appeared untouched though Daphne had pointed out a number of items shifted out of place. Whatever had been moved, Jacob flagged for the forensics team.

Leon's laptop sat zipped up in its bag. Even so, they'd confiscated it as well as Daphne's—under vocal protest from its owner. She'd saved a novel in progress on it and didn't want him to take off with her work. He refused to feel guilty over it. If she didn't back up her stuff to the cloud, it wasn't his fault.

Sure, she'd hate him forever, but he promised her they'd return it as soon as they'd inspected it. From the road, he contacted the tech geek who'd be working on it and made him promise to alert Jacob when they'd finished with the laptop. That was the best he could do for her. He then remembered he'd wanted to send the grief counsellor her way and left a message on the woman's voice mail with Daphne's contact info.

All loose ends tied up for the night, Jacob headed home to his apartment in St. Catharines, a city southwest of Niagara-on-the-Lake. He'd grown up there and preferred the anonymity of city life to small-town living. Each day, he commuted to the Niagara Region Police Station, which also covered the town of Niagara-on-the-Lake. Calls to investigate a homicide in the little town came infrequently, and this one would be high profile.

When he arrived home, he checked the mail compartment for his unit and retrieved two bills and three flyers. The sun had set—in August, the days grew noticeably shorter. The air had chilled to what was, for him, a comfortable fifteen Celsius. He rode the elevator to the third floor and headed for the shower before contemplating food.

Although he always covered up his hands and shoes at a crime scene—as per regulations—his clothes weren't protected. He felt compelled to throw everything he'd worn into the laundry and have a shower the moment he returned home. It meant an extra trip to the dry cleaner's tomorrow for the suit, but so be it.

His routine never varied. The upside to having no one waiting for him was the freedom to come and go. The downside? Wasn't one as far as he could see. No one messed with his stuff. If he wanted to eat at the sink, no one told him not to. Nothing flowery or fluffy anywhere in the place.

After he'd showered and dressed in a T-shirt and jeans, Jacob fixed himself a sandwich. To prove a point, he ate it at the sink while he checked messages. He'd screened his calls while at the Patterson residence and needed to catch up.

The first message was from his mother. A family gathering on Labour Day weekend at his parents' place. He'd go, but it'd be hell without a date. As an only child, he was his mother's last best hope for a grandchild. She pressured him to procreate, and he didn't have a steady girlfriend.

The second message was from Stacy, a woman he'd dated twice. As soon as he heard her voice, he regretted giving her his number. She seemed nice enough but spent a great deal of time talking about her best friend who'd just married and had a baby. Stacy wanted to settle down. He shivered at the thought.

Messages completed, Jacob turned off his phone.

His sandwich consumed, he grabbed a beer from the fridge and strolled into the living room to turn on the television. He flipped to the news and waited. The media would be all over the Patterson story by now. They'd tried to get a statement from him as he left the house, but he'd given them a firm "no comment."

He'd have to give them an official statement sometime soon, but he wanted to wait until he uncovered information helpful to the case. If he found a witness who saw a suspicious car in the area or a piece of useful video footage from the cameras, he'd release the information. Then the media would aid the investigation while getting the ratings bump for which they always scrabbled.

An image of Leon Patterson appeared on the screen, and Jacob turned up the sound. The newscaster, a classy brunette with a strong voice, announced Patterson's death. She focused on the suspicious nature of it and the fact that the police had spent the entire day at the house and still had it cordoned off.

A clip ran, showing Jacob exiting the house and shaking his head at the reporters swarming him. Then they cut to another clip, this time of Warren getting into his car. Before he pulled out, he also shouted "no comment" at the reporters.

Next came Beth and Daphne. The two women had left before Jacob, but the news played this clip last for a reason. To Jacob's irritation, Daphne stopped and appeared ready to spill her heart out. *Shit.* He should have been more emphatic when he'd told her not to talk to the media.

A sinking feeling in his gut, he turned the sound up further.

"The detective told me not to discuss the investigation, so I won't. But thank you for taking an interest in what happened." She paused and stared sadly at the reporters and into the camera.

They're eating it up. A gorgeous woman, grief-stricken. The camera loves her. She looked beautiful. Beautiful and vulnerable. He should have walked her to her vehicle. *Shit.*

Bad enough he'd refused her request to stay until the investigators left so she could lock up the house herself. Jacob sensed fanaticism in her routines. He'd promised her repeatedly they'd secure the doors before they quit for the night.

One reporter, a guy with slick-backed hair and an expensive suit, jammed a microphone into Daphne's face. "Mrs. Russel, what can you tell us about your brother's death? How did he die?"

"I don't know. They wouldn't tell me."

"What happened when you went inside? Did you see Leon?"

She shook her head and pressed her hands to her face. When she dropped them, she said, "They wouldn't let me."

Beth whispered in her ear then, and Daphne said, "Okay. You're right." She turned her gaze back to the reporter. "I'm sorry. We need to go."

"Are you leaving for the night because the police are still in the house?"

"Yes. I have to go. Sorry." She truly looked sorry.

Jacob cursed. At least Beth had cut the interview short. God knew what Daphne would've divulged to the press without meaning to. No more interviews for her. If necessary, he'd lock her up. He took a swig of beer and tried to release the tension that had built up.

Tomorrow promised to be another long day. He'd better go to bed. But first, he'd give Daphne a call and tell her to stop talking to the press or she'd answer to him.

CHAPTER 4

"Here, sweetie." Beth, a perky blonde, held a rocks glass out to Daphne, who accepted it gratefully.

"Thanks." She sipped the amber liquid. Typically, she avoided hard liquor, but she'd make an exception this time. After all, you didn't deal with murder every day.

Daphne couldn't sleep though it was already past eleven o'clock at night. Beth, bless her heart, understood and stayed up to keep her company. Daphne spent most of the evening calling friends and relatives to inform them of Leon's death before they heard it on the news. As the night wore away, the chances of doing so became more remote.

Her job became easier then. No longer forced to tell the horrifying story from the beginning, she simply accepted condolences and received solace. After Daphne retired the phone for the night, Beth suggested using the hot tub to ease tension.

The two women sat in the main house's sunroom by the indoor lap pool that doubled as a hot tub. Both wore bathing suits though they hadn't yet entered the water. So far, the only tension-easing tool Daphne had used was alcohol.

"Thank you for letting me stay here." Daphne tossed back the drink. She set the empty rocks glass on a coaster on the white wicker coffee table in front of her.

"Take it easy. That's your second drink." Beth, a teetotaler, laid a manicured hand with shiny pink nail polish on the fingernails over Daphne's. "Let's go in the hot tub before you get drunk."

Daphne flinched.

Beth's eyes grew large. "I'm sorry. I didn't mean it."

"Yeah, you did." Daphne gave Beth a contrite smile. "And you're right. I have to take a break, or I'll end up with my head in the toilet."

"Not a nice picture," Beth agreed.

They rose and slipped into the heated water. When they'd settled into their seats, Daphne said, "Work gave me the week off, which helps, but I don't know when I'll have permission to return to the house."

"You can stay here as long as you need."

"Thank you." After a pause, Daphne said, "Whoever killed Leon searched through my things."

"How do you know? You said nothing was taken?"

"Things were moved around."

Beth smiled. "You'd know."

She did. For Daphne, everything must have a place, and, when not in use, everything must sit in its exact spot. Otherwise, she became agitated until she corrected it even if it had shifted only a millimetre.

"Did you tell the police?"

"Yes, but then they removed everything I indicated had been touched. They took half the stuff in my room." Daphne huffed out a breath in frustration. "I'll never get everything back in order."

"It'll be okay. You'll be okay." Beth eased out into the water and floated on her back. Her curvy torso breached the surface; her hair floated like golden seaweed around her head. If it weren't for her two shapely legs, Daphne would've sworn she watched a mermaid.

At the tender age of twenty-seven, Beth was already in her second career and striving for a third. As a teen, she'd modelled and had succeeded enough to buy the bed and breakfast at twenty-three. While the reason Beth had quit modelling remained a mystery, rumours speculated it had something to do with her mother's death around that time.

A private person, Beth was even more secretive about the circumstances surrounding her mother's death. She'd died in bed of an overdose of painkillers, and Daphne suspected the woman had killed herself. After that, Beth had gained weight and experienced sleep problems. Add in Robin's fear of leaving the house by herself and Daphne's obsessive-compulsive disorder and you had quite a neuroses cocktail between the three of them.

At the thought of Robin, Daphne said, "How did Robin react when you told her?"

Beth drew her legs down and swam back to her seat next to Daphne. "Devastated, of course."

"Is she okay?"

"No. It's one more death piled on top of what happened to her husband. This blind-sided her."

Daphne fell silent. Poor Robin. She'd lost her husband three years ago. Losing Leon, who she cared for more than she'd let on, would throw her whole life into chaos again.

Beth sighed. "She refused to come over tonight even though I told her we'd come pick her up. I don't know what we'll do if she refuses to leave the house at all after this."

The two women exchanged knowing glances.

"I'd like another drink," Daphne said.

***

The subject of Beth and Daphne's conversation lay awake in bed. Robin tossed and turned, wishing she had the courage to call a babysitter for her two kids and join Daphne at Beth's. Her friends needed her, and she was too terrified to go out.

Frustrated from trying to force sleep, Robin rose and strolled to the bedroom window. She pressed her hands against the cool pane. That and a screen separated her from the outside world. She unlocked the window and raised it so she could touch the screen. Eyes closed, she imagined herself striding confidently to the car and driving to Beth's or to the park with the kids the way they used to when Martin was alive.

Back then, summer meant hiking as a family in the provincial parks or trips to Niagara Falls. Sometimes, she and Martin left the kids with a sitter and rode bicycles to the different wineries nearby for tours. She used to love having dinner with him in a never-tried estate restaurant. He'd take photos of the wines they discovered together, and she'd print the pictures up at home and add them to their scrapbook.

But Martin had died, mowed down by a distracted driver who'd thought texting more important than a man's life. Robin witnessed the whole thing while she waited outside their favourite Thai restaurant. Her heart hurt whenever she recalled his last words to her, said flippantly as she stepped from their car so he could find a parking space: "Wait there. I'll be right back."

He would've been right back.

If only.

If only they hadn't been late leaving the house so Robin could run back inside for her purse and to give the kids one last goodbye kiss while she was at it.

If only the man who'd been texting hadn't headed home from the office just before Martin found his parking spot. It'd been a sweet spot, close to the restaurant. Yes, if only he'd had to walk a little farther, Martin wouldn't have been in that place at that time.

Robin would still have her life, her love.

The fear hadn't gripped her immediately. It snuck up on her, creeping like a thief.

The first panic attack happened at the grocery store. She'd been standing in line with her cereal and bread and milk when her heart trip-hammered. Cold sweat streamed down her back and soaked her blouse. She opened her mouth, taking gulps of air, but couldn't breathe. Her mind raced.

A sudden urge to pee hit her. What if she peed herself in the supermarket? What if she fainted? Dizziness escalated the fear, and Robin dropped everything on the counter and raced to her car. After a heart-pounding fifteen minutes, she drove home and rarely left the house by herself since.

She'd tried many times over the last three years to go out on her own. Three times, she'd made it to the car and then out onto the road. Then the shaking started and the panic and fear hit, and Robin returned the car to the garage and went back inside. As long as she stayed on her property, she held anxiety at bay.

Her children acclimated to the new reality. They stopped asking her to drive them anywhere, and Robin shopped online. Clients accepted virtual meetings—she did exceptional work, and software and web developers often worked remotely.

Wasn't technology wonderful? An agoraphobic's best friend.

Neighbours sympathized, and the closest ones chauffeured her kids when they needed it, or Robin called a cab. Thank God, she lacked pride. But she died a little every time one of her kids stepped into someone else's car.

Six months ago, Beth and Daphne had held an intervention for Robin. They insisted she see a therapist. For her friends, for herself, for her kids, she'd agreed to the demand. As a result, she could leave the house when accompanied by another person. She improved, slowly, painfully, day by day. After Leon's death, she feared the shock would make her backslide.

She didn't want to return to living with constant anxiety and fear—refused to. That he'd died in his home—was murdered in his home—compounded her fears. Home wasn't only where the heart was; it was where safety lived.

Guilt washed over her when she realized she'd made this about herself.

Leon. Oh, God. They'd developed a closeness she'd only ever experienced with Martin. Leon wanted her to work with him on the non-fiction book he planned to write. Flattered, she'd accepted his offer, which included a hefty advance from his publisher.

She didn't understand why he'd chosen her even over his sister. Robin had never published a book, neither fiction nor non-fiction. Sure, she'd published articles in tech journals and wrote a regular column in an online tech magazine, but the two novels she'd written she'd tucked away. Until Leon. He'd prodded her to send them to his agent, who'd promptly sold them to his publisher.

What did it say about her psyche that she feared to release her work to the outside world as much as she feared to go out in it herself? What did it say about her psyche that she feared every man she fell in love with would die?

The opposite of love is fear. She'd heard that once and hadn't agreed. The opposite of love was hate, wasn't it? Now, she thought perhaps whoever had said it was a genius. Didn't fear give birth to everything evil?

Robin closed the window and meandered from her bedroom to the living room where she'd set up her desk. The tiny bungalow contained only three bedrooms and one bathroom, so Robin worked with the space available. The basement, a crawl space, afforded no additional useable room. At least they had an eat-in kitchen, but she couldn't invite more than three people at a time for dinner.

Her cell phone buzzed, alerting her to an incoming text. She glanced at the clock. One o'clock. Who'd be texting at this time of night? Not all her clients were local, but they were in the same time zone, so it couldn't be business.

She snatched her phone from the desk and read the message: *Are you awake?*

The sender was Conrad Barnes.

CHAPTER 5

Why would Conrad text her in the middle of the night? Robin stared at the message, stumped. Sure, they saw each other every month at the writers' group meeting in the local café, but he wasn't a close friend.

After a moment, she responded: *What's up?*

Can't sleep. Thinking about Leon.

Of course. Poor Conrad. He'd been close to Leon. If not for Leon, Conrad wouldn't be so far along on the publishing trail. Leon had helped, encouraged, and supported them all. The group consisted of women and only a handful of men, most of them married. As the only two single guys, Leon and Conrad had grown chummy.

God, learning of Leon's death must have destroyed Conrad. He'd have known how close she and Leon were growing and probably wanted her help to cope with this. She'd let down Beth and Daphne already. Maybe she could comfort Conrad.

She sent him another text: *Me too. You okay?*

Not so much. Want company?

It's late. Kids asleep. Where are you?

Home. Left the convention when I heard. Can't believe it.

Me either. Poor Daphne. Tears she'd tried to hold back escaped her eyes. She swiped at them but why bother? No one could see the tears. Conrad wouldn't know.

He didn't reply for a few moments, and then she got: *How is she? Tried to call but she didn't reply. Sent messages, too.*

27

She's at Beth's.

Tried Beth. Were you there?

No. She wasn't obligated to explain why.

When you talk to her, tell her to call me.

He meant Daphne, not Beth. He'd pursued Daphne from the moment she'd announced her marriage had collapsed, but she hadn't reciprocated his feelings. Too preoccupied with work and getting her ex out of her life, Daphne remained aloof.

This explained why he texted Robin so late. Conrad wanted things to happen instantly. If he'd tried to contact Daphne, and she hadn't responded, he'd do everything to find out why.

Sure. In the morning. Goodnight. Tired of texting, she turned off the phone rather than wait for a response.

He's crazy about her, Robin thought. Would anyone get crazy about her again? With a sigh, she concluded she didn't need the drama and hoped not. She set her phone back on the desk and returned to bed.

***

Startled out of sleep by the realization she'd slept, Daphne sat up in bed as grief, loss, and worry flooded through her. Worry won the toss and all the anxious thoughts from the night before dominated even as tears of grief flowed freely.

A knot in her stomach, she snatched a tissue from the box on the night table and stumbled into the bathroom. She'd have to pull herself together and do whatever needed to be done. She stemmed the flow of tears and grabbed her toothbrush.

Beth planned to take the next few days off and assured Daphne that Robin would too. They'd help arrange Leon's funeral. Daphne depended on her friends for emotional support. Her parents lived too far away, across Canada in British Columbia. They couldn't have moved any farther away without leaving the country if they tried. When she'd called them last night, her dad had reacted with stoicism, and her mother had fallen to pieces.

At the recollection, tears flowed and Daphne sobbed uncontrollably, choking a little as she aspirated toothpaste. She brushed her teeth twice and rinsed her mouth three times.

Her parents would be on the first flight out of Vancouver the day after tomorrow, needing time to put their affairs in order first.

A copy of their itinerary probably sat in her inbox. God, what else waited for her? She hadn't checked voice mail, email, or text messages since she'd hung up from her folks after getting to Beth's.

It seemed as if all of Canada wanted to contact her. Most of the calls came from reporters—even a bunch from the States. She refused to discuss Leon's death with strangers. She'd turned off the phone and allowed her friend to stand in for her mother—and she desperately needed her mother.

This happens when you move away from your kids. You can't help them in a crisis. She pulled on first her left sock and then her right. Next, she removed her nightgown and dressed, finishing the routine by sitting on the bed to pull her jeans onto both legs at the same time.

In her head, her refrain became "she puts her pants on one leg at a time like everyone else. No, she doesn't." When she caught herself doing it, she huffed out a breath in frustration and promised to book an appointment with her therapist. She'd all but eliminated the tension-soothing, repetitive self-talk before Leon died. Now it returned full throttle.

"I won't let it. I won't let it. I won't let it," she muttered and then cursed herself for doing it.

She didn't begrudge Mom and Dad their freedom. Honestly, she told herself, she didn't. That's not what wound her nerves so tight she backslid in her healing. After all, she and Leon were both adults and could take care of themselves. Oh, but Leon couldn't. She couldn't. He was dead; she was divorced.

Why did she act so immature? Didn't her parents have the right to do what they wanted with their lives?

Oh, God, Mom, Dad, why did that have to involve moving to British Columbia? For what? To open a restaurant? Why not do that here? She knew the answer though not because they'd explained it to her.

Her mother had always longed to return to the place where she'd grown up, where much of her family still lived. She'd sacrificed to settle where her husband's family lived when they got married, but her heart always belonged to the west.

"Love you. Love you. Love you," Daphne muttered. "I do. I do. I do."

***

Twenty minutes later, Daphne entered the kitchen where the scent of freshly brewed coffee greeted her. Beth leaned against the counter by the sink, sipping from a mug.

"Hi, sweetie," Beth said. "Did you sleep?"

"Some. How long have you been awake?" Daphne glanced at the time. Already eight o'clock. "I guess I slept more than I thought."

Beth gave her a reassuring smile. "I woke early to verify the B and B kitchen started up okay. The cook has things under control."

"I'm sorry, Beth." Daphne burst into tears, unable to help herself.

"What happened?" At the fear in Beth's voice, Daphne waved a hand in negation and shook her head.

"No, nothing else happened. I'm sorry you must take time off to babysit me." Her tear-filled gaze met her friend's startled one. "You don't have to."

Beth set her mug on the counter and rushed to Daphne's side. "Oh, honey, of course, I'll take time off. This isn't your fault. Whoever hurt Leon put us in this situation."

Daphne continued to sob, shoulders shaking. "You don't understand. Leon left everything to me."

"What?"

"He left me everything. Life insurance, too. A lot. Beth, I told him not to buy the policy, but he did. How can I deal with this? The cops will think ..."

Beth squeezed and then released her. "No, they won't."

"Yes, they will. Most murders are committed by family or friends, for greed or jealousy."

Beth sighed. "Writers do way too much research on murder and have overactive imaginations. Naturally, your mind would go there."

"It makes sense. Why didn't Turner arrest me yesterday?" she asked.

"Did you do it?"

Daphne's jaw dropped and her eyes widened. "How can you say that?"

"I didn't say it. You're talking crazy, so I'm asking: did you do it?"

"No. You know I didn't."

"How should I know? Can you prove it? Talk me through it. Tell me what you'll tell the police."

Daphne dropped to the floor. "Oh, God, Beth, he was alive when I left him. At least, I assume so, because Giselle found him in the kitchen, and when I left for work, it was empty. But if the police find no evidence someone else entered the house, I'm the one they'll blame."

CHAPTER 6

"Don't be ridiculous." Beth held out a hand and helped Daphne regain her feet. "Have a coffee. You'll feel better."

"I'll never feel better. Oh, God, I'm so selfish. Leon's dead and all I can think about is how it affects me."

"You're not selfish. Aside from Leon, you're affected the most." Beth guided Daphne to a chair at the kitchen table, easing the distraught woman into one facing the garden. "Sit, and I'll get your coffee and breakfast."

"I can't eat." Daphne sounded petulant.

"But you must." Beth removed a mug from the cupboard and poured coffee into it. She doctored it with cream and sugar and set it before Daphne.

"Drink."

Daphne grimaced but picked up the mug and sipped.

"Thank you," she whispered. "I'm so sorry. I'll try not to fall apart anymore."

"Relax. I understand." Beth's eyes welled up, and she bit her lip. More tears wouldn't help Daphne. "I've got muffins made and yogurt and fruit. That's not too much for you?" Beth didn't wait for a reply but collected everything from the cupboards and fridge and set them on the table.

"We'll eat," she told a silent Daphne, "and then we'll visit Robin. I've already spoken to her."

"She okay?"

"As well as can be expected, I guess. Her parents picked up the

32

kids and will keep them for the next five days so she can focus on you." Beth didn't mention Conrad had texted Robin during the night. Daphne didn't need to add him to her worries. Beth didn't like how he pursued Daphne even when she'd made it clear she wasn't interested in a romantic relationship. Two casual dates and the guy acted as if he owned her.

"That's so sweet." Daphne placed a raspberry muffin on her plate and scooped vanilla yogurt and fruit salad next to it. "This looks wonderful. Thank you. Suddenly, I'm starving."

When she put none of it in her mouth but only stared at it, Beth at first ignored her. She topped up their coffees and added cream and sugar to both. Then she settled herself in a chair across from Daphne and filled her own plate with food. Daphne still hadn't made a move to eat anything. Finally, Beth had enough.

"Can I bring you anything else?" She tried to keep her tone light.

"If I go to jail, make sure my parents know I didn't do it."

"You won't go to jail." Beth tried not to snap at her, but this fatalistic attitude grated on her nerves. Of course, Daphne hadn't killed her brother. She'd rather go broke than do anything to harm him. Wouldn't she?

Frustrated that doubts crept in, Beth put a hand over Daphne's and, forcing confidence into her voice, said, "Eat. Keep up your strength, and it'll help clear your head. You'll see you worried for no reason."

Daphne had a tendency to worry about everything. Surely, this too was all in her head. Beth speared a strawberry and stuck it in her mouth. She'd better get food in her, too. Who knew what today would bring?

***

In the Niagara Region Police Station, Jacob Turner accessed the network from his computer. He clicked on the file the tech guru had left for him of the surveillance footage from Leon Patterson's home. Motion activated all the cameras on the property, and the ones on the driveway and facing the front of the house had caught activity from the previous morning.

He accessed the first file, and the video played. The footage showed Daphne leaving for work. The time stamp read five thirty-two in the morning. She'd told him the truth about what time she'd left. Jacob watched her walk to the garage, enter, and then drive out three minutes later. The other cameras tracked her journey down the long driveway.

As he viewed the video, he tried to notice any agitation or display of emotion in her gait. She seemed normal—a regular workday where she started a long shift early. Daphne hadn't hurried out of the house, but she hadn't strolled either. Her stride was confident, purposeful. She carried a bag slung over her shoulder, and she wore the same clothes she'd worn home.

Jacob moved to the next clip. This one showed a woman, a backpack strapped to her back, riding a bicycle. The probable killer. He followed her progress up the driveway and to the garage where she parked the bike. Her face remained tilted down, avoiding the cameras. The time stamp said five forty-eight.

He paused the video and pulled up the image of Leon's agent. The woman's blonde hair hung chin-level in a sleek, professional style; the suspect's hair cascaded halfway down her back.

Wait. Beth Holmes's hair was about that length and colour. Jacob studied the image. This could be her, but a defence lawyer would argue it could be any woman with long, blonde hair. The suspect kept her face down, but the hair certainly looked similar. Would Beth have been stupid enough to ride up to Patterson's house, kill him, and then return to comfort the sister?

Stupid? Or clever? He zoomed in on the hands. The suspect wore gloves. Beth had sported pink nail polish on her fingernails when she'd picked up Daphne. She could have applied it after the murder, but it didn't matter, anyway. Gloves hid her fingers.

Jacob rolled the footage and tracked the suspect he forced himself not to refer to as Beth to the entrance. She cast a side glance towards the Niagara River, slightly changing the angle of her face but still not exposing it. After a moment, she slipped into the front entryway. As soon as she stepped inside and the glass door closed, the camera stopped rolling after thirty seconds of inactivity.

If the universe were kind, Jacob would find a better shot of her when she came back outside, but he didn't hold out much hope. She'd been careful to keep her face down. Beth was tall. The person on the video was tall.

His lips pursed as he contemplated. He'd enlist a forensic analyst to help him figure out the exact height. If it matched Beth

Holmes, he'd be one step closer to proving she'd done it.

Jacob went rigid in his chair as a horrifying thought popped into his head. He'd sent Daphne home with Beth.

Okay, calm down. You don't know it's her on the video. But he didn't know it wasn't. He leaned closer to the monitor and ran the next sequence.

The camera rolled again when the suspect exited the glass door of the front entrance. As he watched her slip outside and walk calmly to her bike, the bulky sweater caught his focus.

Much like today, the previous day had been warm and humid. She must have been dripping with sweat, especially after riding the bike in it. Jacob shook his head. No. She'd have stowed the sweater and the gloves in the backpack to put on before she hit the row of cameras on the driveway. On such a warm day, a bulky sweater would've attracted attention.

The sweater covered up her body, gave them less to work with. It gave her a sturdy appearance. Beth was good and solid—a curvy woman. Jacob examined the pants the suspect wore. They were also big and bulky. Sweatpants. Nothing body hugging. The tech people could do something with this, though—identify a brand name, for instance.

They should examine the bike, too. He didn't know bike brands, but if the techs identified it, they might trace it. That information he could give to the media to get people on the lookout for the bike. She may have been able to hide her face, but she couldn't hide the bike. Dark blue, it didn't have a crossbar, making it a woman's bike.

It'd rained the night before, too. The driveway was paved, but the shoulder of the road in front of Leon's house was dirt. They might have picked up a tire impression at the top of the driveway.

Jacob grabbed the phone and called forensics.

***

Satisfied the investigative team would search for bike tire impressions and the lab would keep an eye out for blonde hairs, Jacob retrieved a digital recorder from his briefcase. He queued up the interview he'd done with Beth Holmes in his car before he let the women leave.

His voice floated up from the speaker. "Interview by Detective

Jacob Turner with Elizabeth Rachel Holmes, Monday, August 8, 2017, at seventeen hundred hours. Ms. Holmes, how do you know Leon Patterson?"

"We're colleagues. He's the organizer of the writers' group I belong to. His sister, Daphne, and I are friends." No tremor affected her voice, but her eyes had grown to deer-in-the-headlights size. Shock? Or guilt?

"When did you last hear from Leon?"

"Not since the last writers' group meeting at the coffee shop."

"When was that?"

"First Thursday of the month, so last Thursday."

"Where?"

"Coffee shop in town."

"Which one?"

"Andrew's Books and Café."

"I know it. Never been in." As he listened to the conversation, he made a note to visit the owner.

"How did Leon seem then?"

"Great. Does amazing with his books. Gets great reviews, goes on tours. He landed a large publishing contract."

"Know anyone who'd want to harm him?"

The pause here was substantial. She'd appeared to be wracking her brains on this one. When she finally answered, she said, "Not anyone who'd want him dead. None of our friends. But he's a celebrity and on social media. What if he has a crazed fan or someone's jealous of his success?"

"Did he receive any threats?"

"If he did, he never told me. Detective, I'm not the closest one to Leon. We were friends because of Daphne. Robin Carson knows him better, and they worked together on his recent book."

"What do you do, Ms. Holmes? You a full-time writer?"

She laughed. "No. I have two novels out and a non-fiction book. The non-fiction one sells a decent amount but writing is a sideline. I own a bed and breakfast near the centre of town. Windermere?"

"Oh, yes, I've driven past it. You work there?"

"I live there. In the main house. My father lives in the in-law suite, in a separate building. Another building has eight rental rooms. It keeps me busy from dawn to dusk."

Her way of informing him she had an alibi?

36

"When do you start your day?"

"Early. Most of the time, I'm in the kitchen by six in the morning, making sure breakfast preparations are underway. I always help with cooking and serving. Helps me keep costs down."

"Were you there this morning?"

"Yes." No hesitation and an emphatic response. Well, he'd verify her presence in the B and B kitchen on the morning in question.

When he asked her for a list of the writers' group members, she suggested he get it from Daphne, who co-organized the group with Leon. The interview ended then when Daphne asked if they could leave.

But Jacob wasn't finished questioning Beth Holmes—not by a long shot. If she had anything to do with Leon Patterson's death, Jacob would pry it from her. First, he needed physical proof. If only the autopsy results were available. The autopsy would be completed soon, but receiving the results required time. In the meantime, the killer ran free. What if Leon wasn't her only target?

Jacob called Shayla, the head of the tech department.

"What do you need, Jake?"

He smiled. She'd recognized his phone number on the call display. "Your exceptional graphics skills. Anyone available who can manipulate video?"

"Yeah, Trey."

"Tell him I'm sending him a link to a file. Have him work on enhancing anything in it that might identify the blonde on the recording."

When Shayla gave him the okay, he disconnected the call and sent the link. While Trey worked on the video, Jacob decided to pay Robin Carson a visit. Perhaps she'd lead him closer to identifying Beth Holmes as the culprit.

CHAPTER 7

When Jacob pulled up to Robin's house, he found the driveway blocked by Beth's car, so he parked on the road in front of the neighbour's property. Likely, Daphne was with them. At least they were all in one place, but it might mean they were getting their stories straight.

He sat for a few moments, contemplating whether he should wait for Beth and Daphne to leave before approaching the house. Before he decided, the door opened, and Beth and Daphne stepped out onto the porch. Robin remained in the doorway, waving them off.

Jacob watched from his car, hoping they didn't notice him. All three women wore somber expressions, but they weren't crying. A sad smile flitted across each of their faces as they said their goodbyes.

The two women never looked his way while they walked down the steps to Beth's car as Robin closed the door. He waited for the women to pull out onto the road and drive away before he stepped from his vehicle.

As he walked up a set of cement steps, he gave Robin's house a good once-over. Small. Neat, but not manicured. Landscaped, but not professionally. She did her own yard work, or, more likely, her kids did it, which would explain the weeds scattered around the flower garden. They tempted him to stop and pull a few on his way past. He'd never let his yard get this weedy. Good thing he didn't have a yard.

A wooden deck with two plastic Muskoka chairs on it snugged up against the front porch. Obviously an add-on, the deck, stained a light brown, looked incongruous next to the main cement porch and steps, all painted a glossy grey. Before he reached the door, Robin flung it open, almost hitting one of the hanging flower pots with the screen door.

"You're the cop."

She made it sound like a bad thing. If he wasn't looking for a taller, blonder suspect, she would've put his radar on alert. Even so, he didn't exclude her from being an accessory. Perhaps all three conspired together. Interesting thought.

Jacob held up his badge and met her at the front door. "I am, yes. How'd you know?"

"Saw you on the news last night, Mister No Comment." She flashed hazel eyes at him and gave a toss of her head, which tumbled riot-red curls around her face. Part of him wanted to arrest her on the spot so he could see her in handcuffs.

Jesus, how long since he'd been with a woman? He hadn't reacted this viscerally to either Daphne or Beth, and they were more of what you'd call classical beauties. Something about Robin made him want to touch her. He crossed his arms instead.

"I had nothing I wanted to make public. May I come in and ask you a few questions?"

"Sure." She smiled, and it was as if the sun appeared from behind a cloud.

Jacob followed her into her tiny living room. For such a small house, it was surprisingly uncluttered. She was obviously a minimalist. He appreciated that—his place had the same spartan feel.

"Please, sit." Robin indicated the couch. A large, insulated coffee pot and tray with mugs, sugar, and milk sat on the pine coffee table. She snatched up two of the mugs. "I'll grab a clean one for you. The coffee's still hot, and the milk's still cold."

"Thank you."

An open-concept home, nothing separated the living room from the kitchen except a cooking island. A dining area held a four-seater table and chairs set on hardwood flooring that extended from the living area and stopped at the ceramic tiles of the kitchen floor.

Jacob followed her with his gaze as she set the dirty mugs in the sink and retrieved a clean one from the cupboard.

"I'll be recording our conversation," he warned and set his digital recorder on the coffee table. He stated the date, time, and their names as the interview participants.

She frowned but didn't remark on it. Instead, she said, "What's happening with the investigation?"

"No comment." He grinned when she raised her chin.

"Leon was my friend, Detective. I want to know you'll catch whoever did this." She paused while she poured his coffee. Done, she raised her face so their gazes locked. "Are you positive someone murdered him?" Disbelief drenched her voice. Hope flashed across her face.

Jacob shook his head. "I'm sorry. The evidence points to homicide."

Before she could ask, he said, "I can't provide any details—to maintain the integrity of the investigation."

"I hope you catch the bastard."

"Count on it." He accepted the mug of coffee and added sugar to it. After giving it a quick stir, he set the spoon and the mug down without sipping. "Leon's sister visited you this morning."

"I spotted you in your car, waiting for them to leave." She dropped into the chair across from him and crossed her ankles. If she was tense, it didn't show. "Are you playing a game with me? With us?"

"Why would I?"

Robin leaned forward and picked up the coffee pot, pouring coffee into the mug she'd left sitting on the tray. In silence, she added two teaspoons of sugar and a splash of milk. Leisurely, she stirred it with a teaspoon. When she finished, she tapped the spoon twice on the edge of the mug as she withdrew it from the coffee.

Quite a ritual, he thought.

"Maybe you're messing with me." She sipped from her mug.

"What for?"

"I understand how it works."

Jacob reclined in his seat. "How does it work?" he asked, puzzled.

"You assume someone close to him killed him, so you harass us instead of chasing the real killer."

"I'm doing my job."

Robin stood and went to the living room window. She parted

the sheers with one hand and gazed out. Turning to face him, she said, "I'm sorry. It's crazy. I haven't been able to sleep and can't think straight. He's dead. You must rule out friends and family first, so you start with the closest to him and work your way out. As a writer, I'm familiar with this stuff. I've researched it."

She folded her arms across her chest in a tight hug. Eyes brimming with tears, she pressed her lips together. When she spoke, her voice dripped with emotion. "It all hurts too much. He can't be dead. He was the greatest guy. You don't know. You don't understand."

Robin wiped her eyes with the heel of her hands and sniffled. Jacob glanced around the room until he spotted a box of tissues on an end table next to the couch. He retrieved one for her and passed it over.

"Thanks." She dabbed at her eyes and wiped her nose.

"What exactly was your relationship with Leon?"

"Friends. Daphne's my best friend. And Beth." She returned to her chair and dropped into it.

"The four of you spent a lot of time together?"

"I guess."

He squinted at her. "You guess? Would they say the same?"

"Yes," she said, too quickly. "Of course."

"How long have you known Leon and Daphne?"

"Years. Daphne was a year ahead in school. Leon is two years older than Daphne. We attended elementary and high school together. When we graduated, we went separate ways for university but kept in touch. We've all lived in this town forever."

"What about Beth?"

"She's lived here all her life, too, but she's younger than me and Daphne."

"How did you meet?"

"She joined our writers' group about three years back."

"You haven't known her for long, then."

"We haven't been close for long. I've known her, of her, for years."

"Of her?"

"You don't recognize Beth? Elizabeth Holmes?"

"Should I?"

Robin smiled the sad smile Jacob had observed since he'd arrived. "She was a model—a top model."

"Guess I get little exposure to fashion magazines."

"The local papers made a big deal of it—local girl makes good kind of thing. She acted in commercials, walked the catwalk in fashion shows, starting when she was quite young. Her sister still models."

Jacob considered a moment. "Beautiful woman. Tall." He wanted to phrase the question without revealing he suspected Beth. "Was she one of those large models? Beth doesn't seem to fit the stereotype of a skinny runway model."

Robin's eyes narrowed and her brows furrowed. "She used to be too skinny. Now she's normal. She'd be too light to qualify as a plus-size model."

"No offence intended. I'm trying to get a picture of Leon's intimate relationships."

"Beth wasn't intimate with Leon."

Jacob sighed, his irritation rising. "Must you jump on everything I say?"

"Perhaps you should choose your words more carefully."

"Perhaps I should bring you down to the station and question you there." As soon as the words were out, an image of her in handcuffs flashed through his mind again. His stomach clenched at the visual. *Stop it, numb nuts.*

"If you must. All I care about is catching whoever killed Leon." She pressed the tissue to her mouth as if to stifle a sob, but no sound escaped.

"Cooperate and we can stay here."

She shrugged and turned her face away, but not before he caught the expression of relief.

"I've been cooperating."

"Then tell me about Beth's relationship with Leon."

"She respected and admired him, as we all did. He's an award-winning author. Leon did what all of us aspire to do—hit the best-seller lists without the help of a publishing house. Then publishers climbed all over themselves to give him a contract. His latest novel will be made into a movie. Everything he touches turns to gold."

"Has anyone expressed any jealousy over his success?"

Robin fell quiet, contemplating. "No, but I guess that's not something anyone would admit."

"No sour grapes anywhere? Frustration over not matching Leon's success? Must be tough to be a famous model and then lose it all."

"What?! You mean Beth?" Robin shook her head. "No way. She's our friend. Leon's success thrilled her. Besides, she chose to leave modelling. She wanted out and bought the B and B."

"And her writing? How's it going?"

"Well enough. She has a fan base to draw on. No reason for her to be jealous. She put out a non-fiction book about how to become a top model, and it's sold hundreds of thousands of copies. For God's sake, she's not as focused on making a success out of writing as the rest of us are, but she's successful at it anyway."

"How are your books selling?"

Robin smiled that smile again. "They're not. I haven't published anything yet."

"Do you have something in the works?"

"I do." She paused. "I did. Leon asked me to work on a non-fiction book with him. He'd sold the concept to a publisher, and they gave us an advance."

The implications of what she'd told him reverberated through his skull. Leon's death wouldn't benefit Robin at all. "What happens now?"

"The lawyers will decide. The publisher might cancel. They bought on the strength of Leon's name, not mine. I'm nobody." She said it matter-of-factly, simply stating the truth. If this bothered her, she gave no hint.

"Will you repay the advance?" Jacob asked, genuinely curious. Maybe someday he'd write a book, become the next Grisham or Connelly. He could draw on his years of experience solving murders.

"No. If they cancel, they can't claw it back—it's in the contract. Leon has a good lawyer."

"Why'd he ask for your help?"

She smirked. "I like to think it's because he valued my input."

"But you're unpublished."

"Yes, but he's read what I've written. Just because I never published a book doesn't mean I can't write or have no experience."

"Fair enough." Jacob rose. "Mind if I use your washroom?"

"Sure. Down the hall on the left."

He strolled in the direction she'd indicated. Normally, he'd peek into the other rooms on his way to or from the bathroom, but in such a tiny house, she'd see him do it. Too bad his partner, Skylar Lambersky, wasn't with him, but she'd been assigned to another case.

Unusually, they'd had three suspicious deaths in the last week. One, at least, was established as a suicide—a jumper into Niagara Falls—but that left two homicides. He hoped Skylar would be at the station when he returned. He needed a sounding board.

CHAPTER 8

Robin waited, literally on the edge of her seat, for Jacob to return from the bathroom. Dear God, he thought she might have had something to do with Leon's death. How often did they convict an innocent person these days? It couldn't be often. Could it?

Forensics technology could find the perpetrator and rule out the innocent in what must be a high percentage of cases—almost a hundred percent. She'd put her trust in the system and Detective Jacob Turner.

He seemed to do a reasonable job so far even if he placed her and her friends high on the suspect list. And what a fine-looking man. While she had no interest in ever developing a romantic relationship, she could appreciate a sexy man when she saw one.

Oh, God, what am I thinking? Leon's dead and I'm drooling over the guy investigating his murder. She buried her head in her hands. *Forgive me, Leon.*

To her chagrin, Jacob found her that way when he returned from the bathroom. At the sound of him clearing his throat, she raised her head to find him standing in the kitchen, his gaze fixed on her.

"You okay?" He seemed genuinely concerned.

She averted her gaze. "A little overwhelmed."

"You lost your husband a few years ago, correct?"

"Yes." A lump caught in her throat. Would he pick at that scab now, too? "You know about Martin?"

"I read the file on the investigation."

He didn't say the words but implied he'd checked up on her when he added her name to the list of interviewees, suspects, whatever.

"A distracted driver killed him. I was a witness."

"And now you don't leave the house."

"If your files tell you that, they're incorrect. Yes, I didn't leave the house for a time, but I'm improving, thanks to my therapist."

"Good to hear. Where are your kids?"

"My parents' place. The kids will stay there until after the funeral."

"Anyone else know about Leon's project?" He returned to his seat across from her.

"Everyone in our writing group, plus his agent and the publisher. People at those offices also knew."

Jacob leaned back into the couch and propped an ankle on the knee of his other leg. "Must've made quite a stir in the group when the news got out he'd scored this contract."

"It was exciting news."

"Was everyone aware you worked with him?"

"No, we kept that quiet."

"But some people knew?"

Where was he going with this? "A few. Beth. Daphne, of course. The people involved at the agency and the publishing company."

"You share an agent?"

"No. Well, yes. I haven't signed on as a client with Leon's agent because I have nothing more to sell."

"You haven't written any books?"

"I didn't say that."

"So you've written books but haven't sold them?"

"I didn't try to sell them myself. There's a difference. Leon helped sell them."

"Why did you agree to work with Leon?"

Robin chewed on her bottom lip. "I was flattered he'd asked me. I couldn't say no to working with Leon Patterson. No one would say no to that."

Jacob leaned forward, a flash of eagerness making his blue eyes sparkle. "Had he asked anyone else?"

"I don't think so."

"Did anyone seem upset they weren't asked?"

A look of horror crept across her face. "No. Like who? We told no one. Just us—the people I mentioned before."

"Do you have the contract here?"

"Yes."

"I'd like a copy."

Must she hand it over? "I should contact my lawyer."

He stiffened. "Why?"

She shifted her gaze around the room—anywhere but at Jacob. Her stomach fluttered as if building a panic attack. When her palms grew sweaty and her breath shallowed and quickened, she dropped her head between her knees. Fainting would be the next step.

"What's wrong? Are you all right?" Jacob jumped to his feet and rushed to her side.

"I signed papers agreeing not to show anyone anything."

His hand pressed her shoulder. "This is a murder investigation. I can get a court order, but it'd take up valuable time. If you cooperate, I can work on catching the killer much more quickly."

"I understand." Robin forced hysteria from her voice. Why was she so panicked? What would her therapist suggest?

Breathe. Dr. Marsh would advise her to start with her breath. Robin inhaled deeply and slowly exhaled.

"Okay. I'll make copies. But I'm informing my lawyer and Leon's agent. If there's a problem, it's on you."

"Fine. Can you sit up? Do you want water?"

"Yes. Water."

As he walked to the kitchen, she eased herself to a sitting position.

"No! Not the tap," she shouted when he turned on the faucet at the sink.

Jacob startled, almost dropping the glass he held, and threw her a perplexed glance. "Then what?"

"The purifier. Beside the fridge."

He turned his head towards the fridge, his movements halting when he spotted the purifier next to it.

Robin drew a hand through her hair and leaned back in her chair. A glass of water appeared before her face, and she accepted it gratefully. "Thanks. I'm sorry. Do you have a memory stick?"

Jacob retrieved one from his suit jacket pocket and held it up.

"Right here."

"Okay." She stood and ushered him to the computer.

CHAPTER 9

The first thing Jacob noticed when he turned into the driveway of Beth Holmes's estate was the meticulous landscaping. Neatly pruned shrubs edged the walkways, and flowers bloomed in weed-free beds. The barn behind the house shone with new paint. A vibrant green and red tractor next to it gleamed in the sunlight. The building that housed the bed and breakfast, identified as Windermere by a wooden sign printed in calligraphy, invited visitors up the interlocking stone path onto the homey porch.

Fruit trees grew on part of the property—peaches, grapes, plums, pears—all popular food products of the Niagara region. Maybe she made her own wine, too. Jacob could imagine a woman wanting to spend a romantic weekend here. Thank God, he didn't have a girlfriend.

The second thing he noticed was the activity. Cars sat parked in the lot in front of the B and B. Workers toiled amongst the trees and in the massive gardens. An elderly gentleman with a whisk-broom mustache, probably Beth's father, sat on a porch swing in front of what must be the in-law house. If Beth had left to kill Leon and returned later in the morning, surely someone would've spotted her.

The bed and breakfast units offered an abundance of amenities, which he'd read about online before heading over. If she owned all this, he doubted she needed to kill for money. However, Daphne wasn't so set financially. He'd heard from Leon's lawyer on his way to Beth's. Leon had designated Daphne as the sole beneficiary of his estate, which gave the money motive to her.

Beth and Leon hadn't dated. Something might have brewed between Leon and Robin, but it had been in its infancy—too soon for him to be including her in his will.

Interesting that Leon had shut his parents out of inheriting the estate. They had their own money, of course, and didn't need it. So Daphne stood to gain the most from Leon's death. Would Beth kill for her friend? If so, why? Could the two women be lovers? Daphne supported an ex-husband. Perhaps another woman had caused the split—Beth.

Daphne bunked with Beth while the police went through Leon's house. If the two colluded—he doubted Robin conspired with them—Beth profited if Daphne benefited. She'd then have a reason to go all in on this.

Before heading to the main house, Jacob detoured to the in-law suite. Perhaps the old man would give something away without meaning to.

"Good afternoon," Jacob called out.

"Afternoon," the old guy replied. "If you're after the B and B, it's the building out yonder." He pointed a gnarled finger towards the bed and breakfast building.

"I need to talk to Beth. You Terrance Holmes?"

"Who's askin'?" The old guy frowned and ceased his back-and-forth swaying on the swing.

Jacob flashed his badge. "Detective Jacob Turner. I'm investigating the murder of Leon Patterson." With one hand in his suit jacket pocket, he flicked on the digital recorder.

"Yeah, I'm Terry Holmes. I never met Leon."

"He's been living here all his life. You telling me your paths never crossed?"

"I'm telling you I never met him. I seen him. We ain't formally met."

"He never came to the house to visit Beth?"

"Sure. That's when I seen him. But he never came here, and I mind my own."

"Did Beth ever discuss Leon with you?"

Terry fell silent as he contemplated. "Nothing important."

"It needn't be important. Do you recall anything she mentioned?"

"He's a famous writer. I knew that from the newspapers. She

didn't tell me."

"Did she say why he visited?"

"They were friends. He helped her with her writing. Sometimes he drove her around if she needed to go on a long drive."

"Doesn't she enjoy driving?"

"She enjoys it well enough, but sometimes it puts her to sleep. Bethy knows her limits on account of her problem."

Intrigued, Jacob asked, "What problem?"

"Her sleeping problem. Wide awake one moment, nodding off the next."

"Narcolepsy?" Jacob asked, stunned. He'd known no one who'd suffered from narcolepsy.

"Sure. That's it."

"She had it long?"

"Since she stopped modelling, I guess. She'd know the wherefores of it."

"How long has she owned the bed and breakfast?"

"Four years."

So shortly after her mother died, which was interesting timing.

"I'm sorry about your wife. How did she die?"

"Cancer. Filled up her body and then took her." Grief flooded Terry's face, making Jacob feel like a heel for asking, but he needed to dig.

The swing started it's slow to and fro again and silence fell. Jacob let it linger. In the background, birds chirped, a motor ran somewhere in the fields, and children's voices rose in cheerful play. A light breeze wafted the scent of grass and ruffled Jacob's hair. He welcomed it with relief. The light jacket he wore remained too heavy for the warm, summer air. He needed it not only for appearances but to cover his weapon and hide his recorder.

Before Jacob could ask another question, Terry leaned forward. "Some might've called it a suicide."

"Pardon?" Jacob speared Terry with his gaze.

"By the end, the pain meds were ridiculous because the pain was ridiculous. She self-medicated. The doctor said she'd taken too much morphine, but what do you expect? When she was awake, she was in agony. If I'd had the guts to help her along, I'd have done it." Passion raised his voice until it boomed across the yard.

"I'm sorry," Jacob said. "Must've been difficult for you and Beth."

"Bethy handled it. She's tough."

"Yes," Jacob replied. "I'm starting to understand that." He made a mental note to view the autopsy report on Beth's mother. Perhaps Leon wasn't Beth's first victim.

CHAPTER 10

The doorbell chime startled Beth out of the doze she'd fallen into while talking to Daphne. Wide-eyed and apologetic, Beth leaped from her seat at the dining room table. "I'm so sorry for falling asleep. Oh, Daphne, forgive me."

"It's okay. I understand. Go answer the door." Daphne pushed the food around on her plate with a fork. She'd eaten little while Beth dozed.

Hope I wasn't out for long, Beth thought as she hurried towards the door.

A peek out the front door's peephole made her shoulders slump. *Jacob Turner*. She didn't mind answering his questions, but she had nothing useful to reveal. Perhaps he wanted to talk to Daphne again, but Beth doubted it. With a sigh, she swung open the door but blocked the entrance.

"Detective. Good afternoon. Daphne and I are finishing lunch." No need to mention she'd drifted off and Daphne only picked at her food.

"Ms. Holmes, may I come in? I need to ask you a few questions."

"Sure." Beth stepped aside and allowed him to brush past her. "Come into the dining room. Did you want to speak to Daphne as well?"

"If you don't mind, could we talk in private?" Though he made it sound as if she had a choice, that wasn't the case.

With a sigh, she said, "Then follow me."

52

She led him through the hallway and into the living room. His gaze immediately veered to the French doors leading out to the sunroom. He strode over and threw open the doors.

"May I?" Jacob asked after he'd already done the deed. Without waiting for a reply, he poked his head inside. "Nice pool. Has jets?"

"Yes."

"Cool house." He pulled his head back into the living room and gave the place a once-over. "You play?" He indicated the upright piano against the wall.

"A little. Mother signed me up for lessons when I was six. I didn't go very far." Beth's mother, Eva, had decided Beth would be a famous concert pianist. Something always made her push her daughter until she failed miserably—then she pushed the next thing onto her.

Eva forced Beth to endure piano lessons, gymnastics, ballet, jazz, tap ... there'd been more, but Beth couldn't remember everything. Thankfully, it ended when her modelling career took off. She hadn't wanted to do that either, but at least she'd made money at it. Yet it hadn't satisfied her mother. Eva next set her sights on an acting career for her daughter. Cancer had put an end to that dream. Funny how Eva's dreams had always been nightmares for Beth.

"I'll be right back. Can I bring you a coffee? Tea? Water?" Beth refused to offer him anything else. She wasn't feeling generous towards the detective though she couldn't have said why.

"Coffee, thanks." Jacob set a digital recorder on the glass coffee table and dropped onto the couch. "I'll record the interview if you don't mind."

"Not at all," she lied. Her mood turned nasty, and the day turned heavy and exhausting.

Beth hurried into the dining room and told Daphne to take her time finishing her meal while Jacob remained in the house. "If you're lucky, he won't ask to talk to you. Go on upstairs when you're done. Have a nap or something. I'll clean up later."

Daphne tilted her head and appraised Beth. "You going to be okay? You're tired."

"I'm fine. When he's gone, I'll tell you all about it."

Beth carried on to the kitchen and fixed coffee. As a concession to being a good hostess, she retrieved cookies from the jar on the counter. She'd baked them fresh the previous day. When the coffee finished brewing, she arranged everything on a tray and carried it into the living room.

At least a caffeine hit might help her stay awake. What would the detective think if she fell asleep while questioned about a murder? As soon as the thought crossed her mind, sweat bloomed on her palms. The tray shook, rattling the cups on the saucers, as she set everything next to his recording device.

"Help yourself to the cookies." She poured for them both and then added cream and sugar to hers. To keep herself occupied, she sipped the strong brew. "Are you cold? I've got the air conditioning cranked."

Jacob observed her silently as if recognizing her nervousness.

How did he interpret that? Did he view it as guilt or the normal behaviour of someone who'd had no dealings with the law?

"I'm fine. It's comfortable in here. The jacket keeps me warm." His mouth curved up into a decent approximation of a smile.

He had sexy lips, Cupid's bow lips.

Beth shifted her gaze to the plate of cookies. Afraid she'd drop her cup and saucer, she set them on the table.

"How long have you known Leon?" Jacob asked.

"Right to it. Okay." She paused. "Don't you have to turn on the recorder?"

"Already did."

"Oh." When had he turned it on? Had he been recording her the entire time? She cleared her throat. "A few years, I guess. When I joined the writing group."

"Why did you join?"

"Because I write." The condescending tone in her voice shamed her, and she hoped he'd missed it.

"How does the group help you write?"

"Oh, okay." She'd missed the point of the question. As a non-writer, he wouldn't know. "Support. Knowledge sharing or giving and receiving feedback. Writing is a solitary endeavour, but once the first draft is down, you need a team to help you polish it."

"How do they help?"

Beth explained the various ways other writers assisted to make what she wrote publishable.

"What about Robin Carson?"

She frowned, puzzled. "What about her?"

"When I talked to her earlier, she said she'd published nothing.

54

How does the group help her?"

"Same way. Robin takes workshops. When she shares what she wrote, we give her feedback. It's up to her if she wants to publish. She can either shop it around to agents or indie publish. Anyone in the group can ask for feedback or help. It's up to them to accept it."

"Did you help Leon?"

"Sure."

"I hear you have a successful book. On modelling?"

"Yes, the non-fiction one. I also have two novels."

"I'd be interested to see them. Do you have copies on hand?"

"Yes. I'll give you a copy of each one."

When she made no move to rise, he said, "Would you get them now?" After a breath, he added, "So I don't forget."

"All right." She rose and left the room, heading to her home office. Stomach queasy, she placed a warm hand on her belly. Immediately, it soothed. By the time she returned with her books, her nerves had settled and Jacob's coffee cup stood empty. Two of the cookies had also disappeared from the plate.

Beth handed the books to Jacob. "You can keep them. I could autograph them for you."

"Great." He handed them back. When she glanced around searching for a pen, he retrieved one from his jacket pocket and passed it to her. He asked her to make the fiction books out to him but asked her to make the modelling book out to Skylar.

"Your girlfriend?" she asked, fishing for a glimpse into his personal life.

"My partner. Skye has a daughter who might want to read this."

"Should I make it out to her daughter instead?"

Jacob slid a finger around his shirt collar as though it were too tight. "No, just Skylar. I don't know how she'd react if I gave a book like this to the daughter. Kid's only eleven."

"I started modelling at eleven."

"What was it like?"

"I hated it. My mother pushed me into it." She returned the pen and the signed book to him, and he set them on the coffee table with the other two books.

"Your father said your mother passed away. I'm sorry for your loss."

"Thank you. When did you speak to Dad?"

"Before I knocked on your door. Caught him on his porch swing."

"Must have been quite a conversation if he told you about my mother."

"I know how she passed." His gaze remained riveted on her face as he said this.

"It was horrible." Beth's brow's arched, and her lips parted as her mouth turned down. "We all suffered along with her."

Even though she was close to tears, he pushed her further. "Your father seemed to think she might have hurried it along."

"If she did, I don't know. But I wouldn't blame her. She lived in constant, excruciating pain. Detective, what does this have to do with Leon?"

"Nothing. I'm sorry to hear what happened to your mother; that's all." He glanced at the books she'd signed and then returned his gaze to her.

"What are the novels about?"

"Murder mysteries."

"Both?"

"Yes. I enjoy reading them, so when I wrote fiction, I wrote mysteries."

"Must've been interesting. You do a lot of research for it?"

"Not as much the second time because I'd already learned about police procedure for the first novel."

"You must be good at crafting a murder by now, eh?"

The blood drained from her face. "What are you implying?"

"Nothing. Just interested in the process. Listen, mind if I drop in on the next meeting? I've been tossing around an idea for a detective story. Could help me get started."

"Sure. We gather at Andrew's Books and Café in downtown Niagara-on-the-Lake. He has a back room where we meet. Seven o'clock." She didn't want Jacob Turner to attend the next meeting, but how could she refuse without arousing his suspicions? His suspicions were aroused enough already.

"Great. Did Leon attend all the meetings?"

"Yes."

"When did you last see Leon?"

"At the last meeting." He'd asked her that before. Did he forget or was he hoping to trip her up?

"You never saw him outside of that? Never socialized with

him?"

"Sometimes. I have a business to run. He did too. We're all busy."

"Did you see Daphne outside of the writers' group meetings?"

"Yes."

"But not Leon?"

"Rarely. Daphne and I go out often, shopping or to the movies, or we go out to eat."

"Like a date?"

"A date?" Beth honestly didn't understand what he meant for a moment. Then it dawned on her. "You think I'm gay?"

"Are you?"

"No."

"What's your relationship with Daphne Russel?"

"We're friends. Why would you read anything more into it?"

"I'm not. I want to understand the dynamic here. She's staying with you?"

"Yes. Until the police tell her it's okay to return home. Which, by the way, no one has done. Nor has anyone given her any idea when she can bury Leon."

"I'll check and let her know. In the meantime, you say you and Daphne are just friends. Did you visit her at Leon's?"

"Yes."

"When did you last visit?"

"Friday."

"So, after the meeting on the first Thursday of this month."

Beth leaned back in her chair. "Yes."

"I thought you said you hadn't seen Leon since the meeting."

She gazed up at the ceiling. "I went to Daphne's with Robin for a girls' night. The house is huge. Leon could've been home and our paths wouldn't cross. As it was, he had a book tour."

"You sure?"

"Yes. That's why Daphne invited us over. She hates staying home alone." Beth rested her head on the back of the sofa and closed her eyes a moment.

CHAPTER 11

"Hey, Beth, come on." Jacob wasn't sure if he should wake her. Was it like waking a sleepwalker? If he woke her, would she flip out?

No time for this shit.

"Beth!" He grasped her shoulders and shook. "Wake up, dammit!"

Beth sighed and her eyes fluttered open. "Oh, God, I'm sorry." Her voice dripped heavy with sleep. "That's twice today."

"Was it something I said?" He only half-joked. Later, he'd review the tape to see what they'd been discussing. Not that he knew anything about psychology, but perhaps she'd unconsciously wanted to escape the topic.

"That's not funny." She straightened her posture. "I slept badly last night. When that happens, my narcolepsy acts up. I'm able to manage it, mostly, but it's been stressful."

"What has?"

She glared at him. "Leon's death. Are you being deliberately obtuse?"

"Be specific, Ms. Holmes. I'm investigating a murder, not making a social call."

"Yes, but you're being an ass about it. It's as if—"

"As if, what?"

"You think I killed him, don't you?"

"Did you?"

"No!" She jumped up. "How could you even suggest that?

58

What about me says murderer?"

"I have to explore all angles. You're one possibility." Jacob rose, picking the digital recorder up as he did. "If I find you were involved, I'll be back for you."

"Terrific. Make sure you leave no stone unturned, Detective. I'd hate for you to arrest the wrong person for this, especially if that's me." Beth scooped up his pen and the books she'd signed for him. Handing them to him, she said, "Enjoy the books."

He accepted the items with only a twinge of guilt. She wouldn't shake him off that easily.

Before they could move towards the door, Daphne appeared in the living room doorway.

"Detective, when will they release my brother's body?"

Jacob noted the fatigue around her eyes. Beth wasn't the only one who'd had a rough night. Normally, the loss of a loved one would explain that, but if Daphne had taken part in the murder, guilt and fear might poke at her.

"When the autopsy has been completed. Give them a few days."

"Can I plan the funeral?" Her voice sounded small and soft and timid.

He ignored an urge to pat her hand and said, "Yes. The funeral home will walk you through everything."

"They'll let me have his body for burial?"

"Right after they complete the autopsy and collect any evidence, you can bury him."

"Does it always take this long?"

"It hasn't been long. He died only yesterday morning."

"To me, that's an eternity," Daphne said. She turned on her heel and walked away.

***

The following morning, Jacob arrived at his desk at the station to find a message from Daphne on his voice mail. She sounded frustrated and insisted they let her back into her home so she could clean it.

Jacob understood her desire to return home, but was she more anxious to clean than to get her house back? If so, then she might have an ulterior motive—such as wiping out evidence Beth might've left behind.

The investigative team had returned to the house that morning. They'd need at least one more day. He checked the time and decided he had the few minutes required to return her call. Then he needed to get to the autopsy.

She picked up on the first ring. "Hello?"

"It's Detective Turner."

She got straight to the point. "I want to go home."

"They need today to finish evidence collection. I'll call you tomorrow morning to verify when you may return."

"It's taking a long time."

"I'm sorry. They have to be thorough. If we miss something, we won't catch whoever did this."

Her sigh heaved out of the earpiece. "I understand, but my brother lay in the kitchen for who knows how long? I need to clean it for him. God, we might have saved him if we'd found him sooner."

Something tweaked the back of Jacob's mind. He closed his eyes, trying to catch it.

"Detective? You there?"

"Yes. Who knows your shifts?"

"Sorry?"

"Who knew you were on the day shift that morning?"

Silence blanketed the line while he waited for her to reply. Behind him, the station buzzed with low voices. Skylar waved a greeting as she strode in. She set her mug of coffee on her desk, which bellied up to his so they faced one another. He returned the wave.

"Everyone at work. Leon, of course. Beth and Robin. I know no one else who might. I'll think on it."

"Can you make a list and send it to me?" Whoever killed Leon, whether Beth or someone else, knew Daphne's work schedule. This wasn't a crime of passion. The autopsy would show poison killed Leon, which meant the killer brought it to the house. The perp avoided exposing her face to the cameras, which implied casing the place beforehand to locate them.

"Yes. As soon as I'm off the phone. I'll email it to you."

"Thank you."

"One more question."

"Sure."

"When will they do the autopsy?"

"This morning." He hadn't planned to tell her, but since she asked, he decided not to be evasive.

"Will you call me with the results?"

"I'll tell you what I can. The final results will take days, maybe weeks, depending."

"Weeks." Her voice had become low, dejected.

"Yes. I'm sorry. That's how the system works."

"Will you call me as soon as you have something? I need to know what happened. Please."

"I will."

They said their goodbyes, and Jacob headed out to the hospital for a front-row seat at Leon Patterson's autopsy.

***

Doctor Zane "Spuds" Boone, forensic pathologist, autopsied most of the bodies the Niagara Falls police sent to the morgue at Lakeside Health Sciences Centre. When Jacob arrived, Spuds—who'd gotten his nickname from his love of french fries—had Leon's body on a table attached to a sink. He'd already made the Y incision, which meant he'd already completed the external examination.

Though the doctor was wrapped in protective gear, Jacob recognized Spuds by his bifocals and beady eyes—and his linebacker build. Spuds never said, but Jacob was sure the pathologist had played football in university.

"Sorry I'm late, Doc," Jacob said. "What'd I miss?"

"Jake." Spuds tipped his head in greeting. "You reported you suspect poisoning. I assume you reached that conclusion from the same things I noted at the scene yesterday."

"Probably. What you got?" Jacob drew near the table, his protective suit swishing as he walked. The mask he wore did nothing to ease the odour of formaldehyde, death, and an air freshener that failed miserably.

"The vic spouted from both ends. He might have asphyxiated on the vomit."

"So, not poison?"

"Oh, we'll find poison. But someone wanted to make sure that if the poison didn't kill him, the symptoms would."

"How so?"

Spuds pointed to the bruising on Leon's shoulders. "See this? One on each shoulder."

"Yeah?"

"The killer kneeled on him. The vic couldn't turn over, so the vomit reversed down his throat and gagged him. If the poison wasn't fatal by itself, holding him down to choke on his own puke guaranteed he'd die. And here?" Spuds pointed to bruises on the side of Leon's face.

"I see 'em."

"Held his head so he couldn't turn it."

"So he'd choke?"

Spuds paused, met Jacob's gaze, and held it. "To look into his eyes as he died."

"Jesus." Jacob shuddered. *Sick bastard. Or bitch?*

He tried to visualize Beth Holmes holding down an almost six-foot-tall man, forcing his head still so she could watch the light leave his eyes.

"Could a five-foot-ten woman hold down a guy this size?" he asked.

"It's possible. He's not what you'd call a bodybuilder. More like a skinny rock star. No history of drug abuse?"

"No. Why? You find track marks?"

Spuds shook his head. "No, and nothing in his nasal passages. I've already sent the blood work to the lab, so we'll find out from the tox screen if he had illegals in his system."

"Do I hear a 'but'?"

"Yeah. He doesn't look like a drug user. No smell of alcohol, so it wasn't alcohol poisoning. No discolouration around the mouth, so no corrosives—I'm back to talking poison here, not narcotics. His medical records show he wasn't taking any prescription meds. We'll test for that anyway to verify."

"What else?"

"A range of possibilities. We must check the liver tissue and the stomach and intestinal contents. Liquid chromatography should tell us more."

"The next of kin want to know when they can have the body for burial."

Spuds squinted. "Tell them to book transport for the day after tomorrow."

"Not tomorrow?"

"I'm not rushing through this, and I've got something else to work on before I leave today."

"Fair enough. As long as they can plan the funeral, they should be okay with it."

"You staying for the whole thing, Detective?"

Jacob waved both hands at the corpse. "I've seen enough. You'll send the report tomorrow?"

"The preliminary findings, yes."

"Then I'll book. If you find anything wacky, you'll call me?"

"Of course." Spuds huddled over the table. When he raised his scalpel, Jacob said goodbye and hurried from the room.

CHAPTER 12

Three days after Leon's murder, they gathered at the coffee shop where their writers' group met.

Andrew Winston—of the Thorold Winstons, as he was fond of saying—owned the café. He'd diverged from the path his father expected him to follow. Instead of going into the family landscaping business, he'd studied restaurant management and bought the café with money saved from working two, sometimes three, jobs at a time.

The family didn't complain—they supported his ambitions—but only because they expected him to fail. That he'd stayed afloat for longer than the first five years when most new businesses fail testified to his determination and his father's mentorship. While growing up, Andrew had watched and listened to everything his father did and said. The old man knew his stuff and Andrew respected him.

When Daphne, Beth, and Robin filed into Andrew's Books and Café, Andrew handed the counter over to Gregor, his assistant, and hurried to greet the women. He'd promised them sanctuary in the back room, a place to regroup, grieve with friends, and discuss the funeral.

"So sorry for your loss." He spoke to Daphne first and hugged her. Her bony frame pressed against his, and he relaxed his hold in fear of crushing her. As she murmured her thanks, Andrew turned to Beth and Robin.

"You all must be devastated. Come in; sit down. Go in the

64

back. I'll make a fresh pot of coffee. Would you like anything else? Something to eat? On the house."

"Oh, Andrew, you're so kind." Daphne dabbed her eyes with a tissue she held crumpled in her hand. It looked saturated.

When she said nothing more, Robin spoke. "Sandwiches, please. We haven't eaten lunch yet. Care to join us?"

"Sure. Gregor can put something together," Andrew said. He let Robin lead Daphne towards the back of the restaurant, but as Beth tried to slip past him, Andrew stopped her with a hand to her shoulder.

"The police were here to question me and my staff."

Beth's face blanched at the words, but when she spoke, her voice remained even. "Who's 'they'? More than one came?"

"No. One guy. I used the royal they." Andrew flashed her a grin, hoping to ease her tension.

"Detective Turner?"

"That's the one. He asked about all of you."

She tilted her head to the side and narrowed her eyes. "Why tell me?"

"I thought you'd be interested to know a cop came in asking questions about you."

"Why? It's his job."

"I'm not sure."

"You're not sure that's his job?"

"Don't be cute." And she was damn cute.

Whenever Beth came near him, Andrew felt the pull of attraction. So far, he'd kept his distance. She had a vulnerability about her he refused to exploit. Any other woman, he'd have flirted with, hit on.

Too gentle and sweet, she made him want to protect her from the harsh world even if that meant throwing a nosy cop off her scent. Jacob Turner hadn't said he suspected Beth, but his line of questioning put Andrew on high alert. No way sweet, innocent Elizabeth Holmes was a killer. Ludicrous.

"I'm not trying to be cute." Her brow furrowed and her full lips parted with worry.

He struggled with an urge to stroke her cheek, the skin of which looked petal soft. She yawned and her eyelids fluttered.

Damn. He'd caused her stress. She might fall asleep on her feet, and the fault would be his.

"It's okay, Beth. Go on back and join Robin and Daphne. I'll be right in with the coffee."

A shy smile spread across her face. "Thank you," she said before she fluttered past him.

He watched her until she disappeared from sight into the back room.

Control yourself, idiot. You're worse than usual. Maybe he needed to release pent-up sexual tension. She'd been coming into the café too often and getting his juices flowing. He hadn't been on a date in months either—around the time Beth and her posse started meeting here.

Andrew rejected the thought that he'd stopped seeing other women hoping to develop something more … what? Serious? No way. His main priorities, running his business and having fun, occupied him. Serious was for dweebs such as Leon.

Now, that guy had wanted to settle down. He'd even set his sights on Robin. Shame he didn't get the chance. Robin's husband had also died tragically. A coincidence. Right? Yes, of course. A distracted driver had mowed down Robin's husband. She'd had nothing to do with it.

Ten minutes later, Andrew stepped from the kitchen carrying a tray loaded with coffee for four. Gregor remained behind, putting the finishing touches on a platter of sandwiches and pastries, and would carry them to the back soon.

As Andrew headed up the stairs, the door to the café flew open and a male voice called after him. "Andrew, where's Daphne? Her car's out front."

"In the back, Ian." Andrew threw a glance at the back room and then hollered at the kitchen door. "Gregor, we'll need another cup in the back when you have a moment."

"I'll grab it." Ian knew his way around Andrew's kitchen. He'd worked here during the summer when Andrew first opened the shop. The two had been friends throughout high school, after which Ian went on to study science and math at university. He now taught physics at the local high school.

"Thanks, man," Andrew replied and continued to the back room.

The women had spread out over two tables, Daphne's laptop before them. All three appeared absorbed with whatever displayed on the screen. They glanced up when he set the tray down in front of Beth. He glimpsed the screen before Daphne closed it. They'd been checking flight schedules.

Uneasy, he spoke to Daphne. "Going somewhere?"

"What?"

"The WestJet page you had open." Andrew waved a hand, indicating the laptop.

Daphne shook her head. "My parents are coming from the Toronto airport when they get into Ontario."

"Couldn't get a flight into Hamilton?"

"What they could book will land them in Toronto." She sighed. "They should've waited. My house is a mess."

She'd referred to the house as hers. Had Leon left it to her? None of his business, but that would give her more reason to kill him. Why hadn't the cop asked more about Daphne? Why focus on Beth?

Perhaps Andrew was too sensitive when it concerned Beth, but she was no killer. He studied Daphne for a moment. Slim, petite, the size of a pixie. The cop never mentioned how Leon had died. The news reports avoided revealing a cause of death too. Could such a tiny woman have overpowered a six-foot man? Granted, Leon was a twig, but he outweighed his sister by at least fifty pounds.

Ian appeared with the tray of food, distracting everyone. He set it down on a table and flew to Daphne's side. "Are you okay? I'm so sorry about Leon. What happened, Daphne?"

***

Ian's arrival flooded Daphne with guilt. She should've called him before this. Leon and Ian had been close. Even more than Conrad, Ian had been Leon's closest friend. His was probably one of the many messages she needed to retrieve from her phone. She hadn't had the heart to listen to them all.

"I'm so sorry I didn't call you, Ian."

"I understand. Tell me what happened."

"Someone murdered him." The words, as she spoke them, stabbed her in the heart. "The police still have his body."

"When will they release him?"

"Tomorrow. I'm visiting the funeral home after we leave here."

"Can you return home yet?"

"Yes. Detective Turner called me before we got here."

No one responded. Everyone expected she'd go crazy cleaning. They thought they knew her, but they had it all wrong. Sure, she liked a tidy house, everything in its place, but she didn't have to be the one to clean it. She'd already called in a cleaning crew. Her friends were right about one thing though: the thought of the mess gave her jitters.

"I saw reporters outside," Ian said.

Andrew's head snapped up and he glanced from Beth to Daphne to Robin. "They followed you here?"

"They were parked on the road," Ian answered, while Daphne said, "They've followed me ever since the police found Leon's body."

Andrew rose.

"What are you going to do? You won't turn away customers?" Ian slid into the seat next to Daphne but kept his gaze fixed on Andrew.

"I'm not allowing cameras and reporters in here to pester my customers."

Before anyone else could speak, Jacob Turner appeared. His gaze flitted around the room until he zeroed in on Beth. With a grim expression, he strode towards her.

CHAPTER 13

Breath held, Beth followed Jacob's progress through the room. His gaze held hers until he stood towering over her. She remained frozen in her seat as Daphne rose to greet him.

"Any news, Detective?"

Jacob gave a clipped response though the words' meaning refused to penetrate the roaring in Beth's ears. Her hands and feet grew icy, and a stream of cold sweat trickled down her back. She exhaled and then gulped in another breath. The room became stifling, airless.

Surely he wasn't here for her. A woman trailed behind him, her face as grim as Jacob's. Her attire screamed cop. She wasn't wearing a uniform, but her suit trumpeted detective.

"What?" The shocked question came from Andrew. "What do you mean?"

Jacob ignored the outburst and repeated what he'd said. This time, Beth heard him loud and clear.

"Stand, please, Ms. Holmes." He waved a hand towards his partner. "This is Detective Skylar Lambersky. Please accompany us to the station."

Skylar. The woman to whom Beth had autographed her modelling book.

Beth rose on shaking legs. A yawn escaped her as she did. *Oh, God, please don't let me fall asleep. Not now.*

"Is she under arrest?" Daphne's voice rose in panic. Behind her, Robin stood, face pale, a hand pressed against her mouth.

"We just want to talk to her." Jacob turned to Beth. "At the station."

"I'm coming with her," Daphne said.

"We're coming with her," Robin corrected.

"Your choice. This could take a while." He reached out as if to grasp Beth's arm, but she pushed past him and down the steps. His partner followed her.

When they stepped out into the sunlight, she stopped short at the sight of the camera crew. Reporters rushed towards them, homing in on Beth. One reporter shoved a microphone into her face.

"Are you under arrest for the murder of Leon Patterson?"

"No, I—"

"We have no comment." Jacob grabbed Beth by the upper arm. Skylar took Beth's other arm, and they guided her to a waiting Ford Explorer. The partner opened the back door and ushered Beth inside.

As their vehicle whisked her away, Beth caught sight of Robin, Daphne, Ian, and Andrew racing from the café. Beth caught Andrew's gaze before the car turned out of the parking lot. His expression displayed red rage. In a moment, she lost her friends to view, and Beth turned to face front.

Jacob and Skylar kept their gazes on the road and remained silent. No way was this about asking a few more questions. They intended to arrest her.

"I want to call my lawyer." Fatigue overwhelmed her, and closing her eyes, she slipped into sleep.

***

Jacob snapped up from his chair, sliding it towards the wall behind him, and slammed one hand onto the table. Skylar didn't flinch, but Beth jolted as if he'd struck her.

Good. After two hours of ceaseless grilling, she'd better be ready to come clean. She'd dozed off three times since they'd started the interview. Jacob hovered a knife-edge away from dousing her with cold water if she so much as blinked.

"Do you think we're stupid?" He didn't give her a chance to respond. "Only an idiot would buy this story."

"I'm telling the truth. Please. Why won't you believe me?" Her voice quavered, but the tears remained unshed.

"Why?" Jacob raised his brows and folded his arms across his chest. "How can you ask?"

"Maybe I'm stupid. None of what you're saying makes sense." Her eyes pleaded with him for understanding. "I was at home when Leon died."

Jacob pressed his palms to the table and leaned towards her. "How do you know what time Leon died?"

Beth brushed a weary hand across her forehead, sweeping a lock of hair from her brow. "Daphne leaves for work at five thirty, and she left him alive. I'm aware the cleaning lady arrives in the afternoon."

Jacob opened his mouth to thank her for verifying she knew the comings and goings of the household, but she steamrolled over whatever he planned to say. Her next statement slammed the smug right out of him.

"I also know that between the hours of five thirty and the entire rest of the damn day until Daphne called me over, I was home. Working. I have a business to run."

"Where's your alibi, Beth?" Skylar asked. She'd remained silent during most of the interrogation, letting Jacob lead. She checked her watch as if realizing for the first time they'd been in here for a long time. "Help us clear up this misunderstanding so you can go home."

"People came in and out, and I'm not sure what time I did stuff. I always wake up early and verify breakfast is underway. That morning, the chef made crepes."

"And you spoke to him?" Jacob asked.

"Her." She threw him a bland look as if she expected sexist assumptions from him. "Yes. First, I worked on administrative stuff in my office, but I arrived at the B and B kitchen by six fifteen."

"You're sure."

"We've been over it enough that I know it without having to think about it. Yes, I'm sure." She paused. "Haven't you interviewed my chef?" Beth's voice held exasperation and a hint of *you idiot*.

"A police officer assisting in the interviews questioned your chef." Jacob flipped open the folder an officer had brought in and placed on the table when they'd arrived in the interrogation room.

"Says here your chef, Rayleigh, is it?" He paused long enough for her to nod. When she did, he continued. "Rayleigh said you appeared in the kitchen that morning around six thirty."

"I say I appeared in the kitchen by six fifteen. What difference does it make? I obviously wasn't at Daphne's then."

"Rayleigh said you seemed anxious."

"I don't recall feeling anxious. Just preoccupied with finishing my paperwork for the day so I could get out to the fields."

"You work on the farm?"

"Sometimes."

"Okay, so take me through it again."

She huffed out frustration. "Where do you want me to start?"

"From the moment you woke up."

"We've already been through that."

"Humour me."

"You haven't charged me with anything. I don't have to talk to you."

"Don't you want us to find Leon's killer?" Skylar asked.

"Of course, I do. I want to help you."

"Then humour me," Jacob repeated.

"I woke up at five—without using an alarm clock. I always shower and dress first, which takes half an hour. That means I went to my office by five thirty. I cleared up emails." Beth stopped talking, and a startled expression crossed her face.

"What is it?" Jacob spoke softly, afraid she'd fall asleep if he frightened her with gruffness.

"The emails. I cleaned up emails at five thirty."

"Okay."

"Detective, I responded to messages. Check my provider's servers. The time stamps will be on all correspondence."

"We will. It'll help you, Beth, but it doesn't exonerate you—not yet." Skylar covered one of Beth's hands with hers in a gesture of reassurance. "It's good you remembered that. We need more."

A knock sounded on the door. Jacob answered it and stepped outside to join the police officer who stood in the hallway, shutting the door behind him.

"Find anything?" he asked.

The cops, armed with a warrant, had searched Beth's property while Jacob occupied her with the interrogation. Jacob had shown the picture of the woman on the bike to the staff at Andrew's and at Beth's, and they'd all commented it resembled Beth. This had helped get the warrant. If they found anything to tie her to the murder, he could arrest her at once.

"Yes." The officer read from a prepared list. "A blue bike such as the one in the photo you provided. The shoes you told us to search for, size ten. A backpack like the one in the pictures. A book, autographed by Leon Patterson and made out to Beth Holmes, was tucked inside the backpack. And the date next to the signature?" The officer's voice rose with excitement. "The day of the murder and it looks like it's written in the vic's handwriting."

Jacob forced calm into his voice. "Where did you find these things?"

"Garage attached to the main house." The cop handed the list and an envelope to Jacob. "Photos of all the items collected are in here."

"Excellent work. Thanks." Jacob dismissed the officer and opened the door. Time to read Beth her rights.

CHAPTER 14

Beth opened her eyes. This time, she'd only closed them for a moment, unlike when Jacob had read out her rights. Then, she'd dozed off, and he'd had to start over three times before she listened to the entire spiel. Immediately, she exercised her right to consult with a lawyer, though the lawyer wouldn't be permitted to sit in on the interrogation.

Before the police officer had arrived with whatever news convinced Jacob of her guilt, he'd treated Beth as if she might be innocent. Now, he treated her as if convinced she'd murdered Leon.

After consulting the lawyer, she agreed to continue the interview. After all, she was innocent. With nothing to hide, they wouldn't trip her up because she could answer any question with honesty.

But if that were true, then why was she so terrified? Why did she have the horrible sinking feeling she'd spend the night—perhaps many nights—in jail?

The detectives had given her a bathroom break and a bottle of water, but so far, they'd offered nothing to eat. Her stomach wasn't up to it anyway, but how long did they plan to starve her?

She'd also provided them with a mouth swab DNA sample.

"You're in trouble, Beth." Skylar continued to play the good cop.

Beth wasn't fooled by it. She'd watched too many murder mysteries and cop shows not to recognize the strategy. Hell, she'd written two murder mysteries, researching interrogation techniques to make it as realistic as possible.

If she cooperated, they'd have to believe she'd had nothing to do with Leon's murder.

"We have the bike." Jacob's steely gaze cut into her. He stood as he'd stood for most of the interview: arms crossed over his chest, legs planted hip-distance apart, and a sneer on his face. How had she ever thought him sexy?

"What bike?" She owned no bikes, not even to rent them out. The neighbours across the street offered rental bikes. Perhaps one of the B and B guests had rented one and left it on her property.

"The one hidden in your garage."

In her garage?

"The garage is locked." Trying to puzzle it out, she'd spoken out loud.

"Yes. Your father used the automatic garage door opener inside the house to open it."

"But I don't own a bike."

"Then whose is it?"

"I don't know."

"Are you sure?" Jacob threw her an insulted glance. He opened the envelope he'd tossed on the table when he'd returned to the room after speaking to the police officer. After sliding out a photo, he flicked it at her.

Beth pinched it between her thumb and index finger, wanting as little contact as possible with anything tied to the murder. The image showed a woman's blue bike. She couldn't figure out what kind. It didn't look expensive, but how would she know? She'd never bought a bike in her life.

"What do you expect me to say?"

"This is the bike you used to cycle to Leon's house that morning."

"You think I rode a bike to Leon's, killed him, and then rode home? I told you, I don't own a bike. And I stayed home all that day until I drove over to pick up Daphne."

"We found this in your garage."

"I don't know why." Beth pressed her hands to her eyes and rubbed with her knuckles. God, she wanted to sleep. When she dropped her hands, she clasped them in front of her on the table. "It's not my bike."

"Then who owns it?" Jacob yanked his chair closer to the table and dropped into it. He leaned forward and snatched the photo from her hand. "They found this in your garage."

"I can't explain why. No one I know owns such a bike." She closed her eyes and considered. With a sigh, she opened her eyes and said, "Perhaps it's from across the street. They rent bikes out, but I don't understand how it got into my garage."

"And the backpack? The shoes?"

"What backpack? What shoes?"

Jacob slid another two photos from the envelope and pushed them in front of her. He stabbed a finger on the first photo. "This backpack."

Before she could reply, he stabbed his finger onto the second photo. "These shoes."

Beth studied the photos and bile rose in her throat. "I had shoes like that." She swallowed but failed to clear the terror-filled lump that blocked her throat. "I lost them."

"You might as well come clean. Forensics will prove they're your shoes."

The shoes were hers. The drops of brown stain on the top of the right one were from when she'd worn them to paint her deck.

"Someone stole the shoes and planted them in my garage. They must have. I lost them a month ago." Hysteria bubbled close to the surface, and tears sprang to her eyes. For the first time since she'd been accused, she believed in her heart she might go to jail for a murder she didn't commit.

She came close to begging and pleading when Jacob's expression turned smug.

"Then you admit the shoes are yours."

"They look like a pair I lost." The tears escaped then, and she swiped at them with fury. "I didn't kill Leon."

"Beth." Skylar's soft voice caught Beth's attention. "We've got you on video. At Leon's."

A yawn threatened, and Beth forced it down. *Not now.*

"Impossible." She shook her head. "I was at home. And I don't ride bikes. I've never ridden a bike."

"You expect me to believe that?" Jacob chuckled, but it wasn't congenial. They weren't sharing a joke.

"Yes, because it's the truth."

Skylar opened the folder on the desk and riffled through it until she found the stills she wanted. She removed three photos and handed them to Beth.

Hands shaking, Beth accepted them. Breath held, she examined them.

In the first image, a blonde woman rode the blue bike from the previous photos towards Leon's garage. Her head angled down, hiding her face.

At first glance, Beth's heart skipped a beat as she saw herself in the photo. But only at first glance. After examining the photo, she could pick out differences that might save her hide.

"That isn't me."

"Give up, Beth," Jacob said, his voice kind, patient. "We have people who say it is."

She went rigid, and a scowl crossed her face. "I'll never admit to something I didn't do. You can harass me all you want. If you take this to trial, you're wasting taxpayers' money while letting the real killer go free."

Jacob shook his head and made a "tsk-tsk" sound. "Any idea how many guilty people say that? If we released every person who swore we had the wrong guy, the jails would be empty."

"Look at it." She placed a finger on the first photo. "The hair. Examine it. That hair is thicker than mine. I have fine, thin hair. This woman's hair is so full and thick, it'd be difficult to put into a ponytail."

Her mother's hair had been that thick. While Beth could scoop her hair into a high, jaunty tail, her mother's broke elastics if they weren't large enough.

Jacob picked up the second photo and held it close to his face. After a moment, he passed it to Skylar.

"What do you think?" Though the sneer had left his voice, doubt remained.

"Hard to say. Looks a lot like Beth." Skylar's tone was dubious.

"Tell you what," Jacob said, his voice unexpectedly friendly. "Bail hearing's tomorrow morning. I'll have this examined. In the meantime, I want hair samples from you besides the fingerprints. Cooperate, and you might leave here a free woman."

How could she trust him? Would he have the picture examined? Maybe their experts would notice the subtle differences and verify the woman in the photo wasn't Beth. She started to stammer a reply when her eyes drifted closed and everything faded away.

CHAPTER 15

The scope of the cleanup job overwhelmed Daphne even though she didn't have to do it herself. She stood frozen in the entryway of Leon's house, refusing to think of it as her house. Beside her, Robin remained silent, probably waiting for a cue from Daphne.

At last, Daphne spoke. "I have to see the kitchen first."

"Are you sure?" Robin's soft words made Daphne's eyes well up with tears, but she suppressed them.

"Yes. The cleaning service has been through it. No trace remains of what happened. Giselle assured me it's all clean. I only need to put anything out of place back where it should go."

"Okay. I'll help you however I can, but you know I can't guess where everything belongs."

"I know." She touched Robin's arm with the tips of her fingers. "I'm glad you're here. It'll make the job easier if I have someone to talk to. Besides, if I find something else missing that isn't on the list of items the police removed, you can record it for me."

"Of course." Robin gave Daphne's hand a gentle squeeze. "Are you ready?"

Daphne inhaled, catching the scent of lemons and bleach. "They found blood on the kitchen floor, but it wasn't much. He also soiled himself and vomited."

"Sweetie, are you sure you wouldn't rather stay at my place tonight?"

Ever since Beth's arrest, Daphne felt cut adrift. First, she'd been banished from her own home. Then, she'd been ejected from

78

Beth's house as well. She rejected the notion of returning to Beth's after the police finished searching it. She refused to see Beth's house turned upside down. Difficult as being here was, she had to stay. If she went to Robin's, it would be like abandoning Leon. Staying here would be like thumbing her nose at the killer.

Instead of answering Robin's question, Daphne said, "I can't believe Beth has to spend the night in jail."

"Me too. Don't worry. When they realize they've made a mistake, they'll release her."

"The funeral will be the day after tomorrow. What if she can't attend?"

The two women stared at each other, both wearing expressions of panic.

Robin clutched Daphne in a desperate hug. "It'll be okay. She'll be there."

Daphne returned the embrace. "This is so stupid. How could they think Beth had anything to do with this?"

The chime of the doorbell interrupted them.

Brushing tears from her eyes, Daphne released her hold on Robin and opened the front door.

"Conrad. Hi." Daphne stepped aside and allowed him to enter the house.

As he passed her, he stroked her cheek. "How are you holding up, honey?"

She forced herself not to recoil from his touch—he was being kind—but he'd often touched her as if more existed between them than actually did. Still, he'd been one of her brother's friends. She should be nice to him.

"I'm managing. Robin came over to help me organize the house."

"Can I help?" He strode into the living room. "Looks clean. What do you need to do?"

She had to clear the lump from her throat before she could answer him, and it made her sound nervous. "Straighten, not clean. I want to put things back in their place. Robin will help me. I'm sorry, Conrad, but I'm not up to having company."

He threw a pointed look at Robin but only said, "I understand. Just your girlfriend. If you need anything, you call me, okay?"

She nodded because she didn't know what else to do and then said, "I'll see you at the funeral?"

His face brightened. "Of course."

After he left, Robin pushed the door shut and locked it. "He must be devastated, but I'm glad you told him he couldn't stay. I'm not in the mood for him."

Daphne angled her head to the side. "You don't like him?" If so, Robin had never mentioned it.

"It's nothing like that. He makes me feel as if I annoy him, so I don't enjoy being around him."

"I think I understand what you mean. He's always so intense." Daphne walked towards the kitchen and Robin followed.

Both women halted before they entered. Daphne pointed to the floor near the island, next to the bar stools. "He died there."

"I'm so sorry." Robin took Daphne's hand in hers. "Stay at my place. The couch folds out. Tomorrow Beth and I can come back here with you. We'll do whatever you need done."

"How can I ask you to take even more time away from work? You're always so swamped, and Beth has a business to run." She didn't add Beth might be in jail. The thought of it infuriated her. No way. They couldn't let that happen. "He's not taking Beth."

Robin gave Daphne a startled look and said, "Who?"

"The killer. A crazy killer is on the loose, and Detective Turner nailed Beth for it. We can't let whoever did this ruin her life, too. He's already taken Leon away from us."

"Are you assuming the killer's a male?"

"They almost always are, but I'm not forgetting it could be a woman."

"So what can we do?"

"Catch him." Daphne stalked over to the counter without pausing as she crossed the spot where her brother had lain. From a drawer, she retrieved a pen and a pad of paper. She tossed them onto the island's granite top where they landed with a thud. Robin caught the pen as it rolled towards the edge.

"You make notes while I organize the kitchen. Whoever did this? We'll find them, and they'll pay."

***

At the police station, Jacob settled down at his desk to a tuna sandwich, a ready-made salad from the supermarket, and cup of coffee. In front of him sat the two signed novels Beth had given him. This seemed as good a time as any to scan through them.

With one hand, he held his sandwich while he propped open the first book with the other. A murder mystery titled *Fields of Death*, the story opened with a body found in a meadow by two kids. The condition of the body caught Jacob's interest.

Beth's description resembled the condition in which they'd found Leon's body. Jacob dropped the sandwich onto the plate. He held the paperback with both hands and studied it. After reading a few pages, he flipped through the book, searching for cause of death. Poison. Water hemlock.

He picked up his phone and called the lab. When he reached Spuds' voice mail, he instructed the pathologist to test for cicutoxin, which would reveal water hemlock poisoning. At least, the forensic pathologist in Beth's novel had done that. Spuds would understand what to do. Message delivered, Jacob disconnected the call and leaned back in his chair, his meal forgotten.

Was Beth so stupid she'd kill Leon using a method she'd written about in a novel? So much of the evidence pointed to her, but his gut nagged him every time he spoke to her. The persistent doubt irritated him. Usually, when this quantity of evidence pointed to a suspect, it didn't take long for the culprit to cave. When perps saw the jig was up, they confessed.

Not Beth. She maintained her innocence, and Jacob's intuition whispered to him she was innocent and not deluded or stubborn or sociopathic. So, hypothetically—and, because Jacob continued to doubt Beth's innocence, he only speculated—if Beth hadn't done it, then who else? Whoever it was not only had it in for Leon but wanted to take down Beth in the fallout. Otherwise, why frame her? Just to avoid capture?

That might be enough of a motive for some. Frame someone else to take the heat off yourself. But if the killer had framed her, Jacob and the investigative team would find out and ... and what? So far, the only clues they'd found pointed to Beth.

Earlier, he'd reviewed the death report on Beth Holmes's mother. At least he could conclude Beth hadn't been involved with that death. The woman had died of cancer. Yes, she'd been on an exorbitant amount of painkillers, but nothing indicated she'd been deliberately helped along. The report stated the painkillers masked the excruciating pain. Cancer had riddled her entire body. Death, when it came, would've been welcomed.

A growl from his stomach reminded Jacob he hadn't finished his dinner. The food didn't appeal to him anymore, but he picked up the sandwich and bit into it. As he chewed, he contemplated his next move. Before he could search for another killer, he must rule out his prime suspect.

If someone had framed this young woman, he'd find out who and see to it the person paid—not just for the killing, not just for the frame-up, but for adding to Jacob's workload. Fury kicking frustration to the curb, Jacob tucked into his sandwich and salad with enthusiasm. Soon he'd have the killer in his sights, and then he'd make the asshole regret messing with Jacob Turner.

CHAPTER 16

The asshole in question was, at the moment, sitting at the desk in his home office, pondering his next move. A television across the room, sound muted, spooled a newsreel. Conrad had no time for current events, but he liked the visual distraction. He had a mission and needed Daphne to accomplish it. He'd hoped to catch her home alone, but Robin's presence ruined his plans.

A glance at the time told him it'd been two hours since he'd left Daphne's. He'd arouse suspicion if he returned today, plus it appeared the two women were holed up for the evening. He'd wait until the funeral to make another move on her.

The notes for Leon's book were inaccessible. Leon's private contact lists, his marketing plan, and every tool he used were secured on his laptop or stored in a private folder in the cloud. Even Daphne's electronics had been secured.

Good ole Daphne. Such a sweet little thing. She'd open up to him, he'd make certain of it. Then she'd share Leon's files. Perhaps the two could finish Leon's book together, with Conrad taking the lead role. He'd do the book signings and deal with Leon's agent and publisher.

Robin's image on the television screen interrupted his dreams. He turned up the volume.

"...revealed the identity of Leon Patterson's coauthor. Robin Carson, a software developer from Niagara-on-the-Lake in Ontario was hired to help write Patterson's new book. Patterson recently signed a contract with Trend House Publishing with a rumoured seven-figure advance. A non-fiction book on the craft of writing, a departure from his usual romance and erotica, it was targeted for release in the fall of 2019. Another one on book marketing was scheduled to release a year later.

"Patterson died before completing either book. A spokesperson for Trend House has said they will honour Ms. Carson's contract and allow her to finish the books. They maintain she has all Patterson's notes and is more than capable of completing his books to their satisfaction."

Robin has the files. She has everything. And she was at Daphne's, her home empty and unprotected.

Conrad turned off the television and prepared to head out.

***

Before entering her house, Robin turned and waved goodbye to Daphne, who'd driven her home. Inside, she set her purse in her bedroom closet and returned to the living room. She sat on the couch and reached for the television remote but stopped short of picking it up. The prospect of lounging in front of the television bored her though no inspiring substitute came to mind.

At Daphne's, she and Daphne had made a list of suspects in Leon's murder and a list of investigative clues. No matter how they concentrated, both lists remained short. Everyone loved Leon. His former agent might resent him for cutting ties before success made him rich and famous, but he couldn't have done it because he lived in England now. They'd verified it. As for the list of clues, they didn't know much about what the police had found.

Daphne listed poison as the suspected cause of death but couldn't say what kind. A search on the internet using the signs Daphne recalled got them nowhere. The large results list returned meant the symptoms they'd input were too general.

After watching Daphne putter around in the kitchen and then the dining room for an hour, an urgent need to return home had overwhelmed Robin. Perhaps it was the way Daphne needed to place each piece she touched in a particular location. She'd cleaned off each one whether or not it needed it and then set it in a specific spot.

The room darkened as the sun set, but Robin remained on the couch, wrapped in a cocoon of despair and guilt. She should've stayed with Daphne. Though her friend insisted she'd be fine, that wasn't the case, but no matter how much Robin had wanted to stay, anxiety compelled her to rush home. Worse, after dropping Robin off, Daphne then had to return alone to that giant mausoleum of a house where her brother had died.

A creak from the hallway snapped Robin from her reveries, alerting her to a presence in the house.

Oh, God, someone's in here. How? She kept the house locked even when she was at home. Searching frantically for a place to hide, she dropped to the floor as stealthy footfalls approached the living room.

Unable to think of anything else, she shoved herself feet first under the couch. After squeezing her body underneath, Robin pressed as far against the back wall as space allowed.

Footsteps entered the kitchen and went straight to her desk.

Who'd want to break in here? She didn't have much of value, just the computer and the television. She'd wait for him to steal whatever he'd come for, and then she'd call the police. As long as she kept silent, he'd believe himself alone.

Her heart pounded and sweat drenched her. What if panic attacked her? She wouldn't be able to go for help. Robin tried to calm her breath the way her shrink had taught her. Deep, even breaths. Deep, even, *silent* breaths.

The intruder turned on her computer.

He was booting it up? Why not just steal it?

Robin glanced at her television. It wasn't a big-screen TV. She hated television, preferring to spend her leisure time reading or playing on the computer. Still, she'd assumed if it was a drug addict who needed cash, he'd take whatever he found and leave.

But this person had powered up her computer and rooted through her desk. If he searched for a password, he'd hunt for a while. She'd memorized her password. What could be on her computer that someone wanted so badly they risked breaking into her home? Why not hack in?

Of course, that wouldn't be an easy task either. She'd secured her network. A metallic thud told her the intruder opened her filing cabinet. The glow from a cell phone flashlight app allowed her to see more than shadows, but she wasn't in any position to get a good look at the person.

What if this person had also killed Leon? None of her software development work put her at risk for corporate or government espionage. Whenever she'd worked on anything sensitive, she'd done it on-site. Since Martin's death, she'd refused on-site work, so the break-in must be related to Leon's death.

The news had leaked earlier that she'd partnered on his book. Now someone broke in here searching for … what? Notes? Contracts? Ideas? Why would anyone want their book? It wasn't even written yet. She'd be working from Leon's notes. None of this made any sense.

"Dammit." Said in a low growl, the voice was unmistakably male. She couldn't place it though it sounded familiar. Someone she knew had broken into her house. A man she knew, a friend, maybe, or someone she saw often, had violated her home.

Anger flared, and she almost leaped out to confront him when she realized she'd be confronting not just a burglar, but a murderer. He'd killed Leon. If he discovered her here, he'd kill her, too.

At first, relief coursed through her when he left the living room and headed towards her bedroom.

Thank God, he's leaving.

When she heard her closet door slide open, she stifled a sob. What if he found her purse? Her wallet and her cell phone were in it. He'd realize she was here. She wouldn't leave the house without her purse.

Did men know that?

On the edge of panic, Robin focused her awareness back to her breath. The racket from her bedroom told her the man was opening and closing dresser drawers. He wasn't searching for money. Unless he found her purse, which she'd shoved to the back of her closet, he wouldn't find much, anyway. She didn't keep large quantities of cash on hand.

A new surge of panic washed over her. Should she try to escape while he was in the bedroom? The front door was close. Could she sneak out before the intruder caught her?

Her heart rate spiked at the idea of leaving the house alone, but if she didn't get out, he might find her. What if he searched the living room? It might occur to him to check under the couch for whatever he hunted.

Oh, God. I have to get out of here. Her breath hitched at the certainty she must escape. A lump of terror lodged in her throat, Robin eased herself from under the couch.

CHAPTER 17

The floors in Robin's tiny bungalow were hardwood, polished, and creaked almost everywhere, but she knew the hotspots. Robin rose from the floor on trembling legs and waited a breath to verify the intruder remained in the bedroom.

Thuds and thumps confirmed it. As if she were the interloper, Robin crept towards the front door. She kept the pace slow though she wanted to run. One misstep would betray her presence.

By the time she reached the front door, footsteps in the bedroom headed towards the hallway. He planned to return to the living room—nowhere else to go unless he meant to search the children's rooms or the bathroom.

Swallowing a moan, Robin unlocked the door with a controlled motion to stifle the click of the deadbolt. The footsteps paused in front of the linen closet in the hall, creaking floorboards and a squeak of hinges giving away his location.

Good. Let him search through the towels and sheets as long as it kept him busy so she could escape.

She needed to open the front door fast; otherwise, it too would squeak. Her heart thudded, and her pulse roared in her ears. Robin cringed, anticipating noise, and swung the door open wide enough to slip through. Blessed silence. She was almost away.

With a sigh of relief, she slipped through the door, shut it behind her, and dissolved into the night.

***

One glimpse of Robin's face and her next-door neighbour, Antonia Lacey, activated her cell phone, asking if Robin needed an ambulance.

"No, the police. Hurry, please. Someone's in my house."

Robin locked the front door behind her while Antonia called 9-1-1. When the dispatcher assured Antonia the police were coming, she led Robin towards the couch.

"Sit. You look as if you're about to faint," Antonia said.

The Lacey residence was a two-storey home much larger than Robin's. As she shuffled across the deep pile of the living room carpet, Robin tried to collect her thoughts.

"You're barefoot." Antonia eased Robin onto a soft leather cushion. "Must've been terrified to leave without your shoes."

"There's no space under this couch." Robin sounded horrified. If she'd had the same one at home, she'd have had nowhere to hide. The intruder would've caught her. She tried not to dwell any more on what might've happened.

If only the cops would arrive.

At the reminder the police were on their way, Robin leaped up and ran to the window. She should watch for them and run outside when they arrived.

"It's okay, sweetie. Let me bring you a glass of water, and you can tell me what happened."

"I have to watch. He might come outside." Robin's voice shook.

Maybe fear would be her permanent state from now on. Anger bubbled beneath the fear, which was preferable. If she could draw on rage, she'd ease back the terror. Without the terror, she'd have less anxiety.

The front of her house sat bathed in quiet and stillness. The intruder might've escaped while she was distracted, but Robin hoped not. If the police caught him in the act, they might charge him with Leon's murder, too. The two incidents must be related.

Where were the police? She opened her mouth to ask Antonia what the dispatcher had said when a cruiser pulled into Robin's driveway and a man and woman, both in uniform, jumped out. Robin rushed to the front door and flung it open. She raced down the porch steps and waved at them.

The one closest to Robin, a tall, slender woman with mouseyblonde hair, spoke first. "Are you the one who called nine-one-one?"

"I asked my neighbour to call." Robin halted before she reached the officers. "An intruder's in my house."

The two cops closed in on her, but before they reached her, another police car pulled up in front of the house. A burly man in uniform stepped from the vehicle and approached the group.

"It's okay. She's the homeowner." The woman, who seemed to be in charge, met Robin's gaze. "Tell me what happened?"

"Someone broke into my house while I was inside. He must've thought no one was home." She choked the words out around the lump in her throat. "I escaped before he caught me. He might still be in there."

Antonia stepped from her house and moved towards the group. The officer in charge waved at her to return to the house. When she spoke, she directed her words to Robin and Antonia. "Get inside. We'll take care of this. Is your front door locked?"

"No."

"Is there a back door?"

"Yes. He probably entered that way."

"Go inside and don't come out until I knock on the door." She then spoke to the other officers, directing one to go in through the front door with her and telling the third officer to cover the back door.

"Be careful." Robin didn't know why she said it. They were trained to handle this, but what if the intruder carried a gun? She almost told them not to go, but then wondered what they were supposed to do instead.

She hurried inside Antonia's without another word.

***

As the officers exited Robin's house, Jacob arrived. He'd been working late at the station and heard the call come in on the radio that always played in the background. When he recognized the address as Robin's, he drove out there.

He found her leaving the neighbour's home to return to her own where all three officers had congregated on the front porch. Jacob waved a hand at the cops and met up with Robin as she reached her front steps.

"Are you okay? Are you hurt?" He scanned her as best he could in the dim light of the streetlamps and found no injuries.

"I'm okay. Scared." Robin's eyes were wide, the pupils dilated. She pressed one trembling hand to her mouth. "I'm shaking more now than when I was in the house with him."

"A normal reaction," he replied. "You'll be okay."

She huffed out a sigh as he ushered her up the steps and onto the porch. The lead cop told him they'd found the place empty. They'd checked the entire house, top to bottom, including under furniture and in closets.

"Doesn't look like anything's missing, but the vic will have to verify."

Jacob nodded. "I'll take her through. Thanks for your help. This might be related to the case I'm investigating, so I can take it from here."

After the police left, Jacob led Robin inside and asked her to escort him through the house.

"Tell me what happened." He switched on his digital recorder, identified the date, time, and participants, and turned on a camera.

"You're filming me?" If possible, her eyes opened wider.

"I'll take stills. For future reference. Okay?"

Her shoulders dropped as tension released. "Either would be okay. I'm not sure why I needed to ask."

"It's okay. Tell me what happened."

"I was here." She pointed to the couch. "I'd returned home from Daphne's. The sun was setting, but I didn't switch on any lights—distracted, I guess."

"Distracted by what?"

"Thinking about Daphne. About Leon. She's all alone in a huge house." Robin frowned, her eyes going sad. "I left her there. It just … I didn't want to stay—couldn't handle being out anymore. She drove me home and returned to that house all alone."

Jacob's heart went out to her. "Don't beat yourself up."

"People say that, but what else should you do when you're a jerk?"

"Robin." He stopped, unsure what to say next but positive he wanted to ease her anguish and guilt.

After a moment, she broke the silence. "I was a jerk. My friend needed me and I left her—not only that, but I insisted she drive me home. I should've called a cab."

"Did she complain?"

"No, but it's her brother who died." It came out a wail of agony. "Instead of thinking of myself, I should've thought of her."

"I'm sorry." What else could he say? He wasn't a shrink. She saw one. Would she resent it if he suggested she make an appointment?

To his surprise, she smiled. It was small and a little sad, but it was there.

"Thank you," she said.

He raised his brows. "For what?"

"Your kindness. Patience. You're not letting on if I'm annoying you."

Unable to help himself, he returned her smile. She looked so small and vulnerable. "You're not. Let's get through this, okay? Tell me what happened. Then we'll check the house, see if anything's missing, and figure out how he got in."

After that, Jacob thought, *we'll explore our options.*

CHAPTER 18

Nothing in the house indicated anyone had entered it. With no surveillance equipment, Robin couldn't prove there'd been a break-in. With no sign of forced entry and nothing out of place, Jacob had only her word someone had trespassed.

"Someone broke in." Her eyes pleaded with him.

"I believe you. Could he have used a key?"

"If he did, I'm in trouble. I gave no one a key."

"Do you hide one outside?"

Robin paused.

"You hide a key outside?"

"Who'd want to come in here? I own nothing of value. It's a small town. The neighbours all know each other."

Jacob shook his head. "Show me where." His voice broadcasted exasperation.

She led him to the back door. "It's in the backyard, under a rock."

He groaned. "Please tell me it's not one of those fake rocks."

"Well, yes, but it looks real."

They walked along a path of interlocking stones to a flower garden in front of the back fence. Robin crouched down and plucked what looked like a rock from a scattering of rocks throughout the flower bed.

"See? These others are decoys." She turned the stone upside down to display the hollow underneath. Inside sat a key.

"If he used this key, he put it back." Jacob considered the

implications. "He wanted no one to know he'd been here. You said he disturbed nothing?"

"Correct. If he moved anything, he replaced it. He even powered down my computer."

"I'm calling in a forensics team," Jacob told her. "They should dust for prints and see what traces they can find."

"You can catch him that way?"

He paused, not wanting to tell her too much about the investigation and his suspicion that the intruder killed Leon.

Before he could answer her, she spoke. "I think he's Leon's killer."

Jacob didn't reply. To draw that conclusion required no great leap in logic.

"You can let Beth go now, can't you?" Hope radiated from her eyes.

His expression must have betrayed doubt, because she said, "Beth's innocent. Are you saying you still think her guilty?"

"Come down to the station? I want to show you some pictures." Perhaps Robin would help him rule out Beth as the killer once and for all.

Robin didn't hesitate. "Yes."

***

Across town, Daphne settled in for a long night alone. She could've asked Robin to stay or she could've packed a bag and bunked at Robin's, but neither choice appealed to her. Her friend had been anxious to go home, her neurosis kicking in. Daphne didn't blame her for rushing home. One day, perhaps, Robin would overcome it, but it likely would always be a part of her personality. She was an introvert to begin with.

As for sleeping anywhere other than here, Daphne rejected the idea without even considering it. She'd already been away from her room for days while the police combed the house and while the cleaning crew eliminated all traces of Leon's death. Though the huge house didn't make her crave to be here, her lovely, comfortable room did.

After she'd returned from dropping off Robin, Daphne, who recognized a pending sleepless night, made popcorn. With a full bowl of the buttered puffs under her arm and a glass of red wine on the coffee table, she settled in the family room on the couch. She flicked on the fireplace and the big-screen television embedded in the wall above it. Unsure what to watch—definitely not a crime show or anything depressing or violent—she surfed through the channels.

The doorbell rang as she settled on a sitcom she'd enjoyed watching in the mid-2000s. A glance at the time showed eight thirty—not late, but not the usual time for someone to come calling. She set the bowl of popcorn on the table and stood but didn't make a move towards the front door.

A knot of anxiety twisted her gut. Had it happened this way for Leon? Did he open the door to his killer and let him—or her—inside? Would the caller leave if she didn't answer? Daphne angled her head to stare through the large wall of glass. In the dimness of the recessed pot lights and the glow from the television and the fireplace, she saw only the room's reflection.

Leon hadn't put window coverings on the glass wall because they'd interfere with the view. Daphne always felt vulnerable in here at night with the lights on no matter how much Leon assured her no one would peep in. The single door in the glass led to a covered patio elevated one story above ground level. Beyond that, majestic evergreen trees surrounded an in-ground swimming pool. No one should be out there spying, and the cameras would activate if they drew too close, but she felt exposed anyway.

The chime of the doorbell startled her from her paralysis. She'd at least check the peephole—murder hole, some crime novels called it—and see who wanted in. Shaking off fear, she strode to the front door and peered out.

Ian Fergus. Leon's best friend.

Relief flooded through Daphne and she threw open the door. As she did, it crossed her mind Ian might be the killer. Both she and Leon trusted him.

Of course, we trust him.

Daphne flung off the insane suspicion and threw herself into his arms. A sob escaped her, and she buried her face in his solid chest.

"Are you okay?" Concern laced his voice. "No, you aren't. May I come in?"

"Yes. Please." She raised her head to gaze up at his face. "I hate being here alone, but Robin couldn't stay and Beth ..." A lump formed in her throat.

"They arrested her?"

Unable to speak, Daphne nodded.

Ian stepped inside and closed the door behind him. He slipped off his shoes, and she led him into the family room. On the television, the comedy show played on, the laugh track grating on her nerves. She switched it off.

"Drink? I have red wine on the go or beer in the fridge." Leon's beer. She didn't drink it and now every time she opened the fridge, she'd see it there.

As if reading her mind, Ian said, "I'm sorry. If you want, I can take the beer home."

Daphne almost agreed but not seeing it in the fridge seemed worse. "No, thank you. I'd rather keep it."

Ian accepted the offer of a beer, and she wondered if it was to reduce the count by one or if he preferred it.

"I have water or pop if you like." Why go on about drinks? The knot still tightened her gut and her shoulders hunched. She forced herself to drop her shoulders and slow her breathing.

"The beer's fine." He smiled, and the tension eased from her when it reached his eyes.

Daphne walked to the kitchen and retrieved a beer from the fridge. When she returned, he was sitting on the couch with the bowl of popcorn in his lap.

Happy he'd made himself comfortable, she handed him the drink and plopped down next to him. While having Ian here without Leon felt weird, his presence settled her—once she'd convinced herself he wasn't the murderer. The next time she glanced at him, she caught him studying her face, his expression serious.

"What?" She put a hand to her face.

Ian set his beer and the bowl of popcorn on the table.

"Want to talk about it?"

"What?"

"Anything." He put his arm around her. "I'm sorry I haven't been around much."

"You were busy. Leon was busy."

"That's no excuse, and I should've let you know well before this that you can always call me if you need anything."

She drew away and stared at him. "I don't understand."

"Daphne," he began.

"What?" she whispered.

"How long have we been friends?"

"Ages. As long as I can remember."

"Did you always think of me as your friend?"

"I guess." She was always comfortable with him. He'd never been more to her than Leon's buddy, though. "I wouldn't have called you to chat on the phone, but you've always been there for Leon, so I consider you my friend by default."

"Leon was my best friend. If you need anything—anything at all—you can call me. Promise? Day or night." His expression was earnest.

"Sure."

"You're all alone here, and you didn't call me. I want to make sure you understand I care. If you want, I'll stay with you."

Daphne's eyes went wide, and he spoke quickly as if to reassure her of his intentions. "To keep you company." He faced the glass wall where their images reflected in the glow.

His hair was a mass of auburn curls, and Daphne squelched an urge to run her fingers through it. She'd always thought Ian attractive, but because he was her brother's friend, she'd spent more time taunting him and joking with him than cultivating a romance. He was also five years older and popular with women.

How long since the last time she'd seen him with a woman? She couldn't recall.

He'd had girlfriends, of course, but never anything too serious. Leon mentioned Ian dating but had said nothing lately. That explained why he offered to stay with her. A girlfriend wouldn't approve of an overnighter with another woman no matter what had happened to her brother.

Why in the world should that concern Daphne? Ian was being nice, offering comfort to his best friend's sister. Nothing more.

Yet she couldn't shake the feeling her life had just become more complicated.

CHAPTER 19

Robin studied the photos Jacob had spread out on his desk for her to review. He was right: the woman in them looked identical to Beth.

"Do you have a magnifying glass?"

He opened a drawer and produced a large black-rimmed one with a metal handle.

"Thanks," she said absently. She held it over the first photo, one with the woman standing next to the bike. "I can tell you right off I've never seen this bike. Beth doesn't ride bikes."

"Are you sure?"

"Yes, and I've never seen one in her garage."

"Never mind the bike. The suspect could've obtained it anytime without your knowledge. Focus on the woman."

Robin glanced up at the gruff tone of his voice, but Jacob frowned at the photo, not at her. She huddled over the image again.

"Her hair is too thick."

"So I've heard."

Robin blew out a breath through pursed lips. "Beth has fine, thin hair. Great for putting it up in a high pony, but not thick and full. And the colour is off."

"How so?"

"Well, Beth is blonder."

"I don't know what that means." He leaned in close to her and peered through the glass. She caught the scent of spicy shampoo.

"The colour is darker in this," she said.

"Could be the lighting."

"I suppose. Do you have an expert who can check?"

"Yes, but I wanted to see if you recognize this as your friend."

"I'm trying not to."

He straightened up, rubbing his hands over his lower back. "I'm counting on it. Explain why it's not her."

"The nose." Robin pointed to the second photo. "See? In this one, you glimpse the tip of the nose. When the head angles up even slightly, the nose tip juts out a little beyond the hair. Beth's nose is what you'd call perky. Her dad used to call her 'button nose.' This person's nose is straighter."

She hunched closer.

Jacob examined the photos for what seemed the hundredth time. The killer was good. Her head remained tilted down in almost every shot, but there'd been moments where the angle shifted a fraction.

Robin poked a finger on the photo Jacob stared at. "Here. The mouth. See the lipstick? It wasn't applied correctly. It's outside the lip line. To look fuller, I guess. Beth has full lips. This woman didn't use a lip pencil."

"What does that mean?"

"You can see where the lip line ends and the skin starts under the lipstick. It's lighter there."

He leaned over her. "Yeah. I see."

The techs could run with this. He'd ask the graphics geek to erase the lipstick and reveal the true lips—whatever they could see of them, anyway.

"The sweater. The breasts," Robin said.

Jacob nodded. "The sweater is bulky, probably to hide the breasts."

"Yes, but this person looks flat. When a woman wears a bulky sweater ..." A look of shock crossed her face.

Jacob finished her sentence. "It's a man, wearing a wig and a bulky sweater and riding a woman's bike."

Eyes wide with horror, Robin said, "This proves it. The man who killed Leon broke into my home tonight."

***

98

Time crawled towards the day of Leon's funeral. Daphne's parents arrived the day before and settled into one of the many spare rooms in the house. Ian called Daphne infrequently to check on her and texted more often to keep in touch. He'd spent the night in a spare room the night he'd dropped over. She appreciated it, but since her parents' arrival, no one else need keep her company.

While the house was huge, with her parents around, it felt confining. Daphne's relationship with them made it so, but she couldn't change the dynamic. Both parents looked permanently stricken and in shock and moved as though on autopilot.

As she helped them carry their luggage upstairs to the nicest guest room in the house, she tried to talk to them. Not about Leon—God, no. That subject remained verboten. She'd explained to them what had happened when she'd first called them with the horrible news. After that initial conversation, they didn't want to hear about anything other than that the police had caught his killer. While she understood people grieved in their own way, why couldn't they be there for her as more than a physical presence?

"What a lovely room." Sheila, Daphne's mother, set a carry-on bag on a maple dresser. "I love what you've done with the colours. The bedspread complements the rest of the décor nicely."

"I didn't decorate the house, Mom. Leon hired a professional."

"Oh, yes. Sure." Sheila waved her husband, Frank, over to the walk-in closet. "Set the suitcases in here. We'll worry about unpacking later. I'm starving. Let's eat first."

Frank set the suitcases down. "Shall we order something?"

"I've got food I can reheat. Friends dropped by with casseroles. I could warm one up and add a salad," Daphne replied.

"Don't go to any trouble. We'll order a pizza," Sheila said.

"It's no trouble." Something compelled Daphne to make dinner for her parents even if she only tossed together a salad and stuck a casserole in the oven.

After more debate, her parents agreed, and they all trooped to the kitchen.

As soon as Sheila entered the room, she froze. "Where did they find him?"

"Mom." Daphne's voice cracked.

"Where did my boy die?" Sheila's face was a mask of pain and her voice pitched high.

Unable to help herself, Daphne pointed to the floor next to the barstools at the island. When she spoke, she whispered. "Here."

In her stocking feet, Sheila slid to the spot. When she reached it, she collapsed to her hands and knees, sobbing. Frank dropped beside her, enveloping her in his arms.

"Angel, no. What are you doing to yourself?"

"He died here. Alone." She leaned back on her haunches and wailed. "No one was here with him."

Daphne remained silent. Leon hadn't been alone—his killer had watched him die. Jacob Turner never shared the gory details, but she knew whoever killed Leon had witnessed his death throes. She refused to provide even the smallest detail to her parents. Sheila blew the tiniest things out of proportion, and her son's death had triggered her penchant for drama.

Had Sheila intended to arouse guilt in Daphne for being away from home when Leon had died? If so, she'd succeeded. Daphne's rational mind reasoned that, if she'd been home, either she'd have died with him or the killer would've chosen another time. Her irrational mind dumped guilt all over her. She'd abandoned her brother.

The direction her thoughts took caused a flood of shame in Daphne. What must it be like to lose a child, someone you'd given birth to, nurtured, loved? Both her parents worshipped Leon, sparking jealousy in Daphne until she reminded herself he deserved their pride. He'd become successful beyond their expectations. Rich. Famous. Why wouldn't they be proud?

If she hadn't matched his accomplishments, it wasn't their fault, his fault, or anyone else's fault but her own.

"Mom, please. Why don't you and Dad wait in the living room? I'll light the fireplace and put on the food."

"I can't eat." Sheila ripped herself from Frank's arms and flung herself to the floor. She pressed her hands on the cold ceramic tiles by her face. "He must have been so scared."

"Please." Daphne didn't know what else to say. "Please, Momma. Don't think about that. He's not suffering anymore."

"You don't know. What if he's in pain because they can't find who did this? He might be trapped here."

Now I know where Leon got his imagination. Daphne almost laughed at the absurdity. Dead was dead. If Leon was a ghost, he wasn't hanging around here. She'd seen no sign of him since he'd died, and if he watched from the other side, trying to help them solve his murder, he was doing a crappy job of it.

Her mother's piercing wails continued as did her father's gentle consolations. Neither seemed likely to cease soon. Unable to move or speak, Daphne remained outside the scene. Was this what it felt like to be a ghost?

CHAPTER 20

They gathered for the service in the funeral home's chapel two hours after the final visitation. Conrad slipped in after the immediate family and before extended family and friends. Daphne, her parents, and various aunts, uncles, and cousins congregated in the centre front pews. The coffin already stood in place before the altar. He'd missed the pallbearers marching it up the aisle.

Too bad. He'd have enjoyed that scene.

Conrad scurried to the pew two rows behind Daphne's and snagged a position by the centre aisle. As others arrived to sit in his row, he tucked his knees to the side and waved them past. He wanted to be close to the family, associated with them, but he also wanted to be on the aisle. As soon as the service ended, he'd be right behind them as they left the chapel.

Robin and Beth sat at the other end of his pew. They'd entered from the other side and hadn't needed to sidle past him.

Beth's appearance at the visitation had shocked Conrad. She should be in custody. The sight of her froze him with fear. When his heart slowed its panicked thumping, he'd approached her.

"I'm so glad to see you, Beth. I heard the cops arrested you. Thank God, it's just a rumour." He clasped her hands in his.

"They did arrest me."

When she didn't continue, he prodded her. "You're out on bail?"

"They dropped the charges. I'm sorry, but I don't want to talk about it." She'd extricated her hands from his grip, made a lame excuse about giving her condolences to Daphne's parents, and hurried away.

Ever since then, his stomach churned with unease. If they'd dropped the charges, they'd ruled her out as a suspect. How? He'd been careful. He'd executed the frame-up flawlessly. Sure, the evidence was all circumstantial, but the video footage should have cemented her as the prime suspect.

He'd even worn her shoes, for God's sake.

If she'd had tiny feet like Robin or Daphne, he'd never have pulled that off. Thank God, her height and build made her a big-footed size ten, which was still one size too small for him. The shoes had pinched his feet unmercifully, but it'd been worth the discomfort—or so he'd thought.

What went wrong?

Robin and Beth held hands, and each gripped a tissue in her free hand. He studied them as though searching for tells. What if Robin had deduced someone had prowled through her house the other night? He reviewed the excursion in his head: enter with the key from the fake garden rock, which he'd glimpsed Kaylee retrieving once when she'd thought herself unobserved; boot up the computer; power down the computer—what a wasted effort. Of course, a software developer would have security on her PC.

Conrad continued his review of the break-in: search her room; search closets; search the kitchen. He'd found papers in a banker's box and photographed each one with his cell phone. Whatever related to Leon's work, the contracts she'd signed, anything to do with the new book, was now in his possession as image files.

He'd replaced everything exactly as he'd found it, leaving no trace of his intrusion. Even if something was out of place, surely she'd think she'd done it herself. She wasn't Daphne. Robin didn't have the same obsession to keep everything in a specific spot—a fixation he'd rid Daphne of when they married if he had to beat it out of her. Besides, even if Robin suspected someone had broken in, she couldn't prove anything, and why would she tie it to Leon's murder?

Reassured he was just paranoid, he returned to scoping out the funeral attendees.

The low music, playing since they'd entered the chapel, faded away. "Amazing Grace," volume turned up, replaced it. Conrad faced the front more than ready to say his final goodbyes to Leon

Patterson.

***

Daphne and her parents presented a united front throughout the day, but Beth wasn't fooled. Her friend not only grieved for her brother, but she suffered stress from her parents' presence. It didn't help matters that Conrad hovered around Daphne as if he were her boyfriend. He probably wanted to support and help her—after all, Daphne was Leon's sister and Conrad and Leon had been friends. But Daphne was obviously uncomfortable with Conrad's constant presence.

A short ceremony at the cemetery where they'd bury Leon followed the service at the chapel. Reluctant to allow mourners into the home where her brother had been murdered, Daphne held the reception afterwards in a hotel ballroom.

Beth strategized with Robin, and they urged Daphne to join them at Beth's following the reception. Though Daphne argued she should be with her parents, she didn't take much convincing and neither did her parents. Sheila and Frank even appeared relieved they could have an evening to themselves.

In the late afternoon, the three women donned bathing suits and relaxed around the pool area at Beth's house. Robin sat at a bistro table nursing a glass of wine; Daphne reclined on a lounge chair; Beth leaned against the side of the hot tub, a jet of water pummeling her back.

"My mother's probably moving stuff around as we speak," Daphne said.

"Don't worry about it," Robin replied. "Let's forget about everything horrible for a little while."

"Think of all the fun you'll have putting everything back where it belongs." Beth chuckled and was gratified to hear both Robin and Daphne join her. She couldn't remember the last time she'd wanted to laugh. Or joke.

"Oh, Bethy, I'm so happy you're with us." Daphne rose from the lounge chair and slipped into the hot tub. "God, you were in jail."

"Don't remind me." Beth dipped her head under the water, soaking her hair. When she surfaced and cleared the water from her eyes, she faced Robin. "Thank you for helping me get out. If it wasn't for you, I'd still be in there."

"Jacob said you'd mentioned the hair thing. You'd have found more stuff and gotten yourself out." Robin sipped from her wine and then set the glass on the table.

"Yes, but I couldn't make him accept the evidence. He believed I was guilty."

Robin shook her head. "He wanted to eliminate you as a suspect. That's why he brought me to the station to view the pictures."

"He never asked me," Daphne said.

"After he could prove the person in the photos wasn't Beth, he didn't need to bother you."

"You're awfully defensive of the hot detective." Daphne flicked water in Robin's direction.

"Missed." Robin grinned. "He is hot, eh?"

"But why not start with me? Why drag you to the station?" Daphne asked, frowning.

Robin's expression sobered. "I need to tell you something."

"What?" Beth said.

"Whoever broke into my house likely killed Leon."

Beth and Daphne turned startled expressions on Robin.

"Oh, God," Daphne said. "Why? How do you know?"

"I was home when he broke in." Robin told them what had happened, concluding with her trip to the station to view the photos of the person on the bike. "Once I got the idea into my head that a man killed Leon, I could see it in the photos: a man dressed as a woman," she concluded.

"Who would want Leon dead? Why break into your house?" Beth eased up the side of the hot tub to sit on the edge, dangling calves and feet in the water.

"I can't think of anyone." Daphne turned to Robin. "Can you?"

"No." She paused. "Someone did, though."

"Usually it's someone close to the victim," Beth said.

"That's why the police investigated us," Daphne replied.

"They've ruled us out since they discovered it's a man." Beth hoisted herself up and grabbed her towel from the chair where she'd draped it. She wrapped the towel around her waist and sat at the table across from Robin.

"We can figure this out. We know almost everyone Leon knew." Robin picked up her wine glass but set it down when she saw it was empty.

"I'll get you more wine," Beth said. "And paper and a pen. We'll list the men Leon knew. No discriminating." Excitement surged through her at the prospect of taking action. They could help catch the man who'd not only killed her friend but tried to frame her.

"Women, too," Robin said. "We can make a list of women and then add their associated men to the men's list. Maybe it was a jealous husband or boyfriend or something."

Daphne scowled. "He wasn't having an affair."

"I didn't say he was. But if a woman fan-girl crushed on him, it might make some men jealous."

"Good point." Daphne climbed out of the hot tub.

"All right," Beth said. "I'll be right back. Then we'll find a way to nail him."

"What do we do if we figure it out before the police?" Daphne asked.

Beth clenched her fists. "I want to gift-wrap him and deliver him to Jacob Turner, but that's just the Sigourney Weaver in *Alien* part of me talking. I suppose we'd have to settle for calling Jacob and telling him everything."

"Sounds reasonable," Robin said. "Okay, no matter who it is, we don't take risks. We call Jacob. Agreed?"

"Agreed," her friends replied together.

Beth laughed and punched Daphne's arm. "Jinx," she said.

CHAPTER 21

Robin went home early the next morning, Daphne dropping her off before returning to Leon's house to hang out with her parents. For the first time since her husband's death, Robin hated to be alone. After tossing her overnight bag on the floor in her bedroom, she put on coffee in the kitchen. Her children were due home today, and she looked forward to having them back, but worried about the intruder.

As she recalled the horrible ordeal of hiding under the couch while a strange man rummaged through her things, she shook with anger. No one else would do this to her. Robin marched outside and retrieved the spare key from under the rock.

Kaylee, her twelve-year-old daughter, could carry a key and keep it safe. Nathaniel, Robin's son, wouldn't receive his own key. She and Kaylee would have to make sure he didn't get locked out. How hard could it be? At eight, he wasn't permitted to come and go on his own. In fact, neither was Kaylee.

Reassured she'd taken a step towards securing her home, Robin poured coffee and settled down at her desk to work.

Two hours later, a knock interrupted her. Immersed in a web project, she'd been in the zone and completely unaware of time passing. At the bang on the front door, she startled from her chair. A glance at the clock verified it was too early for her parents to be back with the kids. She hurried to the door and peered through the peephole.

Jacob Turner. What's he doing here on a Sunday?

As her hand reached for the deadbolt, she froze. What if they'd caught the intruder? *The killer.* Robin's stomach churned as she unlocked and opened the door.

"Hi." Jacob smiled. "Sorry to intrude."

He seemed nervous. Who'd they catch? Someone close to her?

"You arrested someone?" *The killer.*

"No, sorry. I guess you'd jump to that conclusion." Jacob focused his gaze past her shoulder into the living room. "Mind if I come in?"

"Sure. I mean, no, I don't mind." Robin stepped aside and let him pass.

He removed his shoes and headed to the couch.

"Coffee, Detective?" Without waiting for a reply, she strode to the kitchen and picked up the coffee pot. "I made it two hours ago, but this thermal carafe keeps it hot."

"Okay, thanks. And call me Jacob. Or Jake. My friends call me Jake. My mother's the one who calls me Jacob."

She wished he'd get to the point of the visit. This suddenly felt like an awkward first date.

As if reading her mind, he said, "This isn't really a business call. I mean, sort of." He thrust a finger into his collar and tugged on it. "I wanted to check on you—see if you're okay. After the break-in."

Robin set a tray on the coffee table as she had the first time he'd visited. To keep busy, she retrieved her mug from her desk though she didn't want another cup of coffee.

"I'm okay. Kind of nervous." She gave him a shy smile. "I brought the spare key in from the garden. I feel so stupid for hiding it there. It seemed safe in the backyard since most people keep them near the front door. I fooled only myself."

"Most people wouldn't go to the trouble of searching the back garden for a spare key." His brows rose. "Who knew you hid it there?"

"The kids. That's all. And they promised not to tell anyone."

"What about Beth and Daphne?"

Robin frowned. "I never told them. You don't suspect either of them, do you? A man entered my house, and a man killed Leon."

He shook his head and waved his hands dismissively. "Someone took the trouble of searching for a spare key. Was anyone aware you had one hidden outside?"

"I don't go around telling people, and the kids wouldn't tell anyone. No one knew."

"Makes you wonder how he'd have gotten in otherwise. Would he have broken a window or kicked in the door?" Jacob's eyes glazed over as he spoke.

Robin remained silent, understanding he wasn't asking her. Since he hadn't made a move towards the coffee, she poured for them both.

Jacob's eyes lost the faraway look and his gaze met hers, sending a shiver through her.

"Thank you." He added milk and sugar to his coffee. "So, you brought the key inside. Good. Have you thought more about what he wanted?"

"I doubt he'll come back. Not much here to steal."

Jacob set his coffee down and leaned back in his seat. "You believe he wanted to rob you? He took nothing."

"Perhaps he wanted files."

"What makes you conclude that?"

"Twenty dollars sat on my dresser and he never touched it, but he riffled through my dresser drawers and searched the file boxes in the closet. He didn't go through my purse, though, and it sat on the floor of the closet."

"You verified he took nothing from your purse?"

"Yes. I own multiple purses, and they were all on the closet floor. He ignored them—fortunate for me. If he'd examined them, he'd have realized I was home."

"How so?"

"I'd left my cell phone and wallet in the purse I used that day. If he'd found them, he'd have realized I was in the house. He might have thought I left without my wallet, keys, and cell phone, but how many women do you know who'd do that?"

"I see your point." He picked up his coffee, but instead of sipping, only stared into the cup. After a moment, he said, "When do your kids come home?"

"After dinner."

Jacob opened his mouth, closed it, and then opened it to say "You should install a security system."

She sighed. That idea had already crossed her mind. The nights since the break-in had been mostly sleepless. A security system would give her peace of mind. No matter what it cost, she could afford it. Robin worked on lucrative projects and she wasn't a big spender. The mortgage on the house was paid off after her husband died. Her biggest expenses were her books and household bills.

"It needn't be expensive." Jacob's face brightened. "I'll help you. We'll take care of it right now. By tonight, you'll be much safer."

Somehow, Jacob convinced Robin to allow him to take her shopping for a home security system. He also convinced her to let him take her to lunch with a promise to return to her place to install everything afterwards.

After an hour of stalking the aisles and grilling salespeople at the local tech store, Jacob settled on a system. He secured it in the trunk of his car, and they headed into downtown Niagara-on-the-Lake. They parked down the street from the Prince of Wales Hotel, but she didn't realize it was their destination until they walked through the front doors.

"Jake." Robin halted inside the entrance, and Jacob took her arm and guided her away from the doors.

"Yes?"

"Isn't this too much?" The restaurants here were expensive. She'd expected they'd pop into a fast food place or Andrew's.

"How often do you get to have high tea at the Prince of Wales?" He flashed a coy smile though his tone had been mischievous.

"You want to have tea?"

"Not just tea. Traditional afternoon tea."

Perplexed, she could only say "But why?"

"We could use a nice outing somewhere where the case wasn't hanging over our heads. Get to know each other a little better."

"This isn't a good idea." Was this a date?

Jacob again seemed to read her mind. "Don't think of this as a date. We're getting away from the mundane. They have a great spread for afternoon tea. If you don't mind indulging me, I haven't had a real break in months. It's as much for me as it is for you."

"For me?"

"Robin, when was the last time you went out with a man?"

When she didn't respond, he prodded. "Have you been out with anyone in the last three years?"

"That's my business."

"It was a rhetorical question. This isn't a date. I enjoyed your company today. We had a nice time, right?"

She grinned. "Shopping for a security system because a man broke into my home."

But she had to admit she'd had fun. He made her laugh more than she had in ages. Daphne and Beth had helped her through the rough times after her husband died, but she hadn't gotten close to another man. Just as it seemed things might develop between herself and Leon, someone killed him.

A wave of shock and fear raced through her. Ridiculous though the idea was, what if she was bad luck to any man who became interested in her? The blood drained from her face.

"What's wrong?" Jacob asked, his tone concerned. When she didn't reply, he said, "Robin? Tell me."

"Leon and I ..." She couldn't continue.

Understanding dawned on his face. "Were you and Leon involved?"

"No. Yes. No." How could she explain they hadn't slept together—hadn't even dated—but they'd been on the verge of an intimacy she hadn't experienced since her marriage?

Jacob's expression softened. "I'm sorry. I didn't realize."

"No, you don't understand." She choked on a sob, unable to continue. "I'm sorry."

He sighed. "It's okay. We don't have to go in here."

"I want to." Perhaps if she told him her irrational fear, he'd find a way to reassure her. Either that, or he'd think her insane and head for the hills. If so, she'd be sad to see him go.

"Tell me."

She inhaled a deep breath, held it, and then exhaled. "Let's sit down in the lobby. I'll explain."

CHAPTER 22

The cozy, dim lobby in the Prince of Wales Hotel had a Victorian feel. An enormous stained-glass portrait of Athena in a grape arbour amongst a garden of lilies graced almost an entire wall. Jacob led Robin to an ornate, brocade couch across from it. Robin sank into the seat, her red-gold hair reflecting the red-gold cloth of the sofa. One of her hands rubbed the back of her neck, tempting Jacob to clasp it.

Worried he'd made her uncomfortable, he took a seat on the other end of the couch so they shared space without touching.

After clearing his throat, he said, "What's wrong?"

"Martin was my whole life—the love of my life, I thought. After he died, I wanted to die. If it weren't for my kids, I'd have— well, you can guess what went through my head." She fell quiet.

Compelled to fill the silence, Jacob said, "I'm sorry."

Did she understand how he regretted she'd lost so much? Did she cling to her grief out of habit or something more? Was it wrong to want to spend time with her?

"With time, I recovered from the loss. While I'm not healed completely, I no longer want to die." Robin tilted her head, the curls haloing her face spilling to one shoulder. "I proved it when I ran outside to escape the man who broke into my house."

"How?" He thought he understood but wanted her to say it.

"I'm afraid to leave the house, afraid I'll have a panic attack. But when forced to decide between staying inside with an intruder and going outside to get help, I mustered up the courage to escape despite the risk of discovery." She sat taller as she spoke of her accomplishment and her eyes shone with pride.

Jacob nodded, his silence urging her to continue.

"Leon and I grew close." She must have read something in his expression because she gave him a shy smile. "I've enjoyed your company. This morning was fun. Even looking at those pictures of the suspect together was fun."

Horror flooded her face and she pressed a palm to her open mouth. "I didn't mean ... Oh, God. It just ..."

He scooted close to her and drew her hand gently away from her mouth, clasping it in both of his. "It's okay. I understand. Did you and Leon date?"

"We liked each other—I'd known him for years as Daphne's big brother. Leon was nice. Attractive. Successful." Robin's eyes glistened with unshed tears. "He was so kind and generous. When he learned I'd written two novels and a few stories I'd never published, he insisted on reading them. He liked them—genuinely liked them."

"Did he suggest you work together then?"

She nodded. "Leon guided me through the process of submitting a joint proposal for the non-fiction book. I wrote most of it, but he oversaw it, critiqued it, and forced me to rewrite it, I don't know how many times, until he approved it. We sent it to his agent who sold it to the publisher."

Robin stared down at his hands, which still enveloped hers, as if realizing for the first time he touched her. She drew her hand from his and hunted through her purse. With a tissue she found, she dabbed at her eyes.

Good cover, Jacob thought. *Made it appear she was going for a tissue instead of getting away from me.* He regretted the thought the moment he had it. Judgment always came easily to him. Perhaps this time he'd give someone the benefit of the doubt.

Fine. She'd only wanted to grab a tissue to dry her eyes. It had nothing to do with avoiding physical contact with him.

"Leon died." Her voice broke, and she pressed the tissue to her eyes.

"Yes, and we'll catch who did it."

"You don't understand," she whispered. "Martin died. Leon died. Because they cared for me."

"Robin, you're a software developer."

She raised her head from the tissue and gaped at him. "What?"

"You aren't allowed to be superstitious."

"I'm not."

"Do you believe your husband and Leon both died because they cared about you?"

"My head doesn't. My inner demons? They needle me with it. What if someone else cares for me and dies?"

Jacob huffed out a breath. "Are you worried I'll fall in love with you and drop dead?"

She smiled, brightening the room. "That's ridiculous."

"Sure is. Tell your therapist. It'll give her something to do for the next three sessions at least."

Robin punched his arm. "Very funny."

He turned serious for a moment. "You didn't kill your husband. A distracted driver did."

"Yes, but if I hadn't run back into the house before we left, the timing would've been different. He'd be alive."

"How do you know?"

"Because we'd have parked elsewhere. Or he'd have crossed the street earlier."

"Or not. Traffic might've slowed you down. The parking spot could've been farther away and put you there, anyway." Jacob draped an arm on the back of the couch, a casual gesture. He didn't try to touch her. "Look, your husband—and you—paid a high price for this guy's carelessness. But it sure as hell wasn't your fault. A thousand things could've changed the timing. Despite that, it played out the way it did. It's not on you or on Martin. We'll never know if changing your patterns might've changed anything."

"I understand. Then along came Leon. He kissed me." She met Jacob's gaze without flinching. "I told no one, not even Beth and Daphne. They'd have made more of it than what it was."

The revelation struck him like a throat punch on multiple levels. For one, she hadn't told him during their formal interview exactly how close she'd been with the victim, which might cause suspicion. For another, if the two had been romantically involved, he may as well forget about developing a relationship with her.

Jacob held still and swallowed to clear his throat before replying. "And what was it?"

"Testing the waters. We'd worked late at my place. The kids were in bed. We always worked at my place. He knew I didn't want to go out, so he came over." The look of horror crossed her face again. "The killer could've been searching for our work." Robin shook her head. "Why?"

"I don't know. A good theory though. I'll investigate the possibility. Show me what you worked on later today?"

"What about the confidentiality agreement I signed?"

"It'll be all right. As with the contract, I could get a court order, but if you show me without that, it'll speed things along."

"Okay, but as before, I'm telling the publisher and Leon's agent."

"Fine. Tell me what happened between you and Leon. What did the relationship mean to you? To him?"

"It felt nice—that's all. We made plans to go for lunch the following Sunday. Two days later, he was dead."

"And you blame yourself?" He held up a hand when she tried to speak. "You didn't jinx him. This had nothing to do with you. The only way this would be your responsibility is if you'd killed him."

Jacob leaned forward, squinting his eyes as though examining her face for tells. "You didn't kill him, did you?"

"Are you serious?"

"Are you?"

"I ... No. You're right. It's not my fault."

"Good." His stomach growled, a long, low rumble, and he chuckled.

"What's so funny?"

"I'm hungry."

She laughed. "Your stomach made that noise?"

"Afraid so."

"Jake?" She placed a hand on his arm. The touch sent electricity to his solar plexus, making breathing difficult and almost killing his appetite—for food, anyway.

"Yes?"

"That offer for tea still available?"

"Sure." As he rose, his gaze strayed behind the sofa to where a console table stood with an open guest book and pen resting on it. He clasped her hand and tugged her to her feet. "Come on. You'll love it. We'll even sign the guest book."

Robin grinned and reached for the pen.

CHAPTER 23

With all the chaos in her life, Daphne appreciated not having to return to work until Tuesday. Hard to believe it was already Labour Day though. She'd driven her parents to the airport the previous Thursday morning, not entirely sorry to see them go. Anxious to return to the restaurant, Sheila had suggested Daphne go to British Columbia with them.

As if. She had a life here and couldn't drop everything to run off to BC. For what? To hang around her parents and have the constant reminder that the better sibling had died? Shame overwhelmed her every time those thoughts intruded, but she couldn't prevent them. While her father remained silent, her mother wailed and whined about Leon.

Not jealous of my dead brother, Daphne insisted as she scrubbed the kitchen floor. She cleaned the kitchen floor daily now. It became a compulsion as much as walking through the house to make sure nothing was out of place or chanting her anxiety-reducing mantras.

As guilt flowed through her, she scrubbed harder, repeating "I love Mom" as she did. As the tension decreased, she eased up the pressure she exerted on the sponge and her muttering ceased.

The doorbell rang, and she dropped the sponge into the bucket. Before running to open the door, she beelined to the bathroom and washed her hands. By the time she reached the front entrance, the bell chimed again.

Daphne threw the door open to Ian.

"Hi." She tilted her head and studied him. "Shouldn't you be

116

getting ready for school tomorrow?"

"I never work on Labour Day. It's the law." He grinned. "Want company?"

"Sure." She stepped aside to let him in. "I was just—never mind."

"What? Am I interrupting something?"

"No. Cleaning."

He strolled past her and headed for the family room. "Need help?"

"No. Let me put away the bucket, and I'll be right with you." She returned to the kitchen and put away her cleaning supplies. That necessitated a dash to the bathroom to wash her hands. On her way to the family room, she veered into the kitchen and grabbed two beers.

She found Ian sitting on the couch.

"I thought you'd want something to drink." She handed him a bottle.

"Thanks. You acquiring a taste for this, or are you using up what you've got?"

"A bit of both. What's up?" Daphne eased onto a loveseat positioned ninety degrees to the couch and angled her body to face him.

"Does something have to be up?"

"You didn't call first. Are you checking up on me?"

"That not allowed?"

"I guess it's all right. Sometimes. I can take care of myself, you know."

He frowned and didn't reply.

"What?"

He took a swig of his beer and set it on the coffee table. Unable to help herself, Daphne shifted the bottle to the centre of the coaster. Ian grinned.

"What?" she said.

"It's cute when you do stuff like that. Drove Leon crazy sometimes, but he's your brother." Ian shrugged. "I prefer to find it endearing."

"I'm not normal."

"Honey, who is?"

She laughed, and tension uncoiled from her solar plexus.

"Listen." He leaned forward in his seat and rested his elbows on

117

his thighs. "I heard about the break-in at Robin's."

Surely Robin hadn't told him. "How?"

"People talking."

"Who knows?"

"Probably the whole town. Everyone's discussing it. She ran to her neighbours' house and called the cops. That'll get around."

Daphne nodded. Small towns had eyes everywhere without even factoring in social media. "Then why the hell didn't anyone see who killed Leon?"

"What?"

Startled, she realized she'd said it out loud. "If a neighbour had seen the killer come here, they'd have arrested someone by now."

Ian moved to sit beside her. "Have the police told you that?"

"No." She leaned into him, putting her head on his shoulder, and he put his arm around her.

"Then you don't know?"

"I'm speculating."

"Why don't you ask them?"

"They won't tell me."

"Doesn't hurt to ask."

Daphne stared into his eyes and swallowed with an audible click. His gaze held hers, and it took all her effort not to run her fingers through the curls in his hair. She pulled herself up and away. Best to keep her distance, but damn, why hadn't she noticed before how sexy he was?

"Love you. Love you. Love you," she muttered under her breath.

"Pardon?" His brows drew together.

"Nothing. I talk to myself sometimes."

Ian flashed her a smile. "Leon used to threaten to pound on me if I made fun of you for it when we were kids."

"Did you guys often talk about me?" The grin she returned contained a hint of flirtation. *Stop it. What are you doing?* She couldn't seem to help herself.

When he answered, his voice was soft. "Often enough."

Something fluttered in her stomach. With her focus on him, she groped for her beer. Before she touched it, he clasped her wrist, stopping her.

"Careful. You'll knock it over." He released her, picked up the bottle, and handed it to her.

"Thank you." Her gaze dropped to his lips, and to distract herself, she sipped the beer. "I hate beer." She sounded astonished.

Ian laughed, breaking the tension between them, which, on her part at least, was sexual.

"You discovering that now?"

"No. I thought I might feel differently this time. Leon always drank it, and you seem to like it."

"Better than wine."

"Are we going to discuss beer now?" The flirtatiousness had returned to her voice. *What the hell? Quit it. He's Leon's friend ... So, who better?*

She rose and turned to walk away, but he gripped her wrist, this time more firmly. "Wait."

"Yes?" Daphne froze and held her breath.

"Shall we discuss this?"

"Could we?"

"You can tell me anything."

"Okay. Just one thing."

"What?"

"If I blurt out I love you, ignore it."

"Pardon?"

Daphne sighed. "It's part of my neurosis. I blurt it out. I've said it to my dry cleaner, for God's sake. When I repeat certain phrases, it eases my anxiety. So, if you overhear me saying it, please don't freak out."

"Okay. Promise." Ian's lips twitched, but to her relief, he didn't laugh at her.

Before she could continue, the doorbell rang.

She rose. "I'm sorry. I wasn't expecting anyone else. Wait here."

"Perhaps I should come along in case the reporters have returned." Ian stood.

Reporters hadn't bothered her for a week—Beth's arrest had diverted their focus for a while—but it wouldn't hurt to be cautious. "Okay."

They approached the door, and through the glass, she could tell it wasn't reporters. It was someone far worse: Warren.

***

While Daphne talked to Warren, Ian hung back to give her privacy.

He remained within hailing distance in case she needed him, and he made deliberate eye contact with Warren. Whatever Daphne's ex planned, he'd have to do it with Ian watching.

The couple's voices remained low, but the discussion became heated. Twice, Warren glanced pointedly at Ian before returning his attention to Daphne.

"I'm sorry." Daphne's voice rose in frustration so Ian heard those words clearly, but then she lowered it again.

"Everything all right?" Ian asked. "Need anything, Daphne?"

She glanced over her shoulder at him and shook her head. "It's okay. I've got it. Warren is leaving."

Ian started to return to the family room when Warren's words halted him.

"Daphne, come on! Come out with me."

"Not now," she replied. "Actually, not ever. I'm tired of this, Warren. We're done."

"Friends. That's all."

Since they no longer tried to keep it down, Ian turned back around and sidled up next to Daphne.

"She's got company, dude." Ian tried to sound jovial but wasn't sure he succeeded.

"I can see that." Warren crossed his arms over his chest. "You can both come. My band's playing tonight. Starts in a couple hours."

"No, but thanks for the invite. Hope it goes well." Ian started to close the door, but Warren stuck his booted foot into the breach.

"Why not? It'll be fun. Daphne would enjoy it."

"Apparently not. She's already told you she doesn't want to go."

"We're not arguing about that. She's just being a grouch. Come on, babe, I'll make it up to you. You can hang out after with me and the guys—like old times."

A huge sigh escaped Daphne. "Go to your gig, Warren. Please. You want anything else, have your lawyer contact my lawyer. Goodnight."

She slammed the door shut, Warren leaping out of the way before it crunched his foot.

"You okay?" Ian asked.

Daphne scowled at the door.

"Love you. Love you. Love you," she said.

CHAPTER 24

With chores and paperwork out of the way, Beth took her afternoon coffee and cake, along with a novel, out to the back deck behind the main house. This might be one of the few remaining sunny days before the approaching fall's cold and rain set in. She wanted to take advantage of it—even if only for half an hour.

She set the items on the patio table and wound up the umbrella in the centre. At this time of day, the sun beat down on the deck where the furniture stood. Though the temperature today read a balmy twenty-three Celsius and lacked the humidity of summer, the ultraviolet light from the sun remained strong. With her fair complexion, she couldn't sit out without gobs of sunscreen even for a short time.

Before she settled in to read, her cell phone rang. Unknown name and number.

"Hello?"

"Beth?"

She couldn't quite place the familiar voice. "Yes?"

"It's Andrew."

Why would Andrew call her? Beth lost her ability to think and didn't know what to say. "Oh."

Oh, my God, genius. Say something else. Quick. "Hi. Andrew." *Good save. Your brilliance must surely dazzle him.*

"Haven't seen you since the police were here. Wanted to make sure you're all right."

Since the police had dragged her from his place, he meant.

"Okay. Thanks."

A soft chuckle floated from her phone. "So, you okay?"

"Yes."

"You don't sound okay. What's going on? They dropped the charges?"

Sweat bloomed on her palms and her mind remained blank. Why did he always make her so nervous? He was just a guy. *Yeah, a hot guy. A hot guy who's smart and sexy and would never pay any attention to me.*

Yet he'd called her.

"Beth?" He sounded concerned, earning her gratitude.

"Sorry. It was horrible."

"I understand. Want to talk about it?"

Yeah, but my mouth won't form words. How telepathic are you? "Um. Sure," she stammered out.

"I thought I'd come by."

That jarred her from her verbal stasis. "Don't you have to work?"

"I've got people who can take over. Unless you have to work? Restaurants and inns are busy today, I know. But if you have someone who can spell you, we could go out. Or I could drop by."

"Okay." She didn't want him to come over. She'd rather meet him somewhere. She'd be far too nervous alone here with him. "Where can we meet?"

"How about Ryerson Park?"

"All right." That was near Robin's house. If she needed to, she'd retreat there. "I'll pack food for us, and we'll have a picnic."

Wow, I'm getting so chatty he might even think I'm normal. She yawned. *Oh, damn, no.*

"Meet in twenty minutes?" Andrew suggested.

"A half hour would be better. See you then." Beth disconnected without waiting for a response and set the phone on the table.

Okay, that wasn't so bad, and I didn't pass out.

She rose, collected her things, and went into the house. Since she'd promised him food, she'd better put something together.

As she worked, Beth reflected on the conversation. Why had he called her? To get the gossip about her arrest? Andrew didn't strike her as a gossip. Sure, as the owner of a business where people congregated, he heard all kinds of news. But she'd never known him to relish digging up the juicy details about other people.

From the freezer, she retrieved a container of home-baked cookies, another of muffins, and, from the fridge, containers of yogurt. Finger sandwiches would be nice. She'd make sliced turkey with lettuce, cucumber, and mustard. Beth's musings continued as she worked.

Perhaps Andrew genuinely wanted to verify she was all right and spend time with her.

Yeah, sure. When he has all those skinny women at his beck and call. The guy must have a black book to rival Hugh Hefner's.

Well, perhaps not Hefner. The point was, Andrew played the field. Was he doing that with her? She shook her head. Couldn't be. She rarely spoke to him. They'd never gotten close, though many of the other writers' group members became friendly with him. He always made her nervous and uncomfortable—not in a creepy way, but because she'd felt attracted to him from the moment she'd laid eyes on him.

It hadn't been love at first sight—she didn't believe in it—but more like lust at first sight. Andrew seemed nice despite the never-want-to-settle-down vibe he gave off. Didn't the fact he'd called to check on her prove he was a nice guy?

Beth grabbed a knife and began slicing cheese. Cheddar would be good and Swiss.

A blast of fear struck her. *Unless he killed Leon.*

She sliced her finger and swooned to the floor.

***

No reply on Beth's cell phone.

Andrew sat atop a picnic table overlooking Lake Ontario in Ryerson Park. Waves crashed against the rocks at the bottom of the steep drop to the water. The table stood well back from the edge but close enough to view the shoreline below. On his right, the slope to a sandy beach was more gradual. Kids and their parents splashed in the water or built sandcastles. Teenagers played with a Frisbee on the grass while dog-walkers strolled along the sidewalk bordering the road.

Beth should've already arrived. Sure, she was late by only ten minutes, but she lived close to the park. Maybe she wouldn't show, which made little sense. They'd made the plans less than an hour ago.

Rumours floated around town about her. She'd fall asleep at weird times. He'd seen it once—possibly. Beth had been in the café waiting for the rest of the writers' group to arrive. Andrew dropped by her table to chat with her. Her shyness and sunlight-coloured hair drew him like the proverbial moth to the flame though he wasn't the one likely to get scorched. He'd forced himself to keep his distance so she wouldn't get burned.

With Beth, he'd gone against type and refused to hit on her— not because she wasn't good enough but because he believed he wasn't. However, he couldn't stay away from her even if he only shared space with her as he socialized with her friends.

On this particular day, she'd arrived at the café first. He'd told himself she'd expect him to drop by her table to say hello. If anyone else were there, he'd have done it without a second thought. Beth loved the scones Andrew's sold. Warm from the oven, they made the perfect excuse to approach her, so he took her one.

"Hey, got fresh scones. Thought since you buy them so often, I'd give you one on the house. To thank you for your business."

Her face was sheet white when she raised her head from her laptop.

Andrew reached her table and set the treat before her. "I've got *Crème Fraiche* to go with it." He pointed to a condiment container filled with fluffy white cream next to the scone.

Beth licked her lips and smiled. "Thank you. That's nice."

They gazed at each other in silence.

Finally, Andrew broke it. "What are you working on?"

"A non-fiction book."

Whenever Andrew spoke to Beth, he found himself pulling words from her. In a way, he enjoyed the challenge of drawing her from her shell. He yearned for the day when she'd be as relaxed with him as she seemed to be with Leon and the others.

"What's it about?"

She yawned, but he assumed she was just tired. He continued to chat her up until her eyelids drooped and then drifted closed. Before he could nudge her, her head bobbed, and she snapped awake.

"Pardon?" Beth's expression was puzzled, her tone confused.

"I'm sorry," Andrew replied. "I need to put more coffee on before the rest of the crowd arrives. You good?" She'd flustered

him. Had he bored her? If it was her thing where she fell asleep—
he didn't recall its name—then he wouldn't take it personally. For
the rest of the night, he'd told himself so, though, damn it, women
didn't fall asleep talking to Andrew Winston.

He withdrew from his reveries at the sight of her car crawling
past the park. From inside, Beth scanned for parking spots.

Andrew relaxed. It would take her a few minutes to find a
space. The park was crowded today. She'd have to walk a fair
distance and would need help to carry what she'd brought. He
jumped off the table and followed her car.

CHAPTER 25

From the desk in his home office, Conrad called Daphne. High time she paid attention to her future husband.

"Hello?"

"Hi, it's Conrad."

"Hi, what's up?" She sounded distracted.

"How are you holding up?"

"Fine, thanks. I'm kind of busy. Can I call you back?"

"What are you doing? You at home?"

"Yes, but I have a friend over."

"Beth?"

Daphne sighed, which irritated him. "No. It's not a good time. I'll call you later."

Conrad sucked in a breath through gritted teeth and forced his jaw to unclench. "Yeah. No problem. How 'bout we meet for dinner?"

"I can't. Why don't I call you after Ian leaves? Okay?"

No, it's definitely not okay. "Yeah. Sure. I'll talk to you then." He disconnected the call.

So, Ian was with her. Again.

Conrad picked up the rock he'd stolen from Leon and hurled it across the room. It bounced off the wall, and he rushed to scoop it up and examine it. To his relief, it hadn't cracked or broken.

Inside, he continued to seethe. She'd invited another man into their home. Daphne would have to learn that what was Leon's should now be Conrad's. He'd worked for it. He'd killed for it. All

126

of it was rightfully his. Only luck had given Leon the advantages.

Stupid, simpering fool. Leon had deserved none of this. Some guys had things handed to them and it wasn't right. Conrad vowed to correct the injustice.

***

When Beth stepped from her car and turned around, she bit back a shriek as she found herself face to face with Andrew.

"Oh, where'd you come from?" Her heart pounded as much from physical attraction as from fear. By the time she'd left her house, she'd convinced herself Andrew couldn't be Leon's killer. Doubts flooded back when he snuck up on her.

"The park. I saw you pull up and thought you might need help to carry stuff." He stepped back and appraised her. "What happened to your finger?"

She followed his gaze to the bandage on her hand. "Nothing. A little cut."

"That's a large bandage."

"I accidentally cut myself. It'll be fine." Beth averted her eyes, hoping he wouldn't question her further. She hated to lie, but telling the truth wasn't an option.

Change the subject, dumbass. "Thanks for offering to help. I've got a cooler in the trunk." She smiled at him as she popped the hatch on her car.

Andrew lifted out the cooler.

Honestly, it wasn't too large or too heavy, but it was nice of him to help her. After she locked the car, she followed him to a picnic table under a large oak tree.

He set the cooler on the table and, looking eager, opened it.

"It's lovely here," she said and sat down. "I brought water and pop to drink."

"That's fine." He held up a bottle of water, and when she nodded, he handed it to her.

"Thanks." Beth watched silently as he helped himself to a can of cola and closed the lid on the cooler.

Did he want to eat now? Should she unload everything?

What's wrong with you? Get up. It's your stuff; play hostess.

God, she sounded like her mother. Eva would be thrilled if she knew her verbal abuse of Beth continued after death.

Ask him what he wants. Relief flooded through her, and she said, "Are you hungry? We could eat and then go for a walk."

What if he's in a hurry? "If you have the time," she stammered.

"Sure." He smiled. "Let me help you."

Andrew opened the cooler and dug in. "This looks amazing. You've gone to a lot of trouble." He pulled out the various containers of food, paper plates, and stainless-steel cutlery wrapped in cloth napkins.

"Glad you like it." She focused on her breathing. If she kept it steady, perhaps it would calm her nerves. The last thing she needed was to fall asleep in front of him. Her anxiety ratcheted up a notch at the thought. By forcing herself to regulate her breath and concentrate on setting the table, she pushed the nervousness aside.

"Did you bake these cookies yourself?" Andrew opened the box and reached for one.

"Uh-uh." Beth wagged a finger at him. "Lunch first, then dessert."

"Okay, Mom." He trapped her finger in his fist. "Whatever you say."

Pulse pounding in her ears, Beth squelched an urge to tug his hand to her mouth and kiss it. No way was this man Leon's killer. He was too nice. Too kind. She met his gaze and returned the smile he flashed at her.

Wouldn't the killer want her to believe he was nice?

Damn it. She'd help Daphne and Robin find him no matter what. If they didn't, she'd never trust any man, and, more than anything, she wanted to trust Andrew.

Beth extricated her finger from his grip and said, "Let's eat. We don't have all day."

***

August raced by for Robin. Jacob helped her install the security system, easing her fears and earning her gratitude. When her kids had returned home from their grandparents' house, they brought with them a reassuring noise and activity. She'd enjoyed the quiet and solitude, but having the kids back brought the house to life.

Today was the first Thursday of September, and tonight would be the first writers' group meeting since Leon had died. She smiled to herself as she powered down the computer to start dinner before the kids arrived from school. The routines associated with fall and the school year's start kept her cheerfully occupied.

She'd barely spoken to Beth and Daphne—they'd all been busy, struggling to return normalcy to their lives. Naturally, Robin spent most of her time at home. Beth had visited Daphne once on Tuesday and once on Wednesday and reported that everything seemed fine with their friend—or as fine as possible under the circumstances. Ian visited Daphne as well, and even Conrad dropped by to check on her.

Robin phoned but couldn't force herself to leave the house and visit. No matter how she justified it, she couldn't convince herself it was anything but cowardice that kept her from visiting Daphne.

The night the intruder entered Robin's house had seemed to trigger a breakthrough. She'd run outside and to a neighbour's. Once inside the neighbour's home, the anxiety had eased, but leaving the house had been the hurdle. In a way, she owed the intruder her thanks for revealing she could handle an emergency.

"I can cope." Robin said the words aloud to try them on. If she continued to progress, she might stop her meds. Maybe she'd be normal.

She chuckled. *Who do I know who's normal?*

Making dinner for herself and her kids was normal. From the fridge, she removed a package of thawed chicken breasts. After beating an egg and dipping the chicken in it, she prepared breading. She coated the meat and laid the pieces out on a pan. While the oven warmed up, she got the rice underway.

As soon as the chicken was in the oven, she checked the time. The kids would run up the walk soon, so she opened the front door to watch for them through the screen. That done, she started work on a salad.

This is good. Robin felt happier than she had since her husband died though the admission brought with it a flood of guilt and thoughts of Leon.

"I'm so sorry, Leon." How could she take pleasure in cooking when he'd died so recently? He'd never make another meal, never eat another meal. Did spirits eat on the other side?

She'd visited a psychic after Martin's death. Beth had dragged her. She'd thought a medium would show Robin Martin existed somewhere and help her overcome her fear of leaving the house.

It hadn't worked. The psychic, who called herself Shambhala, seemed okay, but Robin didn't believe the woman communicated with Martin. The woman said Martin wanted Robin to move on with her life—not exactly a radical insight into the mind of a beloved husband and father. You could say the same about any departed loved one.

Robin froze as a memory popped into her head. The psychic had predicted Robin would meet a man with a badge.

"He'll become important to you; you'll grow close. He'll free you, dearie. Watch for him. When he appears, your life will be in chaos. He'll help you through the turmoil. It's meant to be."

Meant to be. Robin had left the session over a hundred dollars poorer but no more enlightened than when she'd gone in. Beth listened to the recording of the session and interpreted everything Shambhala said to mean Robin would meet a cop. Robin brushed it off and said perhaps the man with the badge was a health inspector.

"I'll bring a health inspector into our lives, and he'll shut down our friends' work places. Daphne and Andrew will hate it."

"Do health inspectors carry badges?"

"They need to have ID. Basically, Beth, it's anyone who carries ID. A driver's license would qualify."

This had annoyed Beth, who visited Shambhala every six months for advice on her life. "You wait," she'd argued. "The man with the badge will show up. You'll see. Shambhala's never wrong."

A tap on the screen door made Robin look over.

"Hey, something smells great. May I come in?"

"Conrad. Sure." She set the knife on the cutting board and waved him in.

CHAPTER 26

Conrad stepped through Robin's front door and strode through her living room as though carefree.

"What's up?" she asked and returned to chopping celery. "Grab a drink from the fridge."

That she hadn't even flinched when she spotted him at the door boded well. Perhaps she hadn't been able to identify him as the intruder. Ever since that night, he berated himself for not knocking on the door first to verify no one was home before entering the house. The place had been dark, had looked empty, and she'd been at Daphne's for what seemed to be the long haul. Was it his fault she'd returned home early?

"Thanks." He helped himself to a beer. "How are you doing? Talk is, you had a break-in. Everything okay?" Concern laced his voice.

"Yeah, fine. They didn't break in. Whoever came in used a key hidden in the garden."

Conrad groaned. "You keep a key in the garden. I don't believe it."

"It's not insane. I needed it for emergencies."

"You mean you were terrified you'd be locked out of your sanctuary."

Robin's eyes widened, and she pinned him with her gaze. He'd hit the mark. She turned her attention back to the salad. "I suppose," she admitted. "But we live in a small town." She set the knife down and picked cherry tomatoes from a bowl on the

131

counter.

"A small town with a recent murder and lots of tourists."

"Leon must have known his killer, Conrad. It's someone we know." She shook her head. "Which means someone we know broke in here."

His heart froze. "Why do you say that? I thought you had no idea who came in here."

"Not his identity, but it was a man."

"You saw him?"

"Kind of. Not well. I hid under the couch when I heard someone in the house."

"You're lucky he didn't realize you were here. You could've been killed." He wasn't sure if that's how it would've played out, but the possibility existed. She'd tied the intrusion to the murder.

"I've removed the key from the garden. He won't enter with it again."

No, from now on, I'll come in through the front door the way I did with Leon. He smiled, but it was more to himself than to her.

Conrad shoved a hand into his pocket and touched the packet of water hemlock powder. It reassured him. He pictured himself sitting down to dinner with Robin and her little family, distracting them and sprinkling the lethal contents into their food.

"No one will get in and out undetected, either."

"What do you mean?"

"I've installed a security system. Strategically placed cameras. They record to the cloud, and you must log in to the account to retrieve the footage. Call me paranoid, but I've got cameras inside the house, too. Leon never had that."

Goddamn it. That one stupid mistake continued to regurgitate on him. If he needed to kill her, he'd have to do it somewhere else—a challenge, considering she never left home alone.

He changed the subject. "Haven't seen much of Daphne lately. She okay?" He pulled a chair out and sat at the kitchen table. Tilting a chin at the salad, he said, "Need help?"

Robin grinned. "Want to stay for dinner?"

"I wasn't angling for an invite. Just feel guilty sitting here while you work."

"You're welcome to stay. The kids will be home soon. Dinner will be ready in an hour."

Conrad glanced at his watch to make it appear he considered

the offer. "No, gotta run in a few. Stuff to do. But thanks. So, what's going on with Daphne?"

Robin set the bowl of salad in the fridge and retrieved a beer. "She's coping, I guess. It's difficult for her. She and Leon were close."

Conrad nodded as if in sympathy. "She's been seeing a lot of Ian Fergus. They got a thing going?"

"Could have. They seem to like each other."

"Daphne looking for a steady relationship?"

"No, but she might get one whether or not she's looking."

Yeah—with me. Maybe Ian should be next on his list—yet another guy who'd snatched away what was rightfully Conrad's. He set the empty beer bottle on the table and rose.

"Thanks for the beer. Glad you're okay. I'd better head. Things to do, places to go." *People to kill.*

"You attending the meeting tonight?"

"Wouldn't miss it."

"Great. See you then."

The sound of children's voices and the thud of feet on the porch floated in through the open screen door.

Conrad hugged Robin on his way out. As he sidled past the kids, he fingered the packet hidden in his pants.

***

The call Jacob made went to voice mail, so he left a message: "Hello, Conrad. Detective Jacob Turner calling. I'm investigating Leon Patterson's death. Please call me back as soon as possible."

He left the station's phone number and his cell number. Jacob and Skylar had slowly worked their way through a list of Leon's family and close friends. They had yet to interview Conrad Barnes, a member of Leon's inner circle.

This would likely be just a formality. Conrad's presence at a convention during the murder alibied him. Still, Jacob needed to verify it. Niagara Falls' proximity to Niagara-on-the-Lake allowed for the possibility that Conrad had slipped away, killed Leon, and returned unnoticed.

Before Jacob dug into the convention alibi, he wanted to talk to Conrad and get a feel for him. The louder the warning bells from the interview, the deeper Jacob would dig.

"Plans for the weekend?" Skylar dropped into the chair beside Jacob's desk.

"Nothing firm."

"A little late to make plans, isn't it? Tomorrow's Friday already."

Jacob shrugged. He hadn't told his partner he was sort of dating Robin. Now wasn't the time to fill her in. He'd wait until there was a relationship to discuss. Skylar always got over enthusiastic whenever he mentioned dating a new woman. And this time, the woman in question was a former person of interest in their investigation. Not an auspicious start. However, he'd waited until he'd cleared Robin before approaching her for anything not pertaining to the case. That ought to be enough, but until the relationship turned serious, he'd keep it off the record.

"Not sure when I'll finish today. I need to interview this Barnes character and tick him off the list."

"What does he do?"

"Masseur. Works from home. I left a voice mail, but if he's booked up for the day, he won't listen to it until much later. I might have to hit his place on my way home if I can't entice him to come in." Jacob lifted his chin up to meet her gaze, but sunlight streaming in through the windows made him squint. "How's your list coming along?"

"I talked to Ian Fergus yesterday."

The way she said it made him take notice. "And?"

"He said something interesting."

"Don't make me pull it from you piecemeal, Skye. You know how I hate that."

She grinned. "All right. He mentioned he's seeing Daphne Russel."

"It's a free world."

"He started seeing her after Leon died. They were close friends, and now he's dating the dead guy's sister."

"You think he offed his friend to date the sister?"

"I've heard stupider reasons for murder. So have you."

"Yeah, nothing surprises me anymore. How did he strike you?"

"Not like a killer, but that could be good acting. He also mentioned Daphne's ex-husband has been hanging around."

"He trying to steer you towards Warren Russel?"

"Sounded like it. You know, whoever lands that fish will be

very wealthy."

Jacob groaned. "Did you really call her a fish?"

"Aren't they trying to hook her?"

"Not a bad theory. We'll see what develops. You're right—she's inherited a shit-ton of money and real estate. Any of these guys sniffing around her while Leon was alive?"

"Warren always hung around asking for money."

"He might have an alibi. Says he spent the night with a woman after his gig."

"Yes, but Ian doesn't know that," Skylar said.

Jacob nodded. "I see what you mean."

His phone rang then, and he held up a finger for her to wait while he answered it.

"Turner."

"Detective, it's Conrad Barnes."

CHAPTER 27

"I'm glad you released Beth," Conrad said.

Jacob nodded in response. They sat across from each other at a small, square table pushed against the wall in Conrad's tiny kitchen. A ceramic mug of coffee sat before each man.

"No reason to hold her." Jacob reflexively picked up his mug and sipped. It took all his effort not to grimace at its bitterness and spit it out. *I hope he's better at giving massages than he is at making coffee.*

"Rumours say a guy did it."

"Could be." Jacob leaned forward. "Tell me what you did that day."

"I'll never forget where I was when I heard the news." Conrad sighed and shook his head. "Like when a celebrity dies. Leon was a celebrity—I keep forgetting that."

"We'll discuss that later. What were you doing that morning at five thirty?"

"Sleeping. I'd slept in. Partied late the night before. Massage therapists can party." He grinned.

"Who'd you party with?"

Conrad rhymed off a few names, and Jacob wrote them down in a notebook despite the digital recorder. He didn't want to have to play it back just to retrieve the data.

"After the party, did you return to your room alone?"

The other man looked sheepish. "Yeah."

"No roommate? No one to split the cost of the room with?"

"Oh. No, not that either. I don't share rooms in case I get

lucky."

"And you slept in?"

"Room service woke me up."

"What time?" This might clear him. Jacob relaxed. He couldn't pinpoint the reason, but he'd been tense. Conrad hadn't done or said anything suspicious, yet something about his story didn't ring true. Probably nothing—Jacob's intuition had led him on a snipe hunt before—but the tickle at the back of his mind persisted.

"I'd ordered the food for eight thirty. The seminars started at nine and I needed to be ready."

"So you saw someone at eight thirty?" That would be easy to verify. It didn't rule him out, but it gave him a smaller window.

"Yeah. He knocked a couple of times to wake me up. I was hungover."

"Did you get to the seminar on time?"

"Ten minutes early."

Jacob rose. "Thanks for coffee."

Conrad stood as well and moved towards the door.

Jacob paused in the foyer. "You work here, eh? Mind if I see your treatment room? I've had back issues. Maybe I'll book an appointment."

"Sure."

Conrad hadn't hesitated; his face never registered alarm. He guided Jacob to a room at the back of the house. A massage table stood in the centre, made up with sheets and towels. An electric fireplace hung on one wall. Along another wall rested a walnut dresser, a tray of candles with staggered heights taking centre stage on its shiny top.

The candles were unlit, but the scent of something flowery lingered in the air. Beside the tray stood a diffuser with a tealight candle beneath it. The lighting was soft, muted, and the walls a neutral tan with a dark wood trim that matched the dresser. A small table under the window held a media player.

Jacob sniffed. "What's that smell?"

"Jasmine. Helps with stress. I used it with a client earlier."

Jacob waved at a tall bookcase next to the window. "Lot of books. You do more than give massages here?"

"Not sure what you mean."

"You've got books on herbs. Do you offer any other holistic practice?"

"I use aromatherapy for some clients. I'm certified. Also reflexology."

"What's that?"

"A technique that works on pressure points on the hands or feet."

"Been doing this long?"

"Ten years. Give or take."

"Nice room. You work from here all the time?"

"Some clients prefer me to visit them, and they pay extra for that."

"Was Leon one of your clients?"

Conrad bobbed his head once but remained silent.

"Did he come here, or did you go there?"

When Conrad replied, his voice remained steady, neutral. "Both. Mostly I went there."

"When was his last appointment?"

"I'd have to check."

"I'll wait."

Conrad left the room, leaving the door to the treatment room open. Jacob strode over to the dresser and opened drawers. He found towels, scrubs and ointments, sheets, extra candles, and a meditation CD collection. Nothing suspicious here, but why would there be?

He continued to snoop anyway. One drawer held essential oils, another, herbs, which made Jacob pause. He examined the labels but didn't see one for water hemlock. Even so, if Conrad understood plants and their uses, he'd know water hemlock was deadly. But so did Beth. Could she have learned about it from Conrad?

Footsteps alerted Jacob to Conrad's impending return, so he closed the drawer and moved away from the dresser. He peered out the window between the horizontal slats of a set of blinds. The view showed a small, fenced-in backyard. A four-by-six patio held outdoor furniture. Nothing fancy. Conrad obviously didn't make a lot of money giving massages.

"August fourth." Conrad stood in the doorway, a leather book in his hand. "I record my appointments in this datebook and then enter them into my phone. I want the hard copy. Don't trust computers."

"Okay, thanks." Jacob started to walk from the room but

paused on his way past Conrad. "You going to the meeting tonight?"

"What meeting?"

"The writers' group. You go, right?"

"I do. And yes, I'll be there."

"You working on a book?"

Conrad averted his gaze and shifted from one foot to the other. "Yeah. I'm always working on a book."

"Fiction?"

"Yeah."

"What do you write?"

"Primarily horror or SF."

"SF is science fiction?"

"Yeah." He gave Jacob a puzzled look.

Jacob held up the digital recorder. "Want to be clear. For the record."

"Right."

"What made you get into writing?"

"I've always wanted to write." His eyes grew distant. "I've always loved to read, and writing is a natural extension of that."

"You ever work with Leon?"

Conrad's eyes narrowed to slits. "No."

"That bother you?"

"Why would it?"

"I don't know. You were friends. Close friends. You never wanted to work together?"

Conrad's jaw clenched. "The opportunity never presented itself."

"Did you want to work on his current project? Why did he partner with Robin Carson?"

Conrad's voice dropped almost to a whisper. "Leon wanted to tap that—it's why he asked her to work with him."

"They were involved?"

The other man shrugged. "They wanted to hide it, but I think so."

"Why hide it?"

"Some people might suspect he used her for sex."

"Did Leon use his influence to garner sexual favours?"

"Robin published nothing. Explain why else he'd partner with her. She's a nobody. No offence, but a woman that gorgeous who hasn't proven herself in the industry has to be selling it to get anywhere."

Jacob forced himself to unclench his jaw and uncurl his fist, which, he realized, was on the verge of socking Conrad in the face.

"Perhaps her work impressed him," Jacob said. He'd heard of a casting couch but never a publishing couch.

Conrad snickered. "I'm sure her work impressed him—but not her written work, if you get my drift. I've read the pap she churns out. She writes romance."

"Leon wrote romance."

"Leon wrote in a variety of genres, including romance. His bestsellers were erotica. Anyone can write romance."

"I can't."

"Do you write?"

"No." Jacob paused for effect. "I catch killers."

He headed for the door before the urge to throw Conrad against the wall and pound his face in became too much to bear.

Back in his car, Jacob called Skylar and set his phone to hands-free. As he pulled away from the curb, he spotted Conrad watching from the living room window.

"Jake?"

"Yeah. I'm leaving Barnes's house."

"Anything shake loose?"

"Nothing specific. I found a bookcase full of books on plants and essential oils. Also on anatomy and similar stuff."

"Hmmm." Skylar's doubt came through the phone.

"What?"

"Poison is typically a woman's weapon."

"Yeah, but this guy disguised himself as a woman. He'd have known that and chosen it to throw us off. Men can use poisons."

"Find anything that ties him to the murder?"

"Nothing concrete. We can't arrest him for knowing his wildflowers. Beth had the knowledge—hell, they all probably do. Anyone can research this shit, and writers are the worst for searching out obscure facts." Jacob tapped the steering wheel with his finger. "Especially about murder. They revel in the details. The more gruesome and unique the better. It makes our job more difficult when the suspect is a writer, and we've got a whole group of them to deal with here."

"You leaning towards one of the group members?"

"The killer thinks he's smarter than we are, Skye. He thinks he's pulled off the perfect murder. Twenty bucks says when we're done it's a male writer we're locking up."

Skylar laughed. "You're on."

CHAPTER 28

Every time the door to the café opened, Andrew glanced over with a mix of anticipation and frustration—anticipation over Beth's imminent arrival, but frustration because he didn't want to care so much if she showed up. Here he was, a grown man, happy with his life, pining away for a woman.

It was close to seven o'clock and almost everyone in the writers' group had arrived except Beth. When Gregor stepped from the kitchen with a loaded tray of pastries and coffees, Andrew intercepted him.

"This going to the back room?"

"Yup."

"I'll take it."

Gregor hesitated. "You sure? I'm okay to do it."

"I know. But I wanted to check in on them."

Understanding lit up Gregor's face. "Okay, boss."

"What's that supposed to mean?"

"Nothing. I notice Beth's not here."

"So?"

"So, I noticed you watching the door. You worried because someone broke into Robin's house and Leon's killer tried to frame Beth for murder?"

"Holy Hell, Gregor. Where d'you get all that?"

His assistant shrugged. "I hear things."

"Framed?" He hadn't heard that. "Who told you?"

"Beth."

142

Andrew froze. "When did you talk to Beth?"

"Relax, man. I had breakfast with my girlfriend at the B and B this morning."

"And that's when Beth told you someone framed her?"

"Not in so many words, but what else would you call it if evidence from the murder ends up in her garage?"

"She said that?" She had mentioned nothing to Andrew when they'd been together on Labour Day. Why? Didn't she trust him? Did she think she couldn't confide in him?

"To Sherry, yeah," Gregor said, referring to his girlfriend.

Andrew relaxed a little. Women talked—mostly to each other. So Beth hadn't been confiding in Gregor. To verify how entrenched his assistant was in his relationship, Andrew asked, "You've been seeing Sherry for a while, eh?"

"Yeah. A few months."

"Gettin' serious?"

"Yeah. She's fun."

The door opened and Beth strode into the café. Andrew's shoulders relaxed, and the tension drained from his innards.

"Give me the stuff." He gripped the tray and Gregor surrendered it.

"You should ask her out, boss."

"What makes you think I haven't?"

"Have you?"

"Saw her on Labour Day. We met at the park for lunch."

"Sweet."

Andrew tried to detect sarcasm in the comment but couldn't find any. "Take her order, smart guy."

"Sure. Anything you say."

As Beth drew up to the counter, Andrew nodded a greeting to her and headed to the back room.

***

It might have been a coincidence that as soon as she stepped through the door of the café Andrew left the room. Beth told herself it was, soothed herself with the idea that perhaps he'd even taken the tray of food and drinks to the back to hang out with them. The "them," of course, included her most of all.

They'd had a nice time together at the park, and the nagging doubt that she didn't trust him had dissipated. She wasn't ready to confide in him—the skeletons in her closet would not only send him screaming but probably have him pulling out the garlic and crosses.

Garlic and crosses are for vampires, not skeletons, she reminded herself. Even so, the point was, she didn't want to scare him off.

"What can I bring you?" Gregor asked as Beth approached the counter.

"Café mocha and a scone, please." Ever since Andrew had brought her a scone, she ordered one every time she came in. She couldn't decide if she really wanted one or if she wanted to show him she loved his scones.

Awesome. I'm proving my love with biscuits. That should have him asking me out again in no time.

Gregor handed her a plate with a scone and a side of Devonshire cream. "Nine fifty-five, please."

As she paid with debit, Gregor suggested she head to the back room. "I'll bring your mocha back for you."

She thanked him and left to join the others.

The group was large tonight. Daphne sat at a round table with Robin and, to Beth's surprise, Jacob Turner. Two other group members—MJ Morse and Leanne Daly—sat with them. The rest of the group sat scattered at various tables throughout the room.

At the sight of Jacob, Beth's mouth went dry and her stomach churned. Why was he here? To spy on the group? Did he suspect someone here killed Leon? Did he think Andrew did it?

Andrew distributed the food and drinks and turned to face Beth as she entered the room.

"Hi." His smile triggered one of her own, and she moved to his side. When she stood next to him, calm seeped through her. He didn't seem bothered by Jacob's presence, which settled her.

"You going to join us?" She hoped he'd stay but didn't expect he could. He had a business to run, customers to serve.

"I'll be in and out. You all right?"

"I'm surprised to see Detective Turner here." She raised her brows and inclined her head in Jacob and Robin's direction. "What's going on?"

Andrew's gaze followed hers. "He gave Robin a ride."

Beth mulled it over. "I guess he doesn't suspect she killed Leon then."

He grinned. "I guess not. As long as he doesn't think you did it."

"No. The detectives cleared me." *But not you.* The thought jumped unbidden into her head. Andrew wouldn't have killed Leon. He couldn't.

"I wish they'd find the person who did it already," she said. "It's frustrating. Everyone is a suspect, but I can't believe anyone I know is capable of doing this."

He nodded. "Any idea who it might've been?"

"If I did, I'd have told Detective Turner."

Conrad's voice interrupted them. "Excuse me, just need to slide by." He gripped her arms and sidled past her.

She flushed, embarrassed she'd been blocking the entrance, and shifted aside. "Sorry."

"No worries."

When his gaze landed on Jacob, he froze, a scowl on his face, but recovered so quickly Beth wondered if she'd really seen it.

Now I'll think Conrad's the killer. At least she could trust the women around her—and Detective Turner was in the clear.

Beth took the seat her friends had saved for her at Daphne's table.

To start things off, Daphne rose and spoke about Leon and the void his death had left in the group. While her friend talked, Beth scanned the faces in the room. They all appeared to pay rapt attention to what Daphne said. All wore solemn, if not grief-stricken, expressions. Of all of them, Beth was the only one more concerned with what the others were doing than with listening to the tribute.

Except Jacob. When her gaze landed on him, he met it levelly. She looked away and nervously sipped her coffee. After that, she focused her attention on whoever spoke, though she spared the detective an occasional glance.

He appeared to take an interest in their discussion topic, a lecture on backstory. The speaker, MJ, provided handouts and read examples from a variety of novels. Beth took copious notes and lost herself in the assignments MJ gave them. Even Andrew's whereabouts slipped off her radar, and before she knew it, the evening wound to a close.

Beth let the others say their goodbyes and hung around until the back room emptied of everyone except herself and MJ. While the other woman packed up her laptop and notes, Beth ordered another cup of coffee and brought it back to her seat.

"Aren't you going home?" MJ asked as Beth pecked away at her current manuscript.

"No. I'll work here a while."

Andrew appeared in the doorway, carrying a plate of date squares. "You ladies want a late-night snack? Only a couple left, so I'd rather give them away than keep them for tomorrow."

MJ pinched a corner from a square. "They look amazing. Thanks."

"Take more."

She laughed. "No way."

Beth envied her friend's self-control. Once upon a time, in her bid to be skinny, Beth would've refused even the morsel MJ accepted. Now, she'd eat both pieces if someone else didn't help her finish them. Why did Andrew insist on bringing fattening pastries over to her all the time?

Oh, God. Leon had been poisoned. What if Andrew had brought Leon something laced with poison from the café?

"No, thank you," she said as he passed her the plate. "I can't eat another bite."

"Are you sure?" He smiled and her heart warmed.

Surely he wasn't capable of poisoning anyone, and he wouldn't do it in his place of business. What an idiot she was.

"Okay, a little bite." She broke off a piece and popped it into her mouth. It flooded her taste buds with comforting sweetness. The oats and brown sugar provided a delicious crunchiness that contrasted with the creamy texture of the pureed dates.

"I enjoy watching you eat." Andrew sat across from her and broke off a piece of date square for himself. He turned to MJ, who'd finished packing her things. "Have some more. Seriously."

"No, thank you. I ate too much already."

MJ said goodbye and headed out, leaving Beth alone with Andrew.

CHAPTER 29

"Daphne. Hey, wait."

Outside the café, footsteps pounded across the parking lot towards Daphne.

She paused at Conrad's shout but pressed the button on her key fob to unlock the car. After placing the bag containing her laptop and other supplies in the trunk, she slammed it closed and turned to face him.

"What's up?" She offered him a smile.

"Want to go for a drink?"

"Can't—have to go home and get ready for work."

"Night shift again." He frowned. "When's your day off? I'd love to take you to dinner. How do reservations at The Cannery sound?"

The Cannery was the restaurant at The Pillar and Post Inn. One of the nicer restaurants, it had always been out of Daphne's snack bracket. Leon had treated her to dinner there to celebrate the sale of his first book. While she'd love to go back, she'd have preferred Ian's company to Conrad's.

However, though she'd seen more of Ian since Leon died, she didn't consider them exclusive. Ian hadn't discussed this with her, and they hadn't even gone on a date.

"What do you say?" Conrad prodded.

"I don't know. That's a date restaurant."

He grinned, showing front teeth that slightly overlapped. "I'm asking you on a date."

"You're Leon's friend." Was this about Leon? He was dead, so his friends crawled out of the woodwork to date her?

"Yes. We have a connection, though, don't we, Daphne?" His brown eyes grew wide, his gaze intense. Conrad sported a scruffy five-o'clock shadow today. Usually, he was clean-shaven no matter the hour. "We could go somewhere less fancy, but I wanted to take you somewhere nice. To relax and escape the stress you've experienced."

He drew close to her, forcing her to tilt her chin up to meet his gaze. Not as tall as Ian, he still towered over Daphne: five-foot-ten to her five-foot-two.

How should she respond? Maybe she should date Conrad again. She didn't get the same physical buzz from being near him she did around Ian, but who knew? If she spent more time with him, that might change.

"Let me check my calendar." She rooted through her purse and retrieved her cell phone. After checking it, she said, "I'm free on Sunday."

"Then it's a date. I'll pick you up at seven. We'll go for a nice dinner and see how things go." He gave her a brief hug and jogged to his car.

After he drove away, she fired a quick text off to both Robin and Beth: *Guess who asked me out? Conrad. We're going to The Cannery on Sunday.*

Before she could put the phone away, she received a response. Daphne smiled when she saw Robin sent it. The message read *Hope you have a good time.*

Since Beth remained inside Andrew's and probably worked on her manuscript, Daphne didn't expect a response from her yet. Happy with her plans, she climbed into her car and headed home.

***

Guess who asked me out? Conrad. We're going to The Cannery on Sunday.

Her manuscript forgotten, and a creeping terror gnawing at her insides, Beth stared at the message from Daphne. Why the hell was she seeing not just one but two of Leon's friends with a killer on the loose? What if Conrad and Ian had conspired on the killing and now set their sights on Daphne?

Calm down. No one's trying to kill Daphne.

Then what did they want with her?

The obvious conclusion was they vied for her attention because she stood to inherit everything Leon owned. But Ian didn't strike Beth as mercenary. Conrad, on the other hand, made no secret of the fact he wanted to become rich from the sale of his books.

What author doesn't? She'd published her books for people to buy and read. What was wrong with making a living from something you loved to do? Conrad often said writing was his passion. He wanted it to become his full-time gig so he could retire from his massage business.

Once again, whoever had murdered Leon forced doubts and distrust into Beth's mind.

Better get back to the book. She scanned what she'd written. She'd been in the zone for a while after Andrew returned to his customers. This resulted in an additional two thousand words to her story.

She responded to Daphne's message: *Cool. Tell us all about it after.*

What else could she say? Don't—the guy you're dating might have killed your brother? Wouldn't Daphne sense it? Wouldn't they all sense it?

Sighing, Beth rubbed her hands over her face. She should pack up, go home, and catch some sleep. *Five thirty comes early in the morning,* she thought and powered down her laptop.

On her way out, Beth stopped to say goodbye to Andrew, and he insisted on walking her to the car. When they reached it, he waited while she put her bag in the trunk and climbed into the driver's seat. Once settled, she started the car and rolled down the window.

"You going to be okay?" Andrew asked.

"Yes, I'll be fine."

"I could escort you home."

She laughed. "I live nearby, my home has an alarm system, and I've got cameras outside the house."

He hesitated, looking doubtful.

"What? You don't believe me?"

"I do, but ever since someone invaded Robin's house, I wonder if you'll be targeted." His frown deepened. "Why didn't you tell me someone tried to frame you?"

Beth gasped, shock rendering her speechless.

"You should have said something." He placed his hands on the lowered window as though ensuring she didn't close it and leaned towards her. "Someone sneaked into your garage and planted evidence."

"Where did you hear that?"

"Word gets around. The cops arrested you for a reason."

"What did you hear?"

"Evidence from the murder ended up in your garage."

"Who told you?" Her hands grew icy, and she balled them into fists. What if Andrew had planted the evidence in her garage? Then he'd be the killer. Sweat beaded on the small of her back and under her arms.

"You talked about it."

"Oh, God." Beth moaned and covered her face with her hands. Gregor told him. That had to be it. In a fit of frustration, she'd spilled the information to Sherry and now Andrew knew.

"Didn't they look on the video and identify the person?" Andrew's voice rose in anger. "What kind of detective is this Turner? Did you check the footage?"

"Yes. It looked like me going to the garage, and then the camera went dead."

"And he thought it was you?"

"At first. Andrew, even I thought it might be me." Beth laughed, but it sounded hollow and forced.

"See? You shouldn't come and go alone."

"What do you recommend?"

He shook his head. "For tonight, I can see you home."

"Don't be ridiculous. You don't need to follow me home. I'm perfectly safe. If he wanted me dead, I'd already be dead."

"That another joke?"

"No. It's logic."

"Wait. I'll tell Gregor and then I'll pull my car around." Before she could respond, he headed back to the café.

"Andrew, I'm leaving," she shouted at his retreating back.

When he continued on into the café without a backwards glance, Beth rolled up her window and buckled the seatbelt. She drove towards the parking lot's exit. If he came back outside, he'd see she'd left and understand he needn't follow her home.

The café's doors remained closed while she checked for traffic and turned onto the road. Satisfied he'd remain behind, Beth headed home.

CHAPTER 30

Robin appreciated Jacob's kindness in driving her to the meeting. Sure, his ulterior motive was to study the group members, but the gesture was nice. Afterwards, she quizzed him on his conclusions about who'd killed Leon, but he refused to discuss it. Rather than annoy her and make her think he didn't trust her, she respected his ethical stand. He never discussed the investigation with her unless he needed information from her.

"Care to come in for a coffee?" Robin kept her voice neutral, her expression non-committal, but inside, her stomach flip-flopped.

"I'd love to." Jacob threw the car into park and turned off the engine.

Neither made a move to open the door.

"The kids should be asleep, so we need to be quiet." Robin darted her tongue out and licked her lips. An urge to draw him to her and kiss him made her lean towards him, but she forced herself to stop.

"No problem. I'll use my indoor voice." His mouth quirked up on one side.

"Okay." She opened her door, signalling him to join her.

Together they walked up the steps to the door.

"I'll pay the sitter and send her home. She lives across the street, but I always watch her until she gets in the door."

"Why don't I put the coffee on?" Jacob suggested.

Robin almost protested and then decided to allow him to make himself at home in her kitchen; her living room, too, was okay. Until the kids approved him, she wouldn't extend permission to the bedroom. Jacob had met her kids, and they all seemed to like each other, but she hadn't discussed their feelings towards him with them yet.

"Sure," she said and gave him her most winning smile.

By the time she peeked in on the sleeping kids and the babysitter returned home, the aroma of fresh-brewed coffee filled the house. Since caffeine kept her up at night, she'd drunk herb tea all evening at the café. But she didn't want to tell Jacob the invitation to have coffee was an excuse to extend their time together. She'd drink it even if it had her wide-eyed and buzzing until dawn.

Truth be told, she didn't want him to leave at all. If her kids weren't here, she wouldn't have trusted herself and would've sent him home. As it was, ever since they'd pulled up in her driveway, she wanted to touch him. Three years of celibacy was enough. Perhaps she wasn't after him but wanted physical release.

Jacob set up the coffee pot on a tray with mugs, milk, and sugar the way she always did when he visited. Robin settled next to him on the couch.

"Should I turn on the television?" she asked. A news station running in the background would fill any awkward pauses or at least give them something to talk about—and keep her mind away from thoughts of kissing him.

She made a move to pick up the remote, but he stopped her, covering her hand with his. The touch sparked electricity through her, charging to her core. Her breathing grew rapid and her face flushed.

"Let's keep the silence." Jacob's voice came out a whispered growl thick with emotion.

"Okay," she breathed back.

"Robin, I've been thinking."

She gulped. "About the murder?"

The amused half-smile appeared. "Yes, always, but also about us."

"What about us?" She held her breath. Did he want to slow things down? If so, she'd misread every cue.

His expression turned serious. "Intense circumstances threw us together, but we're not seeing each other because you've been traumatized."

Robin considered his words. Yes, Leon's death and the break-in had rattled her, but somehow, she'd coped. "You've helped me deal with everything."

Shambhala's words echoed in her head then: *"He'll help you through the turmoil. It's meant to be."*

"I'm glad to hear it." He tilted her chin up, his face close to hers. "I never wanted to pressure you."

"Pressure me?"

"I'm attracted to you. Physically, emotionally, intellectually."

"You really have been thinking."

He sighed. "Perhaps overthinking. But I don't want to make you uncomfortable. I know it's been difficult for you—losing your husband, Leon's murder, your friend's arrest, and then a break-in at your home."

"You haven't made me uncomfortable." But she blushed as she said it and rubbed her suddenly damp palms over her jeans-clad thighs. When she realized the contradiction, she laughed softly.

"What's funny?" The half-smile returned though his eyes showed concern.

"You haven't made me uncomfortable, but I'm uncomfortable."

Without thinking, she reached up and ran her hands through his hair. She loved the white strands sprinkled through the black. It made him appear distinguished. He had kissy lips—they always seemed pursed as if poised to kiss. His face was a perfect oval, his brows wide, dark lines over almond eyes.

Jacob remained silent as her hands roamed down his face and neck to his broad shoulders. His Adam's apple bobbed as he swallowed.

"You can safely conclude I'm attracted to you as well, Detective. On all those levels."

He leaned forward and grazed his lips over hers. She gasped for air when he drew away.

"That okay?" he asked.

The question teased a moan out of her. In response, she drew him by the shoulders to her and kissed him hard. He tasted of coffee and desire. His lips gently pried hers open, and his tongue slipped in to sample her. She pressed her mouth more firmly against his and skimmed her hands across his back, locking their bodies together.

After what seemed too short a time, she pulled away. She raised an apologetic gaze to him. "I don't want the kids to catch us."

Jacob huffed out a breath and ran a hand through his hair, leaving it mussed and sexy. "I understand."

"I didn't mean to get you all worked up for nothing."

He chuckled. "Not for nothin', darlin'."

Robin stroked his face, reluctant to sever the physical connection. "You got me all worked up first. I feel like a teenager—wanting to fool around but afraid parents might walk into the room."

"The same thought crossed my mind." He smiled and glanced at the clock before returning his gaze to hers. "I should go before we get carried away."

She nodded. When he didn't move, she realized he probably needed a minute or two to compose himself. The thought made her insides warm and she grinned.

He responded by pulling her to him and kissing her, a hard kiss that made the room spin and her toes curl. Before she recovered her equilibrium, he rose.

"I'll leave before you make me lose all control."

She stood and took his hand. "Okay. But maybe we could get together on the weekend?"

"Sure. I'll text you." Jacob started to turn towards the door but paused. "You going to be okay? The cameras are on?"

"Always. I check them every morning and night."

"Doors locked?"

"Even when I'm home. Don't worry. No one will break in here again."

Her cell phone buzzed, and she checked it.

Beth.

Robin almost ignored it, but it was late, and Beth never called her at this time of night. She held up a finger, signalling Jacob to wait.

"Beth? What's up?" Robin stroked a hand along Jacob's arm, and he snatched it with his, wagging a finger at her with his other hand.

Naughty, naughty.

She giggled.

"Robin?" Beth's frightened whisper knocked the smile off

Robin's face.

She froze and her fingers gripped Jacob's hand, making him wince.

Concern on his face, he mouthed, "What is it?"

"What's wrong?" Robin struggled to keep the hysteria out of her voice.

"Someone's here. Outside."

"Did you call nine-one-one?"

Jacob snatched the phone from Robin's hand. "Beth? Jake Turner. What happened?"

Robin didn't catch Beth's reply, but Jacob said, "Call nine-one-one. I'm on my way."

He broke the connection and handed the phone to Robin. "Lock the door and stay inside. I'll call you."

Without another word, he was gone.

CHAPTER 31

Jacob listened for reports on his police radio for news on what happened at Beth's and learned two police cars were on the way. When he pulled up in front of the property, he spotted a BMW parked across the street in front of the farmer's fields. Not exactly what you'd expect a burglar or killer to take on a job. Perhaps it wasn't related to Beth, but who'd park this far from any other house on the street?

The police cars hadn't shown up yet, so he waited.

Three minutes later, they arrived. The same posse Jacob had seen during the break-in at Robin's stepped from the vehicles.

Two officers went around the back while Jacob and the woman in charge covered the front. Despite the property's huge size, they focused their efforts on the main house where Beth had spotted a man creeping around.

"Police! Freeze!"

The shouts came from the side of the house. Jacob raced over to see who they'd found, the officer following close behind.

"It's okay," a distraught voice replied. "I'm a friend."

The voiced sounded familiar to Jacob, but he couldn't place it. When he rounded the corner of the garage, he recognized Andrew Winston.

"Hands up where I can see them." One cop trained his gun on Andrew while the other approached him with a pair of handcuffs.

Andrew raised his arms high but continued to protest. "I'm not doing anything wrong. I came to make sure she got home okay.

Ask Beth. She'll tell you."

Jacob pulled out his cell phone and dialled Beth. When she answered, he said, "We've got Andrew Winston here. You expecting him?"

"No. He wanted to follow me home, but I told him it wasn't necessary."

The fear in her voice decided him. "We're taking him in for questioning. I'm coming to the door, Beth. Meet me at the front."

Jacob instructed the police to take Andrew to the station and put him in an interview room. "I'll question him when I get there. This might have something to do with the case I'm investigating."

"Leon's murder?" Andrew's eyes grew wide. "Detective, you've got the wrong guy. I just wanted to make sure she got home safe."

Jacob sighed. "Okay." He turned and spoke to the police officers surrounding Andrew. "Put him in the back of a squad car and wait. First, I want to interview the victim."

"She's not a victim," Andrew said. He held up his cuffed hands. "And you don't need these. I've done nothing wrong."

"Winston, how do you think this looks? You have one murdered friend and one friend who's suffered a break-in. You're creeping around another friend's house. Go sit in the cruiser like a good boy and wait for me." Jacob waved for the cops to take Andrew to the vehicle.

Eyes lowered and shoulders slumped, Andrew allowed the officers to lead him away.

By the time Jacob arrived at the front door, Beth already stood on the porch. She wore the jeans and T-shirt she'd worn to the writers' group meeting. Her eyes were weary, her hair mussed, but she looked gorgeous.

"You okay?" Jacob asked.

"Yes. What happened? What did Andrew say?"

Interlocking stones trailed a path to Beth's front door. A few metres before the front door stood a wrought-iron bistro table and two chairs.

Jacob indicated a chair. "Sit for a minute."

She walked over and took a seat. Jacob snagged the other one and sat.

"Winston said you could explain his presence," Jacob began.

"I can't, though. Not really." Beth rubbed her eyes with her knuckles. "He wanted to follow me home—to see me home safe, he said. I told him it wasn't necessary. He insisted. When he left to grab his keys, I drove home."

"Without saying anything?" If so, it stood to reason that Andrew believed she expected him to follow.

"I shouted at him that I was leaving. It seemed absurd and a lot of trouble for him to drive after me."

"Has he bothered you before this?"

Beth shook her head. "We picnicked together on Labour Day."

"Are you dating?"

"Yes. No. I don't know."

"You don't know if you're dating this guy?"

She sighed audibly. "I chat with him at his café. We saw each other on Labour Day and talked today after the meeting. He gives me scones."

Brows raised, Jacob said, "He gives you scones?"

"Oh, that sounds so stupid." Beth put her elbows on the table and dropped her face into her palms. When she raised her head, she said, "He's nice to me and I like him. Maybe he was concerned. He said he was worried about the break-in at Robin's."

"Does he frighten you?" If this guy was a stalker, perhaps he'd killed Leon over Daphne. The three women were friends. A man had killed Daphne's brother. The same man had entered Robin's home but stole nothing. This visit to Beth's might be the third strike.

Or fourth. The killer had planted evidence in her garage.

"I'll have to take him in."

"Can I talk to him before you do?"

Jacob shook his head. "You can talk to him after. First, I have to verify he didn't mean you any harm."

"Oh, God." She crossed her arms over her chest, hugging herself.

"Go inside, Beth." Jacob rose. "Lock your doors. Make sure the security's engaged. Call Robin, or she'll worry, and tell her I'll call her tomorrow."

"But Andrew?"

"If it's as innocent as he claims, he'll be home in a few hours."

"Can I at least have his car keys to park his car in my driveway so it's not on the road all night?"

"No, sorry." Jacob's tone was grim. "We have to search it."

***

"I was making sure she got home all right. How many times do I have to tell you? What did Beth say?" Andrew half-rose in his seat in the interrogation room at the Niagara Region Police Station. He wanted to kick something. What the hell was this? He'd done Beth a favour and look what it got him. They treated him like a killer.

When Andrew rose, Jacob leaped to his feet, planting them as though bracing himself for a fight. Andrew scowled and opened his mouth to continue his diatribe. Jacob held up a hand, forestalling any further comments.

"Beth told me you'd insisted on following her home even when she said not to."

"I was worried about her, okay? A killer's out there. A killer who planted evidence in her garage."

Jacob frowned and leaned forward, pressing his hands onto the table. "Where'd you hear that?"

"Are you kidding? Don't you live in Niagara-on-the-Lake? One person finds out and the whole town knows. Even the media reported the police removed items from her garage. I'm not stupid. I understand what that implies." Andrew dropped back into his chair and folded his hands on the table. At least he was no longer cuffed.

"I don't live there," Jacob said.

"You work there, though, right? Isn't that why you're investigating Leon's murder?"

Jacob nodded. "I work at this station, which covers the entire region. Why were you at Beth's, Andrew?"

"Jesus Christ, Turner, I told you. My story won't change. Ask my assistant." For the first time in the hour since he'd been here, Andrew remembered he'd told Gregor of his intention to follow Beth home. "Call Gregor. He'll tell you."

"He at the café?"

Andrew paused. "What's the time?"

They'd taken his cell phone when they'd brought him in—they'd taken his wallet, car keys, everything he carried.

Jacob pulled out his cell phone and glanced at it. "Ten thirty."

"He'd be home by now."

"Be right back." Jacob left the room, shutting the door on a seething Andrew.

A while later, the door opened and Jacob stepped back into the room. Andrew jumped up, ready to argue.

"Your assistant backs up your story," Jacob said.

"So you believe me?"

"More than I did before."

"What's that mean?" God, he wanted to go home and go to bed. He'd stay away from Beth Holmes forever if only they'd let him go home.

"It means we'll release you, but you must give me a DNA sample, and we're keeping your car for a while."

"My car? Why?" Before Jacob could reply, understanding hit, and Andrew said, "To search it."

Jacob shrugged. "Part of the process. Sorry. Gotta be done."

"Any damage, you pay for it."

"Don't worry, you'll get it back in one piece. Come on, I'll do a swab and then cut you loose." Jacob held up a swab kit. "Have a seat."

CHAPTER 32

Cricket chirps and rustling leaves, along with the night air's fresh scent, floated in on the breeze blowing through the open windows of Robin's house. In the living room, Robin paced between the coffee table and the television. After she'd heard from Beth, she'd forced herself not to call Jacob. He was busy working—interrogating another one of her friends.

Beth had been frantic with worry over the possibility Andrew could be the killer. No matter how she spun it in her mind, Robin refused to believe it. He didn't have it in him. He was too kind, too sensitive.

"Mom?"

Robin spun around to face her daughter. "What's wrong? Can't sleep?" She glanced at the time. Almost midnight.

"I heard you pacing. Everything okay?"

"Just restless. Want warm milk and honey?" When Robin was growing up, her mother considered this the best remedy for a sleepless night. Whether it worked or was only a placebo, she'd take this opportunity to bond with her daughter.

"Okay," Kaylee agreed eagerly.

Robin strode to the kitchen and hunted out a small saucepan, the milk, and the jar of honey. As her mother stood by the stove and waited for the milk to heat, Kaylee perched on a bar stool at the island.

"How's school so far?" Robin asked.

"Good. I have the good teacher."

"Great. How about Nate? He says he likes his teacher, but he's not as enthusiastic about going every day—not like last year."

"Because Stan isn't in his class this year."

"Oh." Robin should have known. Stan and Nate were best friends. This would be their first year apart. "He never told me." Did she sound defensive?

"He doesn't talk about what bugs him."

"Does he know he can tell me?" Robin stirred honey into the milk as it bubbled and turned off the heat.

"He knows you say he can."

"What do you think? Can you tell me stuff?"

Kaylee hesitated. "It depends on the stuff."

"What do you mean?" Robin sucked in a breath. Was her daughter keeping secrets from her? Robin's gut contracted, and a chill crawled up her spine.

She focused on pouring the milk into two mugs.

"Mom, you have enough on your plate." Kaylee accepted the drink her mother set in front of her and blew on it.

Robin held hers up to her lips and blew. The subtle scent of milk and honey wafted up, soothing her. Steam dampened her nose.

"Where'd you get that idea?" She sipped, peering over the rim of her mug at Kaylee.

"Mrs. Johnston."

Their next-door neighbour, Jean Johnston, pried into everyone's business. Robin had yet to decide whether the woman loved to help or if she got satisfaction from meddling. She was both the biggest gossip and the greatest help in the neighbourhood.

"Did she tell you not to share your problems with me?" If so, she'd give Jean a stern talking to in the morning—even if it meant leaving the house to do it.

"No. I heard her say so to Mr. Johnston when I visited Tara."

Tara, in the same grade as Kaylee, was the Johnstons' daughter.

"Don't listen to her. If you need help with anything, tell me. I'll tell Nate the same tomorrow. Don't keep secrets from me, Kaylee. That does more harm than good."

"Okay." Kaylee's face brightened, which helped ease the stress that had built up since Beth's frantic call.

Noticing Kaylee's empty mug, Robin said, "Okay, it's late and you have school. Break time's over."

Kaylee slid off the bar stool and headed for her bedroom. She paused in the entrance to the hallway. "Thanks, Mom. Goodnight."

"Goodnight. Go pee."

Her daughter groaned. "You don't have to remind me to use the toilet. I'm not a kid."

Robin smiled. "I know you're not. But make sure you wash your hands."

"Mom!"

Robin dispelled her daughter's glare with a lopsided grin.

Silence blanketed the room after Kaylee's departure. With it came the sense of upheaval and lack of control that had kept Robin up so late. Should she text Jacob? What had happened to Andrew, and why hadn't Jacob or Beth sent her an update?

Damn it. If Jacob was her boyfriend—and she wasn't sure she could call him that yet, but he was more than an acquaintance or friend—then he owed her something.

When her cell phone chimed on an incoming text, relief and anticipation made her go weak in the knees. Robin snatched it up, grateful at least one of them had the decency to update her. She glanced at the display and her unease returned.

Conrad Barnes. What did he want at this time of night?

I see you're awake.

For a moment, fear caught in her throat, but she brushed it aside and texted a reply: *How do you know?*

Drove by. Saw your lights.

Why?

Couldn't sleep. Worried.

About?

Daphne. Everything. Want company?

She considered. Did she want to let anyone in during the middle of the night? It was only Conrad. Still, whoever killed Leon must be someone he'd trusted.

Her phone chimed as another text message arrived.

Robin?

Can't. Have to wake up early, so going to bed. Kids asleep.

Okay. Just tell me what happened at Beth's. Saw police.

He'd driven past Beth's? She checked the time. That must have been two hours ago. Why was Conrad cruising the neighbourhoods?

Thought she saw an intruder. That should satisfy his curiosity. She didn't want to mention Andrew. The whole thing must be a misunderstanding. *Why were you there?*

Worried. Killer on the loose. Patrolling. Dumb, right?

She smiled. *No, you're sweet. Have a good night.*

Night.

***

Conrad set his cell phone aside and backed out of Robin's driveway. He'd hoped she'd let him in. She'd been chumming up to that detective, so if she knew anything about the case, Conrad would've pried it from her—gently, of course.

Anxiety had plagued him ever since he'd prowled through her house and had grown worse after the cops cleared Beth of the murder. His plan to frame her had failed, and he blamed Robin. If she became a nuisance, he'd have to eliminate her.

He'd carefully planned Leon's murder, but the visit to Robin's had been impulse. If he'd been more careful, she'd never have known he'd been there, and the key to the house would still be outside. Stupid cow. How was he supposed to know she was home? Who sits alone in the dark? His intention in driving past her house tonight had been to scope things out.

Earlier in the evening, he'd driven by Daphne's. Out of camera range, he'd texted her, asking if he could stop by. She'd told him she was in for the night, getting ready for bed. If it weren't for the cameras, he'd have climbed up her back balcony and watched her for a while. He'd left, promising himself he'd stop by on his way home.

From there, he'd gone to Beth's but pulled into the nearest driveway and turned around when he spotted the cop cars. Before heading to Robin's, he'd gone to grab something to eat. By the time he'd rolled around to her place, it'd been late. Surprised to see the lights on, he'd texted her to try to winnow his way in.

Now back at Daphne's and parked out of camera range, he used binoculars to watch the house. Soon, it would be their house. Then just his house when he got tired of her irritating him. His ultimate goal was to have the place to himself and play the sad widower. He imagined female fans, the beautiful ones, contacting him. He'd invite the hottest ones over, help them with their writing, and take them to bed.

Well before Leon had announced he'd landed a publishing contract with a major publisher, Conrad had seethed inside over his fellow author's successes. Leon's writing was juvenile. Contrived. His characters were one-dimensional. The guy was oblivious to story structure. He'd had a superior editor, that's all. Even then, you could tell the stuff was shit. A polished turd remained a turd.

What kind of guy wrote romance? Leon probably didn't even like the genre. All he did was cash in on the popularity of it. What was wrong with those women who bought his books? Were they illiterate?

Conrad had attempted to write two romance stories and one erotica novel. All had been rejected by agents and publishers alike, and when he indie published, it'd tanked because he simply couldn't get noticed. Every time Leon published a book, it soared to the top of the lists and won awards. Readers snapped up pre-orders as if each book were his last. Well, the joke was on them, wasn't it? The last book released had been Leon's last.

That made Conrad chuckle. With Leon out of the way, his books could get the recognition they deserved. Saturday morning, Conrad would attend the fall craft show at the park in the centre of town. His fans would discover him. The writing group had reserved two tables, and Conrad ensured he'd share one with Daphne.

They'd get cozy. After their date Sunday, he'd accompany her back to her—their—house. He'd spend the night. After a good fucking, she'd know she belonged to him. He'd own her. His cock hardened as he imagined what he'd do to her, what he'd make her do.

The car windows steamed up, and he unzipped his pants to, as he called it, release the kraken. He fondled himself while he stared through the binoculars at the now dark house, pretending his hand was hers—or better yet, her mouth. Close to shooting his load, he dropped the binoculars on the passenger seat and grabbed tissues from the glove box.

His moans filled the car as he finished himself off.

CHAPTER 33

A greeter at the entrance to the Niagara-on-the-Lake fall craft show handed Ian Fergus a plastic bag loaded with promotional materials. Donated by the vendors at the fair, including the writers' group Daphne belonged to, it also provided a map of the tables. Daphne's name was listed next to Conrad Barnes's, the annoying jerk who'd somehow managed to monopolize her for the next two days.

Serves me right for waiting so long before calling.

But he'd wanted to give her space, refusing to appear pushy or needy. Didn't that turn women off? Obviously, he hadn't mastered the art of spacing out calls. When he'd contacted Daphne the day before to see if she'd go for dinner with him on Sunday, she already had plans.

"I wish you'd called sooner," she'd told him, sounding genuinely regretful. "I've got plans with Conrad."

"Where's he taking you?" The question wasn't any of Ian's business, but he hoped she'd answer it anyway. He needed to know what he was up against.

When she told him they were going to The Cannery, his heart drooped. Conrad was making the most of this date. Suspecting that the other man wanted to cap the night off in Daphne's bed, Ian had come here to do damage control.

If he'd read the signs right, he and Daphne had something between them. Ian had no claim on her but hoped to prevent Conrad from moving into the top spot—not that he wanted to jockey for romantic position with another guy, but that's how things stood.

And it's all my own damn fault.

Despite the drizzle in the air, a fair-sized crowd had gathered. At least the air was mild. So far, September had warmed up to mimic the hot and humid summer they'd avoided before this. If the weather continued this way, it might not snow until December.

Ian wove between the tables, avoiding eye contact with the vendors who stood behind them so they wouldn't call to him. In a small town, most people at least recognized one another, and Ian refused to socialize—not until he'd secured a date with Daphne.

If she knew she had him on the hook, she'd hopefully not get physical with Conrad after dinner tomorrow. At least, that was the plan.

Ian spotted her shiny, chestnut waves and petite frame near the back of the park under a tent. The dampness fluffed up her hair, making it curlier and sexier. Her long-sleeve, V-neck T-shirt accentuated her breasts and slim waist. From what he could see of her jeans, they likely showcased her perfect butt. Daphne talked to a prospective purchaser who held her latest book in his hand.

Guy'll probably buy it to cozy up to her.

No sooner did Ian think that than he regretted it with a full serving of shame. He'd never been the jealous type, and he didn't intend to start now. He and Daphne had a connection, chemistry. But if she didn't think so, if she believed she had a stronger connection to, say, Conrad, then Ian would step aside. No matter how grievous her mistake, she was entitled to make it. Perhaps, in time, she'd realize her error.

Impressed with his abundance of maturity, Ian strode up to the table.

"Hi, guys." He saluted Conrad and Daphne first and then MJ and Beth, who sat at another table in the same booth. "How's biz? Selling a ton?"

Daphne's collection included stacks of Leon's books. Those would probably sell well. Leon had more fans after his death than he'd had while alive.

"Hi, Ian." Daphne's grin lit up her face. "I'm so happy you stopped by."

Conrad shot her a look of annoyance, which she didn't notice and Ian ignored.

"I've sold fifteen books since we arrived this morning," Daphne announced, puffing up her chest. "Conrad sold three, MJ five, and Beth eleven. She's rocking it."

"Eight were Leon's," Conrad said.

"Excellent," Ian replied, refusing to let Conrad spoil Daphne's news. "I'll buy one of yours, Daphne."

He picked up the one that looked more like a thriller than a romance. "How much?"

"Fifteen each or two for twenty-five." She beamed at him, making his heart beat faster.

"I'll buy two, then." The hell with it. If romance was what she wrote, then romance was what he'd read. Ian selected the most action-packed of the romance covers. A wolf stood under a full moon in the background. Maybe it was a nature story.

In the end, he bought one from everyone else, including Conrad. Ian loved the excitement in their eyes and voices as they discussed their stories with him. Only Conrad seemed deflated by the whole thing. He sounded happy enough, but his jaw remained clenched, and his mouth drew down in a sneer when someone else talked.

Sour grapes, Ian thought. *Not a good look on an author.*

With his purchases tucked into a shopping bag MJ provided, he focused on securing a date with Daphne.

"Sorry I haven't called," he said. "I've been busy with getting the new school year under control. Always so much to do."

"No problem. I assumed you were busy." She scanned the immediate area, and Ian tracked her gaze. No one else approached their tables, so she sat in the chair behind her.

"Can you take a break?" Ian asked. "Go for a coffee?"

Daphne contemplated for a moment. "Sure. I haven't eaten lunch yet, so I'll walk with you and grab a bite."

"I brought enough food for both of us," Conrad said. "You can eat here."

Ian remained silent, waiting for Daphne to respond.

"That's kind of you. I'll go for a walk anyway. The foot traffic seems to have slowed, and I could use a few minutes away from the table." She gave Conrad a sweet smile and then with a nod included MJ and Beth. "Watch my stuff?"

"Sure," MJ and Beth replied together.

Conrad followed with "Of course." His expression showed

obvious displeasure, but Ian didn't care.

A chip truck stood at the other end of the park, and Ian led Daphne to it, more to be away from Conrad's view than to buy fries. Still, he could get an order of poutine and share it with her.

As they joined the line, he spoke, forcing his voice to remain neutral, conversational. "So, you're going out for dinner with Conrad tomorrow."

"Yes."

Ian glanced at her, but she stared off into space, probably reluctant to look him in the eyes. If she felt guilty, that might be a good thing. Or it might mean he was pushing her away.

"I know you have every right, Daphne. I'm not trying to interfere with your love life, but I hoped to see you again. To ask you out." He paused, but before she could respond, he continued. "On a date."

She smiled. "I understand you meant on a date. Ian, I wasn't sure how you felt. Conrad asked me out, and he was persistent, so I said yes."

"What do you mean 'persistent'? Did he pressure you?"

"No, not pressure."

"Then what?" If Conrad had coerced her into this, then Ian would help her back out of it. Today.

"He suggested we see where it goes. I saw no harm in it." Daphne dropped her head. "You hadn't called or texted."

"Neither had you." Lame, sure, but he couldn't help saying it. When she jerked her chin up and gave him a defiant stare, he said, "Sorry. I'm not helping."

He put a hand on her arm. "I want us to see each other. Exclusively. If you're not ready, I'm okay with it."

That was a lie, but he needed to tell it. Ian had never been a possessive guy, and he wasn't about to start with the first woman who'd mattered to him in years.

"I committed to going out with Conrad tomorrow. He's made reservations."

"He can cancel them."

"Is that fair to him?"

"How fair is it to go out with him when you know it won't go anywhere?"

Daphne dipped her chin while she considered. Decision made, she raised her head to meet his gaze. "You're right. I'll tell him when we return. He'll understand. It's nothing serious. This date was casual."

Ian studied her face, unable to control the twinge of worry. She'd spoken the words with confidence, but her expression betrayed doubt. Odds were high Conrad didn't view this as a casual date. Whatever happened, Ian vowed he'd deal with the fallout.

"Don't worry about a thing. I'll make sure Conrad's okay," he said.

CHAPTER 34

As Ian and Daphne walked away, Beth kept her gaze on Conrad. He glared after the retreating couple. Was Conrad's jealous streak strong enough to compel him to kill? Beth had noticed nothing overt, though, in the past, he'd shown signs of having anger management issues. He hid his displeasure with difficulty when things weren't going his way.

Didn't everyone dislike losing though? Beth hated to struggle, envied other's successes, and wished everything came as easily to her as they did to, say, Leon. Some might argue her life had been easy but only because they hadn't lived it. So just because Leon appeared to have led a charmed life didn't mean he had.

Should she say something to Conrad? Express sympathy about the obvious attraction between Daphne and Ian? Beth sighed. Any interference might make things worse. She'd already alienated the one man who'd meant anything to her.

Andrew hadn't texted her since the night Jacob caught him on her property, and she'd been too nervous to call or go to the café. But she'd have to face him eventually unless she intended to never set foot in Andrew's again.

"You're out of luck, Conrad. Daphne's fallen hard for Ian."

Beth's jaw dropped at MJ's words.

Conrad favoured MJ with a snarl. "That's what you think. She'll change her mind."

"You'd better change your mind."

Was MJ insane? She spoke as if stating facts—probably she

171

was—but was it necessary to say it?

"You don't know how she feels." Conrad studied her face. "Or do you? Did Daphne say something to you about me? About Ian?"

"No," MJ replied. "But they can't take their eyes off each other."

"She'll forget about him after tomorrow."

"Doubt it."

Beth shook her head but remained silent. MJ never feared to speak her mind.

What a risky thing to do with a murderer on the loose.

Conrad rose. "I'm going for coffee. You two want one?"

"No, thank you," Beth said.

"I'll take a hot chocolate if you find one somewhere." MJ dug in her purse for her wallet.

Conrad waved her away. "I'll buy." As she returned her wallet to her purse, he strode away.

***

A hand on her shoulder shook Beth awake. She opened her eyes to MJ's concerned face, close enough to kiss. Behind MJ stood Conrad, arms crossed, a frown on his face.

"What?" Beth pulled away from her friend and yawned. "I fell asleep?"

She must have been stressed. The last thing she remembered was … Conrad going for coffee—and hot chocolate for MJ. Grateful to see MJ alive, and ashamed she'd again suspected one of their friends of being the killer, Beth rubbed the fatigue out of her eyes.

"I'm sorry," she said.

"It's okay." MJ picked up a takeout cup. "Here, have a sip of my hot chocolate. I haven't touched it yet."

"No!" Without thinking, Beth slapped the cup from MJ's hand. When it hit the ground, the lid popped off and liquid chocolate splatted everywhere.

MJ shrieked and leaped backwards, crashing into Conrad, who banged into the table. Books slid across the table, three dropping onto the ground.

"Jesus Christ, Beth, what did you do that for?" Conrad's face contorted into a mask of rage.

"I'm sorry," she stammered. "It was an accident."

She jumped out of her chair and snatched a roll of paper towels from the box under the table. Frantically, she tried to mop up as much of the spill as she could. MJ grabbed more paper off the roll and crouched down to assist.

Beth stuffed used paper towels into the near-empty coffee cup, soaking up whatever remained in the bottom. She snapped the lid on it. The puddle of no-longer-hot chocolate continued its lazy spread over the pavement. While it was impossible to mop up every drop, they soaked up a healthy portion of it. MJ kept a plastic bag on hand for garbage, and they filled it with the saturated paper.

"I'll go throw all this out in a bin." Beth stuffed the coffee cup onto the top of the bag and grabbed the backpack she'd brought to use as a purse. "I'm going to the bathroom and to buy water. Anyone need anything?"

No one did.

Before hurrying away, Beth spared a quick glance at Conrad. He stared at her, his expression grim. She headed towards the public washrooms housed inside a large brick building. Once inside, Beth slipped the coffee cup into her backpack and threw the plastic bag of paper into a garbage bin.

With a nervous glance towards the writers' group table, she hurried into the ladies' room. She was uncertain if she'd call Jacob and ask him to test the remnants of the hot chocolate for poison, but she seriously considered it.

***

"You want to what?" Conrad couldn't believe he'd heard Daphne correctly. He thought she'd said they wouldn't be going out to dinner tomorrow. Surely, he'd misunderstood.

Daphne licked her lips. When she spoke, her voice came out soft and timid. "I'm sorry, Conrad. Allowing you to take me to dinner isn't fair to you. Not now."

"Then when?"

She looked taken aback, but he refused to let her off easy. Ian Fergus hadn't been in Daphne's company more than twenty minutes, and already she was breaking tomorrow's date. And right in front of MJ, who'd predicted this would happen.

"I'm sorry," Daphne repeated. She gave him a weak smile.

An obviously fake smile.

"What happened?"

"I shouldn't have agreed to go out with you. Ian and I"—she stopped talking and swallowed—"we've been seeing more of each other. I'd developed feelings for him. I didn't realize they were mutual."

Daphne placed a hand gently on Conrad's arm. He forced himself not to knock it away.

"We've agreed we want to be a couple. It wouldn't be fair to you if I didn't tell you. I'd be going out with you to be polite, but I'd know it wouldn't go anywhere. I want to see Ian exclusively."

His chest tight, his breathing shallow, Conrad spoke through gritted teeth. "It's okay. I appreciate the honesty."

He forced a smile onto his face and gave her the line he'd heard often from the new age community but never believed. "Don't feel bad, Daphne. It'll work out the way it's meant to be."

This time her smile was open and filled with relief. "Thank you so much for understanding." She opened her arms and waved him in for a hug.

As he wrapped his arms around her, he wondered how long he should wait before taking Ian Fergus out of the picture for good.

CHAPTER 35

The house was quiet without the kids, who'd accompanied the neighbours to the movies, but Robin reveled in it. Back in front of her computer, she accessed each of Leon's book's web pages on the major distribution sites as a separate tab of her browser. She'd called up all the one-star reviews and examined them for similarities.

A few displaying different usernames read as though written by the same person. They also spent more time deriding the author rather than the books he'd written. While this contravened the terms of use on the sites, the sites wouldn't pull them unless someone complained—if then.

If she tracked down the IP address of the user, assuming he hadn't masked it, she might identify him. Perhaps Leon's killer had written these nasty reviews. They displayed a deep hatred towards, and extreme jealousy of, Leon. Both could be motives for murder.

She couldn't trace the user through his accounts, all obviously phoney. The mystery user set them up specifically to troll other authors with one-star reviews. Why the system didn't flag these as bogus reviews, she didn't understand. Perhaps the algorithms weren't advanced enough to detect fake negative reviews. Or perhaps the companies didn't care if nasty reviews hurt authors as long as a glut of other books existed.

That's awfully cynical. Robin hadn't always been so pessimistic, but ever since her husband's death, she found it too easy to slip into negative thoughts. She considered it a good sign she'd caught herself in the act. Maybe her relationship with Jacob had brightened her personality.

Robin kept Jacob unaware of what she was up to, telling only Beth and Daphne. The three women wanted to be certain before informing anyone else, especially the police. Besides, Jacob had no doubt considered this angle and had his best tech guys investigating it. Either that, or he'd think they were nuts and lecture her on meddling.

Earlier that afternoon, Beth had stopped by with a takeout cup containing paper towels drenched in hot chocolate. Robin wasn't sure what to do with it. Beth explained how she'd become suspicious of Conrad and knocked the drink from MJ's hand.

"Yes, it sounds crazy," Beth said, "but what if Conrad murdered Leon? What if he put poison in this?"

Robin pointed out that if Conrad had murdered Leon, he'd be stupid to poison MJ at the craft fair. And for what? Comments about Ian and Daphne? Beth flushed with embarrassment for even considering it, but neither one of them wanted to throw the cup away. For now, they kept it hidden in Robin's kitchen cupboard.

For hours Robin absorbed herself in digging into the mystery user's details. Reluctant to hack his account, she wanted to try more deductive ways to uncover his identity. By the time Kaylee and Nate burst through the door, however, she'd made no progress.

Later, as her kids readied themselves for bed, Robin contemplated her options. Perhaps she needed to approach this backwards. Whenever a logic problem or coding issue stymied her, viewing it from a different angle helped resolve it. This time, she'd work from the end.

She assumed Leon's killer knew him well. Whoever it was made Leon comfortable enough to allow him into the house early in the morning. Leon wouldn't have granted a crazed fan that privilege. Also, the killer was aware she'd kept a spare key in her garden.

How? From watching her kids? Observing Kaylee going around back to retrieve the key? Or did he chance to see it? The idea someone stalked her and her kids nauseated her. Who'd do such a thing? Why?

She shook that off. He must have learned of it through casual observation. Those fake rocks blended in, but if you knew about it, you might pick one out of a lineup of genuine rocks. However he'd discovered the key, the intruder used it to enter the house. The way he moved through her place indicated familiarity—he'd headed straight to the computer.

All this meant she should dig around in the user end of things to find Leon's killer. Perhaps the cops needed probable cause—or whatever they called it—but she could be as illegal as she wanted to be. If she found evidence, then she'd inform Jacob and let him figure out how to legally lay charges.

She retrieved the list of men she, Daphne, and Beth had made at Beth's to use as a guide. She'd scan the list and place an asterisk next to any name she thought belonged to a prime suspect. With a glance at the cupboard where she'd hidden the hot chocolate cup, she placed the first mark beside Conrad Barnes.

***

Annoyed at how often he glanced over to the front doors whenever they opened, Andrew announced he was taking a break. He made himself a latte and headed to the back room. He sprawled out at a booth next to the shelf of books dedicated to the writers' group, one foot propped on a chair. His gaze lingered most on Beth's books.

He picked up his phone and reviewed the text messages she'd sent, which went unacknowledged. There were three.

I'm sorry, but I didn't know it was you.
I stuck to the facts.
Are you okay?

She probably thought he was angry with her when, in reality, he was angry with himself. He should never have followed her home. Or when he'd verified she'd arrived home safe, he should have either knocked on her door or gone back to the café. The last thing he should have done was what he'd actually done: checked the garage to see how someone could have entered it without her knowing.

However it'd played out, the killer had either done a better job than Andrew, or Beth had tightened her security. As if her spotting him wasn't embarrassing enough, the cops had dragged his ass to the station and questioned him. For trespassing. For murder.

This kept him from responding to her. Here it was Monday, and he'd ignored her since Thursday night. It irked him he thought so much of her opinion of him that he avoided her.

Yet he craved to see her. The night before, he'd tried to get her out of his head by going out with another woman. The entire time he'd worried Beth would hear about it, or worse, they'd run into her. After a hurried dinner at the Italian restaurant on Queen Street, he'd taken his date back to her place. When she invited him in, he'd told her he needed to go to work early and passed.

No matter how he tried to spin this, he wanted Beth Holmes.

Was that so terrible? Sure, she had the falling asleep problem, but she'd lived with it for as long as he'd known her. It hadn't prevented her from getting a driver's license. He'd researched how the illness affected driving, worried she'd total her car and kill herself one day passing out at the wheel. Not all narcoleptics couldn't drive. That Beth had her license meant she controlled the problem. According to what he'd read, she probably only drove short distances and only at certain times.

"Hi. Am I interrupting?"

Andrew slowly raised his head to meet Beth's gaze.

CHAPTER 36

"No, you're not interrupting, Beth." Andrew's foot dropped to the floor and he straightened up. He indicated the chair across from him and said, "Sit."

Face tilted down, Beth crossed the floor, her long legs covering the ground in four strides. She pulled the chair out and sat on the edge of the seat as though ready to bolt if the need arose.

He'd better get to the point. "Sorry I didn't return your texts."

She angled her chin up then so their gazes met. "Why didn't you?"

Andrew shrugged to buy time. What could he say that wouldn't sound stalkerish?

"I was worried," she said, her voice soft, calm. Her expression remained neutral, but her throat bobbed as she swallowed, and her shoulders and back went rigid. She pressed her palms against the top of the table.

"That wasn't my intention." He leaned forward and covered her hands with his. When she didn't pull away, he said, "I've been trying to figure out what to say."

"The truth works best."

"I only wanted to see you home safe."

"But you didn't have to." She tried to remove her hands from his, but he tightened his grip, holding her in place.

"Beth, for the last while, I've had feelings for you, but I didn't know what to do with them."

With a look of confusion, she said, "Feelings? For me?"

Andrew nodded, but when he saw she'd averted her eyes, he said, "Yes. I look forward to the writers' group meetings—not only because of the extra business but because you'll be here. Every time the door opens, I check to see if you've arrived."

Beth met his gaze then. "Okay, if you're going to 'fess up, then I will too."

He waited in the silence, giving her whatever time she needed. Finally, she spoke.

"I've always looked forward to seeing you when I come here. It's one reason I visit so often. I've eaten far more scones than I should have because you enjoy it when I do." She laughed, and the sound pierced his heart. He'd missed her delicate laugh.

"Sounds stupid," she said, her face flushing red.

"No. I'm glad to hear it. I feared I'd imagined something had developed between us." This next bit he needed to broach carefully. "Do you have plans Tuesday night?"

"Tomorrow night? Weekdays are quieter than weekends, business-wise, which means I can get away."

"Ditto. Want to do something?"

"Okay," she said. "What did you have in mind?"

"The casino." Andrew grinned. "Tuesdays are date night. We'll go to the buffet and check out the gambling."

"I'm not much of a gambler, and I've never been to a casino. Well, Vegas, but not to gamble. For work."

She was a model before. Once, he'd have dated her for that reason alone. Now, he only cared about who she was, not what she did.

"I'm not a big gambler either and never went to the Fallsview Casino. Might be cool to check it out. Plus, it's open late and we both work long days."

Beth's face brightened, her eyes sparkling with anticipation. "Okay. Sounds fun. What time?"

Andrew pulled out his phone and opened a browser to make plans.

***

"Beer?" Daphne led Ian into the kitchen.

They'd stayed in tonight, and he hadn't dropped by until after dinner in order to finish correcting physics tests. She'd counted the minutes until his arrival, partly because she was eager to see him but also because she hated being alone here.

"Sure."

Ian accepted the beer she passed him, and she poured herself a glass of wine. "Want to watch a movie?"

"Sounds fine." He grinned. "Two hardcore partiers, eh?"

Daphne laughed. "I have to work at six tomorrow morning. This is as hearty as I'll party."

He took her hand as they walked into the family room. Her heart melted at the sweet gesture. Ian was a sweet man. He'd hate knowing she thought that about him, but it was the truth.

They snuggled together on the couch, his arm around her shoulder. Barely a minute into the movie they'd selected, she turned her face up to him. With one hand, she stroked his cheek.

Ian let out a low growl. "Are you trying to start something here?"

Daphne giggled. "Want me to start something?"

"Answering a question with a question. Nice." He nuzzled her neck with his nose.

Instead of replying, she hooked a hand around his neck and dragged him down. She pressed her lips to his, inviting him to taste her. Not normally aggressive, she couldn't seem to control herself this time.

Warren had been the aggressive one, in charge, taking what he wanted when he wanted. She'd been compliant, a willing recipient for whatever he offered. With Ian, she made the demand, and he not only accepted, he made demands of his own.

For a moment, they wrestled for control, and then they both capitulated, one to the other. They forgot everything else—the movie, their drinks, the brutal reality of Leon's death—and focused only on each other. Daphne had never experienced such passion, such emotion, as she did now with this man.

"Oh, Ian, my God." She murmured the words without awareness.

With one hand, he gripped her long hair and tilted her head up, exposing her neck. He trailed kisses down her throat until he reached the scoop of her T-shirt. When he dipped into her cleavage, she moaned from the sensation of tongue on skin.

Shallow breaths, audible gasps, all from her, punctuated every sensual contact. Ian clasped her wrists with his hands and raised her arms above her head. He motioned for her to hold still and then eased her shirt up her torso and over her head. It dropped to the floor when it cleared her hands.

Impatient, Daphne unhooked her bra, dropping it onto the T-shirt.

"Gorgeous," Ian said with a sigh.

He cupped her breasts, tweaking the hardened nipples, which elicited more moans from her. She frantically tugged his shirt from his jeans, running her hands along his hard, smooth back.

Ian pressed her gently down onto the couch.

"Are you okay with this?" His voice was thick and rough.

"What do you think?"

He smiled. "I think you ask too many questions and give no answers."

"My body says yes. My lips say yes." She kissed him on the lips, her tongue tangling with his.

Suddenly Daphne realized where they were and pulled her head back. "Let's go upstairs."

She didn't want to tell him how exposed she felt in this room. He'd either laugh or take her seriously. Neither option was desirable.

Ian didn't reply but rose, pulling her with him. They ran for the stairs, hands linked.

***

From a position in the backyard, far enough from the house to avoid the cameras, Conrad watched through binoculars. The dim light from the fireplace provided enough illumination to see Daphne's naked chest.

Slut. Fury rose like bile in his throat.

She'd turned him down to fuck that loser. A high school teacher, for God's sake. What was so great about that?

Conrad traced the lovers' path up the stairs through the floor-to-ceiling glass. Leon had thought the property private, but he hadn't counted on determination and inventiveness. Conrad found a way through hedges, around cameras and garden beds.

But the victory was small. Compelled to watch the tussle on the sofa, his blood had boiled when Ian forced himself on Daphne. Conrad's perception of what he'd seen shifted. It hadn't been Daphne's fault. Ian Fergus pressured her. He all but raped her. If it weren't for Ian, Conrad would be with her, easing her into a night of love and tenderness. He'd have shown her what a real man could give.

After he eliminated Fergus, Daphne would realize Conrad's worth, and they'd be together at last.

CHAPTER 37

In Daphne's room, their clothes hit the floor, and both tumbled into her bed naked. Their bodies pressed together, hands exploring.

"You're so soft," Ian said.

Daphne reached between his legs. "You're not."

Both laughed, appreciating her humour. Ian silenced the laughter with a kiss, and the mood turned passionate and frantic. Daphne arched into him, her whole body buzzing with the need for him to fill her.

His fingers probed and stimulated her, sending agonies of pleasure through her. She ached for him, but she wanted to give, too, so she used her mouth in ways she hadn't wanted to before. Ian had released her reserve, and she craved to hear him moan for her.

When she ran her tongue down past his navel and up his stiff shaft, he rewarded her with a groan. She encapsulated him with soft lips, and he shuddered and cried out. Her tongue teased and flicked while her hands caressed.

His hands grasping her shoulders, he called out to her, his voice frenzied. "Daphne."

In response, she climbed his body to feast once more on his sculpted lips. Her thighs gripped his, and, in a sudden motion, he flipped her so she lay beneath him.

"My turn to explore," he said, and he did, taking her higher than she'd thought possible.

"You're so wet." He sounded astonished.

"Your fault," she gasped out. "Please, I need you."

A tearing sound made her look, and she watched, unabashed, as he rolled on a condom.

"Hurry. Oh, Ian, hurry."

He obliged, sliding into her and taking her beyond reason, beyond breath. The climax, when it came, tightened her, blinded her, and then unwound and drained her. Daphne's pulse throbbed in her ears; her breath hitched in ragged puffs.

She arched into him further, keeping the rhythm going until he hollered out her name and collapsed onto her chest.

"Now I know why some men have heart attacks during sex," he said, rolling onto his back and drawing her into the circle of his arm.

"You're in good shape. I doubt you're in any danger." She rested her head on his shoulder.

"Don't underestimate your sexual powers." He drew her in closer.

"Ian, why didn't we do this sooner?" Daphne angled her head up to view his face and watch his expression.

He smiled. "I couldn't get here until after dinner."

She smacked him lightly on the chest.

"Cut it out. Why'd we wait so long to hook up?"

"I didn't want to move in on my friend's sister."

"Did you think about me?"

He fell quiet, his eyes growing distant. She waited it out.

"I always thought you were hot. Well, after I stopped thinking girls were icky."

"That's what you'd say about a bug."

He smiled down at her. "Bugs were cool. Girls were icky. Especially little sisters."

Daphne laughed. "Oh, God, I remember you and Leon ditched me every time I tried to follow you." She stuck out her bottom lip in a fake pout. "I only wanted you to play tea party with me."

"Like I said: icky." Ian ran a hand down her arm and touched her breast. "Not so icky now. I'll play tea party with you all night if you'll let me."

The mention of the night reminded her of the morning to follow. "You should go home, I suppose."

"That's it? You're kicking me out? I didn't peg you as the love 'em and eject 'em type."

185

"Not at all." Her expression turned serious, her voice somber. "I don't want you to go, but I'm working at six tomorrow. I wake up at four thirty."

"Wow, what for?"

"To prepare for work."

"For a night with you, I'll wake up at five. You can have the shower, and I'll shower at home."

Daphne didn't reply. If he left with her, he'd see her crazy lock-up routine. Did she want to let him learn about that this early in the relationship? Of course, he was already familiar with her weirdness—they'd grown up together.

"Okay." She stroked her palm along his cheek, enjoying the tickle of the stubble. "That would be nice."

"Excellent. We'll leave together in the morning. While you're in the shower, I'll make coffee. It'll be great."

Daphne pressed her hand to her mouth and whispered, "Love you. Love you. Love you."

***

"Ian and I slept together." Daphne couldn't stifle the grin. Like a cat in the sunshine, she gave a languid stretch.

The three friends met at Beth's in the sunroom, taking an evening to regroup and catch up over drinks.

From the pool, Robin called out, "Wow, that was fast."

Beth, floating beside her, grinned but remained silent.

"If you consider three decades fast," Daphne retorted.

"You've been dating since age four?" Robin replied.

"We've known each other since childhood. It's weird how nothing happened until Leon died." Daphne first met Robin's gaze and then Beth's. "You know how when someone enters a room the dynamic changes?"

When her friends both nodded, Daphne continued. "Something similar happens after someone dies. The dynamic in your life changes. Maybe, unconsciously, you held back from acting on something or the person who died compelled you to do something you wouldn't have otherwise done. Then, when they're gone, you change your life."

"Interesting," Beth said. "When my mother died, I stopped modelling. It's no secret she pushed me into it and kept me in it."

186

"Would she be angry you quit?" Daphne was uncertain if she should ask, but she needed to know. She'd always believed Beth had wanted to be a top model even when her friend had insisted she didn't.

"Oh, definitely." Beth glided to the side of the pool and hoisted herself out. She wrapped a towel around her waist and sat across from Daphne at the bistro table. "Mother was horrible, but I desperately wanted to make her proud of me. I'd have done anything to please her."

Her eyes grew teary. "She pushed me to do whatever the men in power wanted me to do to succeed—and it was always men. God, she was like a pimp."

A lump grew in Daphne's throat, and she covered Beth's hand with her own. "I'm so sorry."

Wrapped in a towel, Robin appeared at Beth's side. "I'm sorry too, sweetie. We didn't realize."

Beth hung her head, and a sob escaped. "No one did. She'd send me to meetings in hotel rooms. Rape was my first experience with a man."

Daphne sucked in a breath as if desperate for air, and her extremities grew cold. How must Beth have suffered all these years? *Her own mother.*

"Did you report it?" Robin asked, taking a seat between the two women.

Beth shook her head. When no one replied, she continued. "Who'd believe me? When I told my mother, she said ..."

"It's okay. You don't have to tell us."

Beth raised her head and met their gazes. "It's about time I did. When I told my mother, she said I should go along to get along. She was my mother, but all she cared about was living her dream through me."

"Your mother wanted to be a model?" Robin's voice vibrated with compassion.

Beth shook her head. "An actress. She did well until she got pregnant with me."

Silence fell, and the obvious next question went unspoken.

"I know what you're thinking," Beth said. "Why didn't she have an abortion?"

No one else spoke. Daphne couldn't think of anything helpful to say, so she remained silent. She stole a glance at Robin, who sat with her gaze focused on the hands she clasped in her lap.

With her voice even, Beth spoke. "Sometimes, I think she wished she had, but then other times, she saw this as an excuse not to continue. Let whoever she gave birth to finish the journey. I found her journal after she died. She used me as soon as I was born."

"Oh, Beth." Daphne squeezed her friend's hand.

"Know what she wrote about every day? Me. About how I'd failed, the mistakes I made, and how she'd push me to do better. When I succeeded, when I became the famous model, she set her sights on the next goal. She never allowed me to enjoy the moment, and she never told me she was proud. It didn't occur to her. I was a means to an end."

"What did your father say? How could he go along with it?" Daphne asked.

"Daddy worked all the time, and Mother managed my career." Beth spat that last part out. She hung her head. "I don't blame him. She controlled us both."

She raised her head and turned her gaze from one to the other. "He apologized after she died. Her death freed us from her control."

"Honey, it's okay," Robin said. "I'm sorry we didn't understand, but we're here for you now."

Beth gave them each a wan smile. "Yes, I know. Wanna know what else?"

When they both nodded, she said, "I got through telling you without falling asleep. That's a good sign."

Beth turned to Robin. "What do you think about Daphne's theory? Your life changed after Martin died."

Daphne and Beth studied Robin while she contemplated the question. Finally, she said, "My life changed for the worse. You were freed to act, but I've become trapped."

"Did your freedom depend on your husband's presence?"

Robin shook her head. "I was independent before we married. The relationship didn't make me whole. Yes, he completed me—at least, that's how I felt—but he didn't make me something I wasn't already. I never felt as though I needed to be different for him to love me. When he died, I couldn't trust anything anymore, so it narrowed my world."

She picked up her glass of wine but set it down without sipping.

"I'm terrified my life could shatter at any moment. Leon's death enhanced that sense of impending doom. We worked together, helped each other—even fell for each other. Then, someone came along and destroyed everything."

Tears slid from Daphne's eyes, and she swallowed around the lump in her throat.

Robin shrugged. "What am I supposed to do after this? I'm attracted to Jacob, and he's attracted to me, but, my God, he's a cop. That's a high-risk job. How can I let myself love him? What if …"

When she trailed off, the room fell silent. This time, Daphne filled the void. "We're supposed to find who killed Leon. The clues are all there. We just need to put them together. Let's do this. It's why we're here, isn't it?"

***

Beth heaved out a ragged sigh and sipped from her cola.

"Okay, what've we got so far?" she asked.

Robin leaned in. "I did some digging on the internet." Her voice dropped to a whisper. "I started with Conrad." She glanced at Beth. "No reason except you gave me that cup."

"What cup?" Daphne asked.

Robin filled her in on the details about the hot chocolate incident.

"We won't ask Jacob to test it unless we find a reason to do it. Conrad would be insane to poison someone at the craft show with witnesses," she concluded.

Beth flushed with embarrassment when Daphne stared at her.

"It sounds crazy when I hear Robin explain it," Beth said.

"Perhaps not." Daphne frowned. "Conrad sometimes gives me a vibe. It's as good a place as any to start. We'll investigate everyone on our list. We've even added Andrew and Ian to it. They'd be hurt if they found out, I guess, but someone we know killed Leon. We have to be as objective as the cops to find out who."

"Conrad's first even if we did this in alphabetical order," Robin pointed out.

Daphne grabbed her purse and retrieved their list of names. "I haven't put it into any kind of order, but we can work from this."

Robin rose and went to the bag she'd left sitting at the back of the room. When she returned with it to the table, she set up her laptop. While the machine booted up, she said, "I've tracked down Conrad's accounts on the major book review and distribution sites. Also his social media. The reviews he's done for other authors are very politically correct and positive—until I retrieved cookies from his computer that revealed other accounts."

"I don't know what that means," Beth said.

"Conrad created other accounts so he can log in as an anonymous user and post negative reviews for other authors and positive reviews for his books." Robin leaned back in her chair. "I also found evidence he did a lot of his posting from Andrew's."

A surge of fear made Beth lean over to inspect the laptop screen. Nothing helpful displayed.

"Are you saying Andrew had something to do with it?" He couldn't have. She'd spent a wonderful date night with him at the casino the night before. He'd been kind, attentive, fun—the opposite of a homicidal maniac.

"Not at all," Robin replied, soothing Beth's fears. "The activity was on his network, that's all. People log in to the café's network all the time. Andrew posts the password so anyone can get on it. Publicly accessed networks aren't secure, but most people don't worry about security. They think they're safe and anonymous. If you target someone, you can get on the system and track whatever he's doing—or worse if your intent is theft or sabotage."

"So Conrad's trolling. Doesn't mean he's a killer," Daphne said.

"I agree. But he's the only one in our writers' group doing this," Robin replied.

"Keeps him on the suspect list for sure. Professional jealousy is a motive for murder," Beth said.

"And he asked me on a date," Daphne pointed out.

"So did Ian," Robin said.

Daphne rose, shivering. "Yes, but somehow, what's happening between me and Ian feels natural, as though it's developing organically. With Conrad, it's forced."

She picked up her bag. "I'm cold."

A sinking sensation in her gut, Beth stood and faced Daphne. "Are you okay?"

"Yeah. I need to get dressed." Looking stricken, Daphne rushed from the room.

CHAPTER 38

As Daphne dressed, her breathing returned to normal and the awful gnawing in her stomach subsided. At first, she refused to accept Conrad might have killed Leon. She refused to accept any of their friends capable of murder. Everyone loved Leon. Yet when she reflected on the days after Leon's death, Conrad's behaviour and pursuit of her took on a more sinister flavour.

She shrugged a sweater over her T-shirt. The change room off the side of the pool room was dim and silent. Neither Beth nor Robin had followed her, and she appreciated the space they'd given her. They were concerned about her, but she didn't want to talk about it.

What was there to discuss? Conrad's guilt wasn't certain, so they couldn't tell Jacob anything. If they were wrong, they'd turn the focus on an innocent man while the real killer escaped.

But what if we're right?

If they were correct, someone should tell Jacob so he could investigate.

Daphne hurried back to the sunroom.

Robin and Beth still sat at the bistro table. Beth's glass was empty of the cola she'd been drinking. Robin's wine glass remained half full, but it looked as if she'd stopped drinking it. An almost-empty bottle of water stood next to it.

Daphne returned to her seat at the table, and as she sat down, something occurred to her. "Conrad attended a conference the morning Leon died."

191

"Only in Niagara Falls. How easy would it be to slip back here, kill Leon, ditch the evidence, and return to the hotel?" Robin asked.

Silence fell as each of them mentally calculated.

Beth spoke first. "It's tight, but it's possible."

"I agree," said Daphne. "If he did it that way, it shows planning and premeditation."

"Poisoning him already shows that." Robin sipped from her water.

"We should tell the police," Daphne said.

"And say what? We have a gut feeling Conrad killed Leon? They'll laugh at us." Beth shook her head. "The police need evidence."

"They'll find evidence when they know whom to target," Daphne replied.

"Jacob would take us seriously," Robin said.

"He'd need evidence," Beth insisted. "The police can't arrest someone without a good reason."

"No, they can't." Robin crossed her arms over her chest and leaned back in her chair. "But they can question him."

"And tip him off they're looking at him?" Beth frowned.

"So? All he can do is hope they don't bust him. You think he'll run?" Daphne shook her head. "He's got nowhere to go."

"So what do we do, then?" Robin asked.

Beth hesitated, but then said, "If we book appointments with him, one of us can go in the room with him for a massage while the other searches the place."

"Are you crazy? What if he catches us?" Robin shouted the words.

"He won't." Beth put a hand on Robin's arm. "He tried to frame me. I want him busted and locked up."

"What would we search for?" Robin replied.

"Anything to prove he did it." Beth frowned. "There must be something."

"The stone he took from Leon," Daphne suggested. "I'd recognize it."

She removed Beth's hand from Robin's arm and held it. "Why do you suppose he targeted you? Did you do something to him?"

"Not that I recall."

Robin turned to Daphne. "Good question. Why Beth? Why not

Daphne? She lives with Leon. She'd have made a good suspect."

Daphne shook her head. "The video cameras. They showed him arrive."

"So why Beth?" Robin asked.

"Oh, my God." Daphne shuddered. "Beth and Conrad are the same height. They have a similar build. The baggy sweater and track pants hid his gender."

Beth rose. "Who wants to book a massage?"

***

At the station, Jacob sat at his desk and reviewed his notes on Leon's murder. He'd stayed late, working in the peace and quiet. The case had stalled. None of the evidence recovered so far pointed to anyone specific.

Leon had a wide circle of influence, many friends, millions of readers. Anyone could've done it, but no one Jacob had spoken to seemed happy Leon was dead. Jacob pulled up the results of the analysis on the poison. Cicutoxin—found in water hemlock, which he'd read about in Beth's novel.

It always came back to Beth. *Why Beth?*

He opened the images they'd gotten from Leon's surveillance cameras. The perpetrator looked so similar to Beth, anyone viewing the photos would think of her instantly. That, of course, was the killer's intention.

Similar size. Similar height.

That narrowed it down. They searched for a Caucasian male similar in height and build to Beth Holmes. From Leon's and Daphne's inner circle, the possibilities narrowed to Warren Russel, Ian Fergus, and Conrad Barnes.

Andrew Winston was too tall, and other men in the writers' group either provided solid alibis or had the wrong body type. Jacob could also rule out Warren Russel.

He'd told them he'd been with a woman. It'd taken a while to track her down because he hadn't known her name. They'd met at the bar where his band played and she returned with him to his place. Lucky for him, she'd spent the night, but it took two days to find her. When Skylar finally identified her, and the two detectives interviewed her, the woman confirmed she'd been with Warren Russel.

193

Ian Fergus claimed he'd been home alone and now dated Daphne Russel. No solid alibi. Conrad Barnes had also sniffed around Daphne after the murder, and he too fit the physical profile. But you couldn't arrest a man because his height and build matched a picture, and Barnes had been at a convention.

The tech guys had worked on the images from Leon's surveillance records, attempting to pull any facial features out of the recordings. The killer had been too careful. He never slipped up and angled full-face towards the cameras.

They'd pulled a hair that likely came from the killer's wig, but they needed a wig to match it to. So far, no joy on that front. They searched for where the killer might've purchased it, which would take a while.

Jacob spent the rest of the day scouting out the hotel in Niagara Falls where Conrad had stayed for the convention. They'd retrieved surveillance tapes from the hotel at the start of the investigation. After viewing them, Jacob found no sign Conrad had left the hotel that morning.

Unless he'd dressed as a woman then, too.

Crazy as that sounded, he needed to investigate the possibility. Jacob glanced at the time. Too late to stop by Robin's on his way home. He sighed. Oh well, he'd see her tomorrow.

CHAPTER 39

The start of the school year was always an exciting time for Ian Fergus. He enjoyed meeting his new students, getting to know them, and encouraging them to learn. By Christmas, the freshness would fade and his students would be more than ready for a break. He worked them hard from the first day, but he made up for it by giving them their holidays free of homework.

At this point in September, they had miles to go before anyone resented the pace, including himself.

He arrived at his apartment building in downtown Niagara-on-the-Lake shortly after four in the afternoon. It was a squat, four-storey building housing sixteen units with Ian's on the top floor, and he used the stairs to get there.

The aroma of simmering chilli from the slow cooker hit him in the hallway, making him salivate. Too bad he'd have to wait another two hours. His stomach growled in protest, but he ignored it.

After unlocking his door, he dropped his briefcase on the floor by the desk in his home office and made his way to the kitchen. Time for a cold beer while he marked assignments before dinner.

Tonight, Daphne planned to spend the night at his place. Sure, it was tiny compared to the palace she inhabited, but he wanted her in his home. She continued to work the day shift, and he'd told her she could head to work from here. In another week, she wouldn't be working at all. She'd already given the diner her notice.

The apartment buzzer sounded. Puzzled, Ian rose to answer it.

He wasn't expecting Daphne until six.

"Yes?"

"It's Conrad. Barnes."

"What's up?"

"Can I come up?"

"Is it important?" Did this have something to do with Daphne? Conrad had seemed okay when Daphne broke their date.

"Just wanted to talk. Won't take long."

Not knowing what else to do, Ian buzzed the other man in.

When he opened the door to Conrad's knock, a takeout coffee was pressed into his hands.

"Thought I'd bring a peace offering," Conrad said.

"Are we at war?" Ian replied.

The other man shrugged. "Hope not. I wanted to discuss Daphne."

Ian backed up to allow Conrad into the apartment and led the way to the living room. He wasn't in the mood for coffee. This late in the day, caffeine would keep him up all night. Ian set it on the coffee table and sat on the couch, arms folded, legs crossed at the ankles.

"I don't have a lot of time," he told Conrad. "I've got assignments to grade before dinner." He left the part about Daphne coming over unsaid—none of Conrad's business. "What can I do for you?"

"I didn't know you two were involved when I asked Daphne out." Conrad sipped on the coffee he held. "Don't know how you take yours. I added one milk and one sugar."

"Okay." Ian glanced at the cup he'd set on the table. Had Leon died this way? Conrad and Leon had been friends. Leon had trusted the massage therapist, gave him business—even helped him with his writing.

Paranoia, Ian decided. Still, it wouldn't hurt to be cautious.

Conrad sipped from his cup. "Hits the spot. I need a jolt." He nodded to the cup on the table. "Try it."

"I'm okay, thanks. I'll drink it later while I'm doing my marking."

Did he detect disappointment in Conrad's eyes? Or was that more paranoia talking? If only the cops would arrest someone, they could all return to normal. As it was, with no knowledge of who'd killed Leon and why, everyone was under suspicion.

"We weren't involved," Ian said. "Not then, which is why she agreed to go out with you. But we talked and decided to take it to the next level. She told me you'd asked her out, and after we discussed it, we thought the ethical thing to do was tell you."

Not that we need to explain ourselves. So why go into that long-winded justification?

"Okay. So we're good?" Conrad held out his hand.

"Sure." Ian gripped it and shook. Conrad's handshake was firm, but his palm felt fleshy, warm, and sweaty. When they disconnected, Ian wanted to rush to the bathroom and wash his hands.

Daphne would appreciate that.

He glanced pointedly at the time displayed on the DVD player and rose. "I hate to rush you, but I have work to do."

"Sure. No problem." Conrad stood and walked to the door. "Tell Daphne I say 'hi,' okay? You're seeing her tonight, I assume?"

Ian shrugged, unwilling to reveal their plans. "Later, I guess."

After Conrad left, Ian dumped the coffee into the kitchen sink and tossed the cup in the trash.

***

At precisely one o'clock the following Monday afternoon, Daphne and Robin arrived at Conrad's for their massage appointment. Robin would get her massage first, allowing Daphne to do the snooping.

He welcomed them into his home, ushering them into the living room, which doubled as a waiting room. "If you wait here, Daphne, Robin can get changed, and we'll start. Help yourself to the tea or water on the cart." He waved a hand in the general direction of a tea trolley. A thermos labelled "Green Tea," a jug of water with lemon wedges, and teacups, water glasses, and honey were arranged on it.

"Sure," Daphne replied. "Thanks."

Daphne tracked their progress by their voices. Conrad showed Robin the treatment room and told her to remove whatever clothing she wanted and climb under the sheet on the table. A door closed. Minutes later, the door swung open.

"Ready?" Conrad's voice floated into the living room from down the hall.

Robin made a short and affirmative reply. The door closed. A lock snicked into place.

Daphne rose and stood motionless a moment, listening to the house. She slipped her cell phone from her purse and slid it into her jeans' pocket. Each appointment lasted an hour, so she'd give herself fifty minutes. Hopefully, she wouldn't need that long. If she found anything incriminating, she'd call Jacob immediately. If Daphne and Robin didn't call Beth by four o'clock, she'd call Jacob.

The hallway stretched out in full view from where Daphne stood. She tiptoed to the washroom and pushed the door open wide. If she needed to scurry back for any reason, it would be easier to duck into the washroom than head all the way back to the living room.

Probably.

A semi en suite, the bathroom had a second door that opened onto the master bedroom, making her job much easier. She closed the bathroom door on the hallway side and slipped into the master bedroom through the other door.

Whatever Conrad was, he wasn't a packrat. The bedroom was uncluttered and simply furnished. The king bed took up most of the room. Across from it sat a dust-free dresser with a large mirror. On the dresser's shiny surface sat a black leather jewellery box and family photos collection.

She didn't touch the photos but studied them.

Conrad, his brother, and his parents stood smiling from a studio shot. The portraits had been done fairly recently by the look of it. Why wouldn't he have gotten a large one for the wall?

Doesn't matter. Get on with it.

The next photo showed Conrad alone. Another professional shot. She recognized the photo from the back cover of his books. His author headshot. Another framed photo, a black-and-white wedding photo, stood next to it. The couple in the shot resembled Conrad's parents, only much younger.

Should she check the jewellery box? Daphne hated snooping through other people's things, but she didn't know what she searched for. What would be in his bedroom that could tie him to the murder? Clothes, maybe, but she wouldn't know what clothes he'd worn, and she couldn't check for forensic evidence.

This idea now seemed stupid, but she forced herself to keep

going. She peeked into the jewellery box. With a gasp, she plucked a ring, a sterling silver band with a square onyx centre, from the display case. Leon owned a ring like this.

She tried to recall whether she'd seen it at home after his death. When Jacob had escorted her through the house, she'd noticed nothing missing—except the smoky quartz rock Leon kept on his desk. She couldn't be certain about the ring, but if she found the stone, she'd know Conrad was the one.

Quickly replacing the ring in the box and closing it, Daphne crept from the room. She made her way to the last room before the treatment room.

Dammit, she berated herself. *I should have started here.*

The tiny room was as neat and clean as the bedroom. Light streamed in from the backyard through the open curtains. A television hung on the wall across from the desk. She'd start at the desk and work her way around from there. On the wall behind the desk hung a large portrait, the duplicate of the author photo from Conrad's bedroom.

It didn't take long.

The smoky quartz rock sat in plain view next to his computer. He'd put it where he could look at it as he wrote. She reached for it but stopped before she touched it. They might find fingerprints on it.

Daphne stifled a sob. She'd call Jacob and tell him what they'd done. *From the living room. I can be on the phone in the living room. I don't have to be here.*

Priding herself on her quick thinking, she headed back out through the bedroom door and almost crashed into Conrad.

"Find what you needed?" He leaned against the wall, arms crossed, a smirk on his face.

"No, I meant to find the washroom."

"Did you confuse the desk with a toilet?"

Her mouth went dry and her hands grew cold and clammy. "Of course not. I'm sorry. I shouldn't have intruded."

Suddenly, she realized she'd neither seen nor heard from Robin. "Where's Robin? Shouldn't you get back? I'll just head to the bathroom if you'll point me to the correct door."

He shook his head. "Tsk, tsk. Still trying to sell me the innocent act, Daphne? We both know you weren't searching for the bathroom. You two came here to snoop."

CHAPTER 40

"Where's Robin?" Terror gripped Daphne by the throat, making the words difficult to say. What if he'd already killed Robin? Daphne's breathing grew rapid and for a moment, dizziness threatened to overwhelm her.

Pull yourself together. If you faint, you're dead. That did the trick. She inhaled a slow, deep breath, forcing calm into her system.

"She's in the treatment room. Join her." He gripped her by the arm and tugged her along the corridor.

As they approached the door to the treatment room, Daphne reviewed her options.

Option one: go into the room and verify Robin was okay. If yes, they'd be two against one. Perhaps he'd used an excuse to sneak out of the room and Robin lay on the table awaiting his return.

Option two: rip her arm from his grasp and race for the door. The tightness of his grip told her he'd anticipated such a move. If she tried and failed, though, what did she have to lose? To stay was certain death. They might talk him out of killing them, but she doubted it.

She couldn't think of an option three, and if she wanted to act, the time was now.

Daphne chose option two and failed to yank her arm free of his grip. Conrad rewarded the attempt to break away by shoving her against the wall. The back of her head slammed into it, and she saw stars.

"Listen, you stupid cow. Don't try anything. I'm stronger than you. Got it?" His stale breath fumed in her nostrils.

She averted her face and nodded.

He gripped her chin and turned her face so they were nose to nose. "I didn't fucking hear you. Do you get it?"

"Yes," she shouted, almost gagging from the fetid onslaught of his breath on her face.

Why hadn't she studied martial arts? Why hadn't she at least learned women's self-defence strategies? If she escaped this horror, she'd learn how to hurt an attacker. That was a promise.

Oh, God, please get us out of here.

She forced herself not to think about Leon and his last moments alive. He'd suffered. She knew without a doubt he had.

Conrad grabbed her by the arms and frogmarched her into the treatment room.

For a moment, Daphne saw only the sheet on the table and not the form under it. The light in the room was dim, a variety of tea candles adding ambience rather than illumination. The warm air hinted at a spicy and soothing scent. Gentle meditation music floated from the media player sitting on the table at the side of the room.

"Robin!" Daphne shattered the room's peace.

When there was no movement on the table, Daphne struggled against Conrad's restraining hands. Rage and panic took hold of her. "Let me go, you stupid ass. Robin!"

Conrad gripped her hair with one hand while he held her against his chest with the other.

"Shut up. Stop." Frustration leaked from his every utterance.

Without thinking, Daphne slammed her foot down on the top of his. The arm around her loosened as he cried out. She lunged towards the table but his grip on her hair yanked her backwards. Her head throbbed where the hair anchored her to him.

"What have you done to her?" Daphne, mind focused only on getting to her friend, elbowed him in the gut. Freed at last, she launched herself at the table and draped herself over the limp body on it.

Robin's pale face, turned to the side, felt warm to the touch. Her breathing, when Daphne had calmed down enough to see the rise and fall of Robin's back, was deep and even.

"Did you poison her?" Daphne whirled on Conrad, hate and fury twisting her features.

"She wouldn't accept anything to drink. You've made sure no one will accept anything from me. Not Beth. Not Ian. Not anyone." His voice held bitterness laced with fury.

Unsure what he meant, Daphne said, "What did you do to her then?"

"Relax. I injected her with a mild sedative."

"How did you get your hands on that?"

He shrugged. "I have my sources."

"How long will she be out?"

"Not long." He backed up, his gaze steady on Daphne, until he bumped against the walnut dresser. Reaching behind him, he opened a drawer and removed a gun. He pointed it at her.

"Sit on the floor against the far wall. When she wakes up, we're going for a little drive."

When Daphne hesitated, he said, "I insist. Obey or I'll use this. I'd rather avoid the mess, but it'd be quicker, so don't tempt me."

Without a word, Daphne crossed the room. Back against the wall, she eased to the floor. She checked the clock on the wall above the dresser. Not even two yet. It would be another two hours at least before Beth called for help.

***

Beth kept herself busy all afternoon so she wouldn't worry about Robin and Daphne, but she constantly glanced at the time. It crept by. As three o'clock approached, Beth told the manager she was quitting for the day and left the bed and breakfast for the main house.

As soon as she entered the house, she pulled out her cell phone and checked for messages—something else she'd done frequently. Nothing from Robin or Daphne.

You'd think they'd have at least updated me.

Why hadn't they agreed on updates? A quick "nothing to report" would be reassuring. Beth berated herself for not thinking of it.

Well, live and learn. Next time we stalk a killer, we agree on updates.

The attempt at humour didn't help. She walked into the kitchen and opened the cookie jar filled to the top with shortbread cookies. Beth had baked them the previous day in cute Halloween shapes of ghosts, pumpkins, witches, and scarecrows.

Even though more than a month remained before Halloween, she'd wanted to test the recipe. It had worked out well, and she planned to use it to bake cookies for her bed and breakfast guests.

Beth snatched up a ghost and bit off its head. She paced as she chewed. Every time she walked past the clock on the stove, she glared at it.

Couldn't they have agreed on three thirty? Why four? Naturally, she knew the answer. They didn't want to call the police too soon and have them storm the house to find Conrad innocently finishing up a massage that had started behind schedule. The women had estimated an hour and ten minutes for each massage and another ten minutes for the women to take their leave. They added a final half hour as a buffer in case they'd underestimated.

She glanced at the clock.

Three oh one.

Paced for what felt like ten minutes. Checked the time.

Three oh two.

Oh, God, why hadn't she gone with them?

She'd wanted to. But someone needed to stay behind and call Jacob if something went wrong. Robin and Daphne had both insisted Beth stay home. Conrad might distrust her if she visited his home after she'd smacked away the hot chocolate he'd bought at the craft fair.

Yes, she'd acted as though she suspected him, but Daphne had rejected him for Ian. Wouldn't he hold that against her? Beth admitted that was different. It wouldn't make Conrad believe Daphne suspected him of killing Leon.

Should she call someone? She checked the time. Three ten.

Oh, God, why did she agree to this?

Screw it. I'm going to Conrad's. I should have been watching the place from the start.

Beth grabbed her purse and stormed out to her car.

***

Jacob reviewed the images of Conrad's hotel the tech guys had analyzed and cleaned up. They'd highlighted all the females in the photos, and there were quite a few. Who'd have thought the hotel would be so busy that early in the damn morning?

He clicked the mouse and moved to the next image.

This woman was obviously too short and skinny. Conrad could make himself appear larger, but not skinnier or shorter. So far, Jacob hadn't found any women who resembled Beth or Conrad. He took frequent breaks from the tedious job, afraid fatigue would make him discard evidence by mistake.

He'd been itching to check for a woman ever since the idea popped into his head but interviews distracted him. His suspect list had diminished as a result. No one popped for this more than Conrad. Frustratingly, hotel room service verified he'd been in his room at the time he'd specified. Conrad had ordered breakfast for that morning and signed for it. If he'd been the one to kill Leon, the schedule was tight—not impossible, but rushed.

There. A woman fitting the general height and build. A brunette wearing a trench coat.

Jacob squinted. The track pants looked similar. Perhaps he'd swapped out the wig after.

Since Conrad would've needed to drive to where he'd biked from, Jacob requisitioned recordings from traffic cameras that might've picked up his vehicle. This assumed Conrad hadn't rented a vehicle. His credit card records didn't indicate that, and no reports of stolen vehicles lined up with this time frame.

Techs had packaged it for him as a slide show. He started the long, difficult search through the new set of images.

The phone on Jacob's desk rang, and he glanced at the time and the caller ID. Three twenty-two. Elizabeth Holmes. A sinking sensation in his gut, Jacob answered it.

CHAPTER 41

Conrad forced the two women into the car at gunpoint. First, he made Daphne bind Robin's hands in the back seat and then ordered her to drive. They headed south on the Niagara River Parkway, and Robin suspected he intended this to end at the Falls. Cliché as it was, Niagara Falls remained the ideal place to dump a body. Even if the police found them, the raging water would destroy any evidence. Beth was their only hope.

The binding scraped and bit into the flesh on Robin's wrists, but she ignored the pain and struggled to slip out of it. At least her hands were tied in front of her. A way to escape the restraint existed, but she couldn't remember it. Too much time had passed since she'd researched it for a story, and she'd never expected to need the skill.

Since Daphne drove, her hands were free. Conrad sat in the passenger seat with the gun held low so no one glancing through the windows would see it. He made it clear that if Robin interfered, he'd shoot Daphne first.

He'd buckled Daphne with the lap belt behind her, so only the shoulder strap kept her in place. This would make it appear to any patrolling cops she wore a seatbelt, but if she caused an accident to try to escape, she'd be injured.

Conrad had instructed Robin to lie down in the back and hold still. She wasn't wearing a seatbelt at all and would suffer the worst injuries. Though they weren't on a major highway, they travelled at eighty kilometres per hour on this stretch. A sudden stop, especially into a solid object, would do damage to all of them.

Robin peeked between the seats at the clock on the dashboard. Not even four o'clock. By the time Beth called Jacob, even if he took her seriously, he'd search for them at Conrad's house. He'd never know where to go from there.

***

"Detective Turner." Jacob's voice sounded rough, so he cleared his throat.

"It's Beth Holmes. Something's gone wrong, and I need help." Her desperation came through like a shotgun blast.

Jacob glanced at Skylar's empty chair. She investigated another case. Should be okay. Beth probably just wanted to relay information.

"What's up?"

"It's Robin and Daphne."

At the mention of Robin's name, Jacob's heart skipped a beat and his stomach did a flip.

"What about them?" He struggled to keep his voice calm and even.

"I'm supposed to call you if I haven't heard from them by four." She sounded near hysteria.

Should this mean something to him? Robin had said nothing about going out with Daphne.

"It's not four," Beth shouted as if he couldn't figure that out. "They went to Conrad's, and he has them in Daphne's car."

Jacob's gaze veered to the images he'd been reviewing. His body grew stone cold, his hands moist.

"Why'd they go to Conrad's?"

"They … We … To get massages, but that was a ruse. They wanted to find proof he killed Leon."

"What are you saying?" But he knew. "For God's sake, why didn't you call me if you suspected that?"

Robin hadn't told him anything about Conrad or visiting his place, and he'd spoken to her the night before. Jacob thought about how often she'd told him she was busy working the last few days. She'd never said on what—he'd assumed on software development or a writing project.

He should've known better. No one was that dedicated. She'd

been working late into the night. He scowled. Wait till he saw her. She should never have meddled. What the hell was she thinking?

"Detective?"

Jacob realized he'd spun out into full-on panic mode. If he didn't control himself, it could cost Robin her life, assuming Conrad was what they suspected.

"What happened, Beth?"

"I don't know. I've called them both, but they don't pick up."

He rose, patted the gun at his side to verify its presence, and snagged the jacket off the back of his chair. "Where are you?"

"Following them."

Jacob swore. "Don't go near him, hear me? Where are you?"

"On Niagara River Parkway." Beth paused, and when she spoke, the words came out in a shrill shriek. "They're heading south towards the trailhead south of the Falls—that bushy area from my novel. Understand?"

"Yes." Thank God, he'd read her novels when he'd suspected her as the killer. "Is Daphne driving her old car or the one she inherited from Leon?"

"Leon's."

"What's the license plate number?"

She told him.

"Listen." Jacob pushed through the double doors and into the hallway, heading for the elevator. "Stay well back and wait for the police. I'm hanging up and sending out two cruisers. When the police arrive, go home and leave everything to them."

When she didn't reply, he said, "Beth! Do it. I have to go." He disconnected without waiting for her response.

CHAPTER 42

"You've ruined everything." It wasn't the first time Conrad screamed that at Daphne. He didn't harangue Robin as much, probably because Robin hadn't been the one to reject his advances. Daphne shuddered. What were his plans for her if she'd fallen for him?

When she didn't reply, Conrad continued to rant.

"You thought you'd keep everything for yourself. It should've been mine. It would've been mine." His voice lowered, and he mumbled, more to himself than to either Daphne or Robin, though Daphne caught the words.

"I can salvage something. Not the house. The cars. But the book." Conrad turned his attention to Robin. In the rear-view mirror, Daphne caught only glimpses of her friend, who huddled below window level.

"Robin, I need to get onto your computer." He pulled out his cell. "Tell me the password. I want everything you have from Leon about the book."

"Are you insane? No." She spoke as though to an idiot.

Daphne held her breath. Conrad had worked himself up to dangerous levels of jealousy and rage. If Robin goaded him, he might shoot her regardless of what information he needed from her.

"You'll tell me, because if you don't, I'll kill your kids, too."

"Oh, God." Robin moaned.

The kids would be with Robin's parents from the time they left school until she arrived home. If she arrived home. It would be simple for him to find them there. Maybe he'd kill her parents, too.

"You sick bastard. Leave my kids out of it."

"Sure—if you give me a reason to be kind. I'm a reasonable person, and I don't want to hurt children. Give me your network login information and your computer login information. Now." His fingers poised over his cell phone, ready to enter the data.

Robin's bravado ended when Conrad threatened her children. She gave him what he wanted, and he typed the data in awkwardly with one hand.

"Turn left here," he instructed.

Daphne eased her foot off the accelerator and slowed to forty kilometres per hour. The dirt road he'd directed her to follow traced a path towards the river. On either side, trees and brush provided shelter and seclusion. Only a few kilometres north, the bustling tourism that never ceased near the Falls would've made it difficult for him to do what he intended.

As a local, he knew the secret spots. Daphne recognized this one from Beth's novel.

Her thoughts became frantic, desperate. If she jammed on the brakes, he'd drop the gun. She could jump out and run for help, and she'd be away before he reacted. If he gave chase, he might leave Robin free to escape. Daphne slowed the car to thirty clicks, then twenty-five.

"Pull over here." Conrad indicated a bare patch in the foliage on the right along the road up ahead.

Daphne slammed on the brakes. The car skidded about seven metres and smashed to a stop against a tree on the shoulder at the west side of the road. Robin hit the back of the seats, a scream tearing from her throat. Daphne, expecting the impact, had braced herself. The seatbelt strap helped restrain her upper body, but her face hit the airbag as it deployed. Conrad hollered a curse his airbag muffled.

As soon as the car stopped, Daphne wrenched open the door and slid out from under the seatbelt. In a daze, she staggered into the road. She heard another car door open. Without looking, she knew it was Conrad. Then another car door opened. Robin?

Daphne stopped listening to the noises behind her, forced her legs to move, and raced across the road. She'd draw Conrad away from Robin. In the brush, she could hide. He'd waste time searching for her, perhaps giving Robin a chance to escape.

A shot rang out, and a tree in front and to the right of her spit bark.

"Stop!" Conrad shouted. "If you leave, you're leaving Robin to me. I've got her, Daphne."

Daphne stopped. Slowly, she spun around to face him. Robin hung from his shoulder in the fireman's carry.

"The police will arrest you."

"Let's go." He waved the gun towards the river. "I'm a good shot. That first one was a warning. The next one won't miss."

She hesitated, scanning the road in both directions. Deserted. In the fresh silence, Daphne heard the rustle of wind in the trees and the roar of the Niagara River.

"You'll be the number one suspect no matter what you do." Perhaps if she kept him talking, a car would come along. She glanced at her car. He'd closed all the doors.

"We're going for a little walk. Hurry. Not much traffic along here, but I'm not taking more chances than necessary."

Fortunately, the sun wouldn't set for a while yet, and the crumpled car stuck out on the shoulder. Daphne released any hope Beth would find them. Even if she called Jacob, they wouldn't know where to look, but if the police searched for her car, they might be found in time.

Conrad had almost caught up to her. Robin hung limply across his back.

"What are you thinking? You'll kill us? Throw us in the river? They'll suspect foul play. How will this get you anything you want?" He'd lost his mind—he must have. Why else would he do this?

"You should've picked me, Daphne, not that loser Ian."

"I think you've demonstrated I made the correct choice."

"Shut up." He fired another shot, this one zooming past her head close enough for her to feel the breeze.

How many bullets did the gun have? If she irritated him enough, perhaps he'd use them up in warning shots.

"Here." He stopped walking and waved her over to an area where the land sloped down to the water.

The current was fast, the waves choppy. The water would be freezing. While the days had been mild, the nights grew chilly. Weak sunlight brightened the orange, yellow, red, and green leaves.

A wind gust made Daphne shiver.

Conrad stood a metre from her. Did he plan to shoot her and then throw her into the water, or did he expect her to jump in? If he shot her and they found her body, it would be obvious she didn't kill herself.

Only one way out: take the gun away from him. She inched a step towards him.

"Stop."

She froze.

He held the gun on her. "Don't move."

With a fluid motion, he dumped Robin onto the ground, but as he did, the gun dipped away from Daphne. She stole the opportunity and leaped at him.

***

The world spun when Robin regained consciousness. For a moment, she thought she hung from a tree. Confusion gave way to horror when she realized she dangled over Conrad's shoulder.

The sound of Daphne's voice reassured her. If Daphne could speak, it meant she was alive.

Unless she's a ghost. Robin shook off the ludicrous thought. She needed to think. Figure out what to do. The gun fired, and Conrad shouted at Daphne to stop, to not move.

Robin's body slid downward as Conrad shifted to set her on the ground on her back. The moment his arms released their hold on her, Robin seized the moment. She kicked at the hand holding the gun.

It went off.

Since Robin felt nothing, she assumed it'd missed her. Throwing herself at Conrad's legs, she tackled him as best she could with her wrists bound. He landed across her body, but when she tried to push him off, he kneed her in the gut.

Winded, she lay helpless, gasping for air, as he struggled with Daphne for the gun. The fight shifted them closer to the riverbank. A wild light flared in Conrad's eyes as he overpowered tiny Daphne.

He gasped great sucks of breath and shoved her towards the edge. Breath recovered, Robin rose to her feet and lunged after him. Daphne's scream cut the air, her body rolling towards the

211

water.

She grasped at roots, bushes, anything that might stop her forward momentum. Her legs splashed into the water, but she grabbed onto a root and hung on. Conrad reached her then and stomped on her fingers, and she slid farther into the water.

Robin reached the pair and kicked Conrad in the back. The sound of feet pounding across the earth behind her alerted her to the arrival of others, but she couldn't spare a glance to see who approached.

"Help," she screamed. "Please help me."

Conrad snarled and spun around to face Robin.

"At least I'll get you." His face twisted with hate, and he raised the gun, aiming at Robin's chest.

CHAPTER 43

At the sound of the gunshot, Robin dropped to the ground. She checked her body for a bullet wound even though she felt nothing. In front of her, Conrad lay bleeding. She stared at him, unable to take her gaze off the seeping blood, unable to make a move. Daphne's shout broke the spell.

"Help me!"

Robin raced to the water's edge where her friend clung to roots and branches, unable to hoist herself from the raging river.

"I'm slipping," Daphne choked out.

"Hold on." Robin knelt and grasped Daphne by a wrist though the zip ties made it awkward.

Thank God, Daphne was a wisp of a woman or they'd both end up in the water. Robin yanked and landed on her butt. She dug her heels into the dirt and dragged Daphne out of the water. The progress was excruciatingly slow, but she managed it, centimetre by centimetre.

The next instant, Jacob appeared and, grasping Daphne by the waist, hoisted her into his arms. Robin collapsed in the dirt and grass, sobbing with relief. She remained curled into herself until a hand touched her shoulder.

When Robin raised her head, her gaze met Beth's.

"Jacob asked me to make sure you're okay. He's putting Daphne into an ambulance. Conrad's already on his way to the hospital."

Robin opened her mouth, but nothing came out.

"Are you hurt?" Beth's tone betrayed her concern. She knelt down next to Robin and stroked her back.

Robin shook her head but remained silent.

"Come here." Beth put an arm around her friend's shoulders, and Robin allowed the other woman to draw her in close.

Finally, she spoke. "I was terrified. Conrad wanted to kill us. How did you find us?"

Beth explained how she'd left the house early and followed them when they left Conrad's. "I called Jacob from the car, keeping my distance so Conrad wouldn't realize I tailed you. The moment I recognized where you headed, Jacob called the police and ordered me to stop. I hung back, but I couldn't leave you two. When I saw they had him, I raced over here."

A shadow fell over them, and Robin turned to find Jacob standing before her. He offered her his hand, and she let him pull her to her feet. With a pocket knife, he cut the zip tie from her wrists.

"I should be angry with you," he said softly as he stroked her cheek with the back of his hand.

"For catching the bad guy?" Robin tried to sound teasing but failed when her voice hitched on a sob.

"Easy," he said. "You're lucky you weren't killed. Why didn't you call me when you figured it out?" He turned to Beth. "Or you?"

Beth sent a sideways glance at Robin. "I'll let her explain while I call Ian and Andrew to tell them what happened."

"Traitor," Robin said but without the tension in her voice.

With a smile, Beth walked towards the road, pulling out her cell phone.

***

Both Robin and Daphne ended up in the hospital to get checked over at Jacob's insistence. By the time she arrived home, Daphne longed for sleep. She didn't want to deal with guilt and remorse for not telling Ian what they'd been doing, yet here he stood on her doorstep.

"Hi." She stepped aside to let him in—the least she could do no matter how reluctant she was to do it.

"Beth called and told me the police arrested Conrad for Leon's murder." His voice sounded normal. Perhaps Beth hadn't told him everything.

For a moment, Daphne considered not revealing what they'd done.

"Yes. They have evidence he's the one." She led him to the family room without a detour to the kitchen for a drink.

"Thanks to you, Robin, and Beth?"

Damn. He knew.

Daphne studied his expression. His brows furrowed and his mouth turned down, but concern showed in his eyes.

"Yes." She waved at the sofa. "Sit. I'll explain."

He sat, and she took a seat beside him.

"Okay, I'm listening."

She huffed out a breath. "We suspected Conrad might be the one responsible."

Before she could continue, he interjected. "The killer, Daphne. You suspected him as the killer. Instead of calling the police like normal people, you played detective."

"We needed to make sure we weren't accusing an innocent man," she protested.

"That's Detective Turner's job." Ian glared at her. "Why didn't you confide in me?"

He hurt, which was at the crux of it. They'd been intimate, had agreed to be a couple, and she'd excluded him from a serious, and possibly fatal, decision.

"I'm sorry. I should've told you." She gave him a beseeching look. "I was afraid to."

He opened his mouth, perhaps to retort, but she barreled on. "I feared you'd think us crazy for suspecting Conrad killed Leon."

"Why? You can't make assumptions about what I think."

"I understand. But at the time, I just wanted to find the proof, and it seemed so simple." Daphne shook her head. "He already suspected us. When I snooped in his office, he spied on his cell phone. All his rooms had cameras."

She grinned, sheepishly. "Dishonest people trust no one. I didn't know he watched, and when he spotted me snooping, he came after me."

Ian dropped her hands and rose. He stalked away from her and paced in front of the fireplace. "You should've told me." He stopped the back-and-forth movement and returned to his place on the couch. "I had no idea you were in danger."

"I'm not your responsibility," she said.

"If something would've happened to you—"

"But it didn't." Daphne clasped his hands. "Look, Robin and I took a risk much larger than we'd anticipated, and it could've gone badly."

When he fidgeted and opened his mouth, she said, "Okay, it went badly, but we recovered."

"Because Jacob found you."

"No." She shook her head. "Because we had a contingency plan. Beth was our backup." She skipped the part where Beth disregarded the plan and left her house early. "Ian, I'm fine. We're all fine."

"Thank God." He pulled her to him and held her.

She tilted her face up to gaze into his eyes, and he leaned down and brushed her lips with his. The kiss deepened as she pulled him to her, and she ran her hands along his back, verifying his solidity.

Daphne pulled back after a moment. "I want to sell this house."

"You do? Why?" He sounded genuinely puzzled.

"Leon loved this house. I didn't." She rose and turned towards the wall of glass. "All this glass and open windows make me feel vulnerable."

"You could buy curtains." When she gave him a puzzled stare, he said, "A simpler solution than moving."

Daphne shook her head and turned back to face him. "I don't want to cover it up. It looks fabulous. But this place is huge. I don't need it, and I don't want it." She sighed. "It doesn't feel like mine."

"All right. If that's what you want, I'm all for it." He drew her into his arms. "You could move in with me."

"With you?" Her shock must have shown on her face because he laughed and squeezed her tight.

"If you want to." Ian held her at arm's length. "We've known each other for years. It could work. We already know so much about each other, and we know we've got chemistry." He grinned. "If not, you move out."

"Nothing to lose?"

"Everything to gain. It'll work out. What do you say?"

Love you. Love you. Love you. "Can I think about it?"

"Sure," he said and pulled her in for a kiss that would lead to more.

216

CHAPTER 44

Beth summoned all her courage to enter the café the day after Conrad's arrest. Robin had used the café's network to identify Conrad as the troll who'd harassed Leon, and that morning, Jacob had questioned Andrew about it—Robin had told Beth so. After Conrad's arrest, Jacob had interviewed each of the three women, and Robin had informed him of the activity on Andrew's network. Would Andrew resent that the women never told him their plans to uncover the killer?

"Beth, hi!" Andrew waved and smiled as she made her way to the counter.

His greeting seemed friendly enough.

"Hi. Got a minute?"

"Sure. Want something to drink? Eat? I'll buy."

"A latte. Thanks." Beth didn't feel like putting anything in her stomach, but saying no would be rude.

He fixed her drink and led her to the back room. MJ sat at a table near the windows, her laptop before her, papers spread out on the table. An empty coffee mug and a half-eaten brownie on a ceramic plate sat next to the laptop.

The women greeted one another, and Andrew guided Beth to a table in the corner farthest from MJ.

"This okay?" he asked.

"Yes." Beth sat, and he set her coffee in front of her.

After taking the other seat, he gave her a questioning look.

"I guess you heard what happened?" She had to start somehow,

217

and this opening was as good as any.

Andrew dipped his head in a single nod.

Since he remained silent, she continued. "I'm sorry I didn't tell you what we were doing."

"Robin did the snooping," he said. "I didn't think it was your idea."

Was he making excuses for her or laying all the blame on Robin? If so, Beth decided to set him straight. "Robin didn't do it alone, so you can't blame everything on her."

"I'm not." Andrew took her hand. "Do you think I don't understand what you did and why?"

"I don't know. Do you?"

"From what Jacob tells me, you helped catch a killer. Good thing you're too level-headed to take the chances Robin and Daphne took. You saved them."

"Level-headedness had nothing to do with it," she protested. "Robin and Daphne refused to let me go to Conrad's because the killer wanted to frame me. I'd also already let on I suspected him when I knocked a hot chocolate he'd bought onto the ground. They figured if Conrad was the killer, he'd get suspicious if I went." Beth hung her head. "As it was, he was already paranoid. Ian refused a drink from Conrad too, but we didn't know that then."

Andrew put a finger under her chin and tilted her face so they gazed into each other's eyes. "A coincidence. Everyone around here was a suspect. Conrad wasn't the only one from whom people would've refused a drink. But he was the guilty one, so when people acted jumpy around him, he got nervous."

"I suppose that might be true." She'd even suspected Andrew at one time, but she refused to tell him.

He rose and drew her from the chair into his arms. "The thought of what could have happened terrifies me. I'm glad you're all okay."

His mouth dipped to hers and he kissed her, a deep, soul-satisfying kiss. Her head spun, and she lost all thought but that she wanted this moment to last forever. When he raised his head, he locked his gaze on hers. "I've wanted to do that since the last time I saw you."

Beth wanted to do that every time she thought about him. In a soft voice, she said, "Me too."

"There's something else." Andrew stroked his fingers through her hair, sending shivers down her spine. "I want us to be a couple. Exclusive. What do you say?"

Self-conscious, she glanced over at MJ's table. Empty. Grateful to MJ for giving them privacy, Beth returned her attention to Andrew.

"I'd like that," she whispered, but she stifled a yawn. *Damn.*

"Do I make you nervous?" He drew her closer and rested her cheek on his chest. His kiss fluttered on the top of her head.

"Sometimes," she admitted. "I have to be honest: all men make me nervous."

"Why?"

She gazed up at him with wide eyes. What should she tell him? "I've had awful experiences. Some people in the modelling industry enjoyed exploiting young girls."

"Beth, I'm so sorry." He kissed her forehead, her nose, and her lips delicately.

"It's not your fault." She smiled, but her eyes glistened with tears.

"No, but I'm sorry, anyway." He put an arm around her. "Leon told me before he died that he wanted to spend more time with Robin. They never got the chance. I want to spend as much time with you as possible. I hope you want that too."

Beth pressed her hand to his cheek. "Yes, I do."

"Will you trust me?"

Her heart swelled with affection and love. "Yes."

"We'll take it slow, okay? Your pace."

"Won't that be too slow?" He'd become frustrated and tire of waiting. "Won't you get blue balls?" She only half-joked.

Andrew laughed. "We'll work around it. Beth, I love you. I'll do whatever it takes to show you a physical relationship can be pleasurable for you, too."

"That's the hottest thing anyone has ever said to me." She beamed with delight. "Would a kiss be okay?"

In reply, he captured her mouth with his, sweeping her away once more on a wave of desire and passion. Something shifted in her. Tension released; fear fled. She'd never felt this way about any man before—never expected to fall in love with any man. Andrew accepted her no matter how she looked, what she weighed, or what she did.

For the first time in her life, she could relax and be herself around a man without wondering about ulterior motives. He'd never asked more of her than she could give. Patient and kind, he'd helped her come out of her shell.

Happier than she could remember being, Beth made plans with Andrew to have dinner at his place. As she walked to the car, she almost skipped.

CHAPTER 45

October started off sunny and warm, but by the third week, the air chilled. Rainy days outnumbered the dry ones, and Robin spent most of them huddled in the warmth of hearth and home. News about Conrad filtered out through the media. He'd been charged with murder, kidnapping, and a host of other things. So far, Robin hadn't asked Jacob for more than the media reported, and he didn't offer anything.

She and Jacob saw each other often, always at her house so he could spend time with the kids, too. Both children said they liked him, and she could see Jacob felt the same. Kaylee and Nate enjoyed his company and always asked when he'd be coming by again. Her heart warmed at the sight of him showing them his badge and even letting them hold it. Both kids displayed a genuine interest in his police work, and he chatted with them about investigative techniques.

One night, Nate told Robin he wanted to be a detective when he grew up. That stopped her heart for a moment, but then she reminded herself that last year, he'd wanted to be Spiderman. At least if this new career aspiration didn't change, he'd have Jacob to guide him.

Over the last few weeks, they'd become like a family, though Robin understood the kids loved their father and no one would replace him in their hearts. The thought that they'd missed having a male role model in their lives while she'd wallowed in grief nagged at her. Had she waited too long to bring a man into the equation?

Then again, if she'd moved on sooner, she wouldn't be with Jacob now. Or she'd have had her heart broken. Or she'd have broken the man's heart by dating him too soon, which would've affected the kids.

Robin pushed those thoughts aside with a sigh. She'd overthought things again. None of that mattered. Only now mattered and what she did with the time she had. She'd survived two threats to her life, one of them in her home, a place she'd always considered her haven.

Then Jacob asked her to take the next step: he invited her to his apartment, offered to make her dinner, and told her to bring an overnight bag.

She'd said yes more easily and quickly than she'd have believed herself capable—she'd even declined his offer to pick her up. At last, she felt competent and capable enough to drive somewhere alone. That Jacob's apartment was her destination proved her readiness for this step.

Robin arrived at the apartment in St. Catharines and slid the car into a spot in the visitors' parking area. The four-storey building wasn't new but appeared well-maintained. She stepped into a brightly painted foyer both welcoming and functional. After she pressed the button for Jacob's unit, he buzzed her into a lobby decorated with warm tones and plush furniture.

Jacob met her at his door, greeting her with a kiss and a hug. He ushered her into the apartment where the scent of something savoury made her salivate.

"Smells amazing. What's cooking?" Robin craned her head towards the kitchen. The enticing aroma came from a slow cooker on the counter.

"Made a stew. It'll keep until we're ready. Let me give you a tour."

She kicked off her shoes, and he led her through a small, sparsely furnished living room done in neutral tones to the bedroom. The same wall-to-wall carpeting as in the living areas of the apartment cushioned her stocking feet and warmed the room.

Robin set her bag on the floor next to Jacob's dresser, the only other piece of furniture besides the bed. The queen bed rose from a steep foundation with handles she assumed pulled open for storage. An enormous headboard with an end table incorporated on each side dominated the wall behind it.

"What a monster," she remarked. "I'll need a boost to climb into it."

"It's practical. Lots of storage underneath." Jacob grasped her arm and steered her to the bed.

Before she could react, he circled her waist with one arm and whispered in her ear, "How hungry are you?"

When she giggled, he said, "Nervous?"

She snorted a little as she smiled in response. "Yes. Are you?"

"Not at all. We could start the evening here." He spun her around. "I've wanted to be with you for so long I can't wait another minute. Tell me it's what you want. Tell me you're ready."

Inside, the fear tried to take control, but the delight on his face pushed it away.

"Jake," she whispered, wrapping her arms around him. "I'm all yours."

Everything became hazy then. The room flipped as he picked her up in his arms and hoisted her onto the bed. Before she could catch her breath, he joined her. In a heartbeat, he pinned her beneath his body and locked his lips to hers.

Robin relished the taste of him and savoured it. For a moment, she felt only his lips on hers. Then his hands drew her attention when they fluttered through her hair, down her blouse, and under her blouse. They were by turns rough and gentle. When one of them snapped her front-closing bra open and skimmed her nipple, she moaned.

He raised his head. "You're so damn beautiful."

"No time to talk." She gripped his face in both hands and pulled him back for another hungry kiss.

Now her hands did the roving. She ran her fingers through his hair and then down his back. His wiry body rippled with muscles, evidence of his dedication to his workouts.

Jacob pulled back and rose on his elbows. "Gotta say something."

"What?" It came out a gasp.

"We're wearing too much."

She clawed at his shirt, tugging at the buttons. "We should fix that."

Their back and forth made her comfortable. The kiss had knocked the nerves right out of her, but this banter was so thoroughly Jacob it flooded her with affection for him. How could she help but love this guy?

As soon as all the buttons on his shirt were open, he shrugged out of it, exposing a smooth, taut chest. Robin almost swooned at the sight. His dextrous fingers made short work of her clothes, and soon they both lay naked.

"I want to explore every inch of you." He traced his way down her body with his lips, letting her sighs and moans guide him.

When he reached her thighs, he spread them and continued his explorations. Like lightning, the sensations speared through Robin's core. She cried out and arched her back, unable to control her body. Tears leaked from her eyes, and she noticed only when one of them trailed down to her ear.

How had she gone three years without this? Without him?

"Jake." His name caught in her throat.

He scrambled up and concern flashed in his eyes when he saw her face.

"Robin, what is it?"

"It's all good. Oh, I need you, Jake. Jacob." She loved the sound of his name. "I need you to make love to me. I need you inside me. Now."

He required no more urging. After donning a condom, he pressed her wrists into the bed with his hands and then nudged his body between her thighs. His stiff shaft pressed against her sex, and she strained to welcome him in.

The first thrust sent a cannon fire of need and lust through her.

"Don't be gentle," she pleaded, closing her eyes to shut out sight and heighten sensation. "Hard, Jake. Make it hard. Make it fast."

He obliged her, pumping, pushing, thrusting. A bead of sweat fell from his forehead onto hers like warm rain from Heaven. An overwhelming desire to look into his eyes made her open hers. Their gazes locked, and she saw her love mirrored in his clear blue eyes.

She wanted him to fill her and matched his thrusts with a violent passion, giving as he gave. The wave inside her swelled, carrying her to the top.

"Oh, God, Robin." He merged with her perfectly. They fit together perfectly.

A spasm wracked her body as she crested the wave. She cried out in ecstatic agony and triggered his release.

"Oh, God, Robin." He couldn't find words for anything else, and panting from exertion, he dropped onto her in exhaustion.

"Too rough?" He nuzzled her neck with his nose.

Spent, she gave him a satisfied smile. "No, Jake," she said. "It was just perfect."

CHAPTER 46

After dinner on a chilly October night, the three friends congregated at Beth's in the sunroom. The mood started out light and jovial. Daphne hadn't seen her friends this relaxed in a long time. Inevitably, though, the talk turned to Leon's murder and Conrad's arrest.

"Conrad admitted breaking into my house," Robin announced as she floated on her back in the pool next to Beth.

"Oh, Robin," Beth said.

"He was jealous I got a contract and hadn't ever published a book." Robin spun around onto her stomach and lazily kicked her way towards Daphne, who reclined against the whirlpool jets.

"But you'd written books. The publishing company bought those as well, didn't they?" Daphne said.

"Yes, but Conrad didn't know." Robin frowned. "I had no idea you knew."

Daphne's face went red. "Leon told me and asked me to keep it a secret, so I did." She turned a beseeching eye on Robin. "He was so proud of you—so thrilled he could help you. He said you have enormous talent."

Robin's eyes welled up with tears. "I'm sorry he's gone. I miss him so much."

"We all do." Beth swam up to join them. "Even though he worked all the time and travelled constantly, he gave his time and expertise to everyone. I'd believed Conrad was his friend, his number one fan. Leon helped him as much as he helped anyone

226

else." Her tone carried outrage.

"Envy." Daphne shook her head in disgust. "He wanted everything Leon owned. Marrying me would get him Leon's house, his cars. If I'd have fallen in love with him, he'd have murdered me too one day. Then he'd have it all to himself."

"He'll go to prison for a long time," Robin said. "Let's forget about him. We're letting him spoil the mood."

"Excellent suggestion," Beth replied. She swam to the side of the pool and hopped out.

At that moment, the doorbell rang. Beth smiled mischievously as she wrapped a towel around her shoulders and left the room.

When Beth returned, she had company. Ian, Jacob, and Andrew accompanied her, and all wore bathing suits and carried towels.

"Now we'll have a real celebration," Beth said, sounding freer and more confident than Robin had ever heard her sound. "It's about time we kicked back and had fun."

Daphne hoisted herself from the pool and ran into Ian's arms. "What a great idea." She giggled when he groaned and stepped back, water trickling down his bare chest.

"Oops," she teased. "My bad."

Robin paddled away from the side of the pool and watched Jacob quietly take in everyone and everything. He always scoped out every room he entered, his gaze picking up the smallest details. She loved how aware he always was.

Barefoot, he walked to the side of the pool and crouched down. "Where's my welcoming committee?" The grin on his face made him appear boyish.

"Climb into the water." She paddled over to the side and clung to it with one hand.

"Kids with your parents?" he asked, melting her heart.

"Babysitter. I'm not staying over."

He raised his brows. "Daphne give you a lift?"

She smiled. "I drove myself." And it had felt wonderful, liberating. "I doubt I'd want to drive on the highway, but around town is all right. I drove to your place alone, and I've been taking the kids places."

"That's great news. You know," he said, his voice low and soothing, "I'll want you to meet my family."

"Sure." Touched, she couldn't say anything else. She understood what it meant for him to suggest that.

Jacob sat on the edge of the pool and slid into the water. The instant he was in, Robin seized him and wrapped her arms around his neck.

"I'm so glad you're here and we're all together." Her gaze scanned the room.

Daphne and Ian strolled hand in hand to the pool, happy faces glowing in the dim light from the wall sconces. Andrew and Beth sat at one of the bistro tables. She'd handed him a beer, and she held out her glass of cola for him to clink.

"I never thought our lives could change so much in such a short time," Robin said, thinking out loud.

Jacob enfolded her in his arms. "A short time ago, I was a bachelor and loving it. Now I've got a girlfriend and children in my life."

"And I was terrified to leave the house," Robin replied, shaking her head. "I didn't realize I could take care of myself. Not only did I take care of myself, I helped others in trouble." An image of Daphne clinging to the banks of the Niagara River flashed through her head. "I know I must keep seeing my therapist and taking my meds, but I'm improving—I trust myself, my capabilities."

"You were always capable, Robin. When you needed to save yourself, you did."

"I've felt like half a person for so long it's nice to feel whole. I have you to thank for that. You don't complete me," she said. "You help me complete myself."

Jacob tilted his head, indicating the two other couples in the room. "We've all come through this with our perspectives changed," he replied.

Robin couldn't agree more. He drew her into his lap and reclined against the jets. Content, she leaned her head on his chest and sighed. Tonight, they all celebrated new tomorrows.

The End

Thank you for reading my book. If you enjoyed it, won't you please take a moment to leave me a review?

SAMPLE CHAPTER: *GILLIAN'S ISLAND*

Today, my life changes forever.

Gillian Foster unclipped the last clothes peg and hauled the crisp, white sheet from the line. It went into the laundry basket beside her with the rest of the bedding, all of it done for a man she'd never met.

As resort owner, she'd often done laundry for strangers when an extra pair of hands was needed, but this time, it was different. This time, it was for Daylin Quinn, the resort's new owner, and that made her every motion heavy and reluctant.

The heat didn't help put a spring in her step. The day was uncharacteristically hot, the air oppressive. It was the first of May and felt like the end of June.

Gillian sighed and ran her fingers through her hair, which always frizzed up in humidity. She bunched it into her fist to let a passing breeze cool her neck.

The wind that had dried her sheets so quickly would also blow in a cold front. The puffy, white clouds overhead now showed hints of grey. Sooner or later, a storm would blow in. Hopefully, it wouldn't be until after Daylin had arrived safely on the island—unless it rolled in fast.

Then she could use it to her advantage and delay the visit until tomorrow. Sure, it put off the inevitable, but a storm was a legitimate reason to procrastinate.

Gillian hefted the basket onto her hip and walked from the garden through the sunroom to the large living room. She set the basket on the floor and arched backward, rubbing her lower back.

A stereo system in the corner next to the fieldstone fireplace had a radio, and she switched it on. Eventually, there'd be a weather report.

Damn it, if she was forced to sell her home, why did it have to be to an arrogant developer like Daylin Quinn?

When he'd made the offer through his real estate agent, Gillian had researched him on the Internet. That had been both enlightening and infuriating.

He had a history of buying up properties, demolishing the buildings, and redeveloping the lots. It had made him a wealthy man, but the prospect of her beautiful century home being torn down nauseated her.

She envisioned a cheesy souvenir shop and tacky cabins; the porch swing gone, a snack machine in its place; the quaint restaurant preparing home-cooked meals replaced by greasy fast food. Her blood boiled as she imagined what he might do, and Gillian wished this city boy had stayed there despite how close to her asking price he'd come.

Most of the photos she'd found of him showed a stunningly handsome man with a variety of gorgeous women on his arm—sometimes one on each arm. No mention of a wife or steady girlfriend. Not that it was any of her business, but it was a reflection of his character.

Worse still, he was an American. A New Yorker.

The locals weren't pleased when the news that the Fosters had sold the island to a foreigner had spread. Most of them admitted no one living in the area had the millions required to buy the resort. Still, they considered it a betrayal that the purchaser not only wasn't from Ontario but wasn't even a Canadian.

No matter that Daylin's had been the only offer in the two years it had been on the market. Nor did anyone care that Gillian's ex-husband had forced her to sell so he could get his half of the money. Folks simply expressed their resentment at what she had done without regard to the extenuating circumstances.

Now Daylin was coming to claim what was legally his.

Gillian carried the laundry basket into the master bedroom to make the queen bed, one of the many pieces of furniture she was leaving here.

She'd already moved most of the possessions she was keeping

into a storage unit on the mainland in the town of Fiddlehead. The meagre wardrobe and personal items she'd need for her month here had been transferred into a room in the staff quarters.

Daylin had contracted Gillian to stay on for two months to show him how the resort operated. She planned to live on the island for the first month and then move to the mainland and commute to work for the second month. This would help her transition to life without her island.

The scent of the outdoors wafted from the freshly laundered sheets as she worked. The cozy comforter she spread out on the bed would provide warmth for the remaining chilly nights ahead. She arranged the decorative pillows and stepped back to survey her handiwork.

All was ready.

Daylin would probably claim this room for his own until he destroyed the place.

Stop it. You don't know that's what he wants to do. She shook her head. It wasn't being cynical if history showed that's what he'd always done.

The weather report caught her attention. She cheered and did a skip-dance when the announcer upgraded the storm watch to a warning.

Gillian rushed to the kitchen where she'd left her cell phone and called Daylin's office.

His assistant answered and took the message. She assured Gillian she'd notify Mr. Quinn to stay in his hotel tonight and head out to the island the next morning.

Relief flooded through Gillian as she disconnected the call, and she sent a quick thank you to whatever weather god might be responsible for this turn. Admittedly, it was silly to get so excited over a one-night reprieve. Nevertheless, the rescheduling made her heart soar.

When Daylin stepped foot on shore, the place would be his. Until then, she'd spend tonight blessedly alone, curled up in front of the fireplace with a book and a glass of wine.

First, she'd better batten down the hatches before the storm hit.

***

Daylin Quinn ended his call and started his Mercedes-Benz E-Class sedan, which sat in the hotel parking lot. He gazed up at the sky.

The sun speared through grey-tinged clouds devoid of menace. His assistant had caught him in time to abort the trip to the island, but Daylin wouldn't let a little rain spoil his plans.

Rain seemed a remote possibility anyway, judging by the sky. If he was wrong, it might hit while he was crossing the channel between mainland and island, but so what? His boat was sturdy and would get him across.

He'd waited long enough to visit his new place again. The quick walk-through before he'd bought the island was a faint memory. He had big plans to implement, and the desire to get started was an itch he had to scratch right now.

To hell with rain. Most forecasts were wrong anyway.

Light traffic on the highway ensured he'd quickly get to the marina where he'd leave his car and pick up his boat. From there, it was ten minutes to the island.

Daylin looked forward to meeting Gillian Foster. He'd investigated the former owner of Loon Island Resort and liked what he'd seen.

She'd lovingly cared for the place even after her marriage had broken down and she'd been left to run it alone. Her insistence on putting into the sales contract a clause to honour the reservations she'd taken before the sale had impressed him. He'd agreed to it readily.

If he ran the resort this season, he'd get a feel for the land before he made any changes. The bonus was that her pictures showed a fit, sexy body despite her hiding it under sweatshirts and baggy pants.

As he sped toward the turnoff to Loon Island Marina Road, Daylin cranked the radio and burst into song. Anticipation and joy surged through him, and it was all he could do not to bounce on the seat like a kid on Santa's knee. The start of an important new project always gave him a thrill, and he was on his way to meet with an intriguing new woman.

Could it get any better than this?

ABOUT THE AUTHOR

Val Tobin lives in Newmarket, Ontario with her husband, Bob, and Scully, their cat. She spends her days writing, reading, and searching for the perfect butter tart.

Her educational background includes a diploma in Computer Information Systems from DeVry Toronto, a B.Sc. in Parapsychic Science from the American Institute of Holistic Theology, a M.Sc. in Parapsychology from AIHT, Reiki Master/Teacher certifications, and Angel Therapy Practitioner® certifications.

CONNECT WITH VAL TOBIN

Facebook: https://www.facebook.com/valtobinauthor
Twitter: https://twitter.com/valandbob
Blog: http://bobandval.wordpress.com/
LinkedIn: http://www.linkedin.com/in/valtobin
Web Site: http://www.valtobin.com/

OTHER BOOKS BY VAL TOBIN

Poison Pen
Three wannabe authors suffering from various mental disorders find love in unexpected places when they interfere in the investigation of a colleague's murder. Part of the *About Three Authors* series, which includes *Whoever Said Love Was Easy?* by Patti Roberts and *Stolen Hearts & Muddy Pawprints* by Georgina Ramsey.

The *Valiant Chronicles* Series
Prequel: *Earthbound*
A spirit becomes earthbound after refusing to cross over in order to solve her murder and prevent more deaths, some of which might be predestined.

Book One: *The Experiencers*
A black-ops assassin atones for his brutal past by trying to help an alien abductee escape her fate.

Book Two: *A Ring of Truth*
A rogue assassin returns from the dead to rescue alien abductees
and triggers Armageddon.

The Valiant Chronicles books are also available as a box set.

Injury
A young actress at the height of her career has her personal life
turned upside down when a horrifying family secret makes front-
page news.

Gillian's Island
A socially anxious divorcée confronts her greatest fears when she's
forced to sell her island home and falls for the dashing new owner.

Walk-In
A young psychic woman fights an attraction to a handsome but
skeptical novelist while she battles a power-hungry sorcerer
determined to make her his next conquest.

www.ingramcontent.com/pod-product-compliance
Lightning Source LLC
Chambersburg PA
CBHW011434240626
47153CB00011B/2991